I0804918

Storm Testament III

Storm Testament III

Lee Nelson

Council Press
Springville, Utah

ISBN 13: 978-1-55517-374-6

Published by Council Press, an imprint of Cedar Fort, Inc., 2373 W. 700 S., Springville, UT, 84663
Distributed by Cedar Fort, Inc. www.cedarfort.com

LIBRARY OF CONGRESS CATALOGING-IN-PUBLICATION DATA

Nelson, Lee.
[Storm testament]
The Storm testament I / by Lee Nelson.
p. cm.
Originally published: Storm testament , 2001.
ISBN 978-1-55517-374-6 (alk. paper)
1. Rocky Mountains—Fiction. 2. Ute Indians—Fiction. I. Title.

PS3564.E4675S76 2007
813'.54—dc22

2007026687

Cover design by Nicole Williams
Cover design © 2008 by Lyle Mortimer
Edited by Annaliese B. Cox

Printed in the United States of America

10 9 8 7 6 5 4 3 2 1

Printed on acid-free paper

Prologue

Brigham Young didn't drive the final spike that eventful day of May 10, 1869, as many Mormons believe. When it came time to put the golden spike to rest to mark the completion of the first transcontinental railroad, it was the directors of the Central Pacific and Union Pacific railroad companies who moved to center stage. Brigham Young wasn't there.

I wasn't there either, it being planting time in Utah Valley, but my two oldest boys, Patrick and Samuel, were on hand to take in every detail. Patrick, my adopted son, was six months old when I married his mother, Sarah, on the old pioneer trail between Fort Laramie and Fort Bridger. I married Caroline, Samuel's mother, the same day. The two women gave me eleven children over the years, with three children dying in infancy. Of the eight remaining, four were boys. At the time of the golden spike ceremony, Patrick had just turned twenty-two and Samuel was almost twenty.

The two boys had been working for the Union Pacific Railroad for almost a year as part of a Mormon construction crew laying track westward across the Wyoming Territory and down into Utah. They each received thirty-five dollars a month for their labors. After the automatic 10 percent was taken out for tithing to the Church, the boys could do with the rest as they pleased; food and lodging were provided on the job. During the year on the railroad, Patrick had saved nearly three hundred dollars toward a college education back east. He wanted to become a doctor. The frontier was badly in need of doctors, and we encouraged him at every opportunity. Pat was tall and strong, physically capable of the strenuous railroad work, but he had a gentle disposition and didn't mix very well in the rough-and-tumble atmosphere of the railroad crews—mostly Civil War veterans, Irish immigrants, freed slaves, Shoshones, a few Gosiutes and, of course, the Mormon workers sent out by Brigham Young.

Samuel wasn't like Patrick. He didn't save his money and was always broke. Occasionally he would send a ten-dollar gold piece home for his brothers and sisters, and somehow he managed to hang on to his horse, saddle, and Spencer rifle, but his money slipped through his fingers like water, mostly by wagering on fist fights, dog fights, cock fights, and horse races.

Samuel was a fierce competitor, and a fighter. Or at least he thought he was. On payday at the end of his first month with the railroad, a burly Irishman offered to fight any man in the camp on a five-dollar wager, winner take all. There were only two takers on his offer, and one of them was Samuel. The Irishman whipped my son soundly before taking his five dollars.

The other man to fight the Irishman that day was a curly-headed Gosiute half-breed by the name of Lance Claw, son of the Gosiute war chief Ike, the black man who had accompanied me to the Rocky Mountains in 1838. Lance was about twenty-five and a drifter with a chip on his shoulder, not fitting very well in the white man's world, though he was very good at fighting and playing cards. Unlike Samuel, Lance was not fighting for money. The Irishman had called him a half-breed, and any man or group of men who dared call Lance Claw a half-breed or a nigger invited a fight whether they wanted one or not. The Irishman licked Lance, too.

Lance and Samuel had met occasionally as boys, but I suppose because of the age difference had never become fast friends. On that day when both of them were whipped by the Irishman, however, they became inseparable companions. Whenever there was a fight around camp, a rather frequent occurrence, Lance and Samuel weren't far away, and more often than not one or both of them was involved.

On the second payday the Irishman whipped them both a second time, but never again. The two fearless young men learned quickly, and as rust eaters their muscles became tempered like steel. The rust eaters were the crews of men who pulled the five-hundred-pound rails from the two-wheeled carts, carried them forward, and dropped them exactly in place on the bed of ties where they were spiked down permanently, the last step in the rail-building process. Patrick, on the other hand, was employed in the commissary, working with purchasing agents and issuing supplies to the men.

The golden spike ceremony wasn't the sober, patriotic event historians make it out to be. It was fully intended to be that way, but things just didn't work out. First, there was the rivalry rather than camaraderie between the Central Pacific and Union Pacific work crews. The men building track from California didn't like the men who were building track from the other direction, and men working from the east felt the same way about the Californians. While the Central Pacific crews were composed mostly of free-spirited Californians and subdued Chinese, the Union Pacific crews were composed mostly of Civil War veterans, freed slaves, and Irish immigrants. Whenever the crews came in contact—first the surveyors, then the excavators and bridge builders—there were always fights. And when the main work crews finally came head to head at Promontory, a regular battle was brewing, with Samuel and Lance Claw two of the most enthusiastic supporters on the Union Pacific side.

Up until the pounding of the final golden spike, the threat of dismissal had kept a lid on most of the fighting between the two crews, but once the last spike was driven, the work would be finished and the threat of dismissal would no longer carry any weight.

Then there was the Valley Tan, Utah whiskey, flowing freely in both camps on the day of the celebration. First the men became bold, then loud, then nasty. Except for the Chinese, who stayed pretty much to themselves.

The Chinese were in the white man's world to earn money. Otherwise, they wanted no part of it. They wore dishpan straw hats, pigtails, and blue pajamas. They slept in their own tents, where their own cooks prepared boiled tea and rice. Most of them made little effort to learn the white man's language beyond the bare essentials of getting the work done. Most of them, after several years of work on the railroad, still called the foreman bossyman.

But the Chinese weren't dumb. They could see the makings of a confrontation between the two work crews and wanted no part of it. But they weren't about to leave, not as long as there was a dollar to be earned.

Perhaps it was the sober, obedient nature of the Chinese that earned them the honor of laying the last two rails as part of the celebration. Perhaps it was the heroics of the Chinese as they lowered themselves over cliffs in baskets to blast away the granite cliffs of the high Sierras. Perhaps it was the fact that the Chinese were the only workers in camp sober enough to be depended on during the celebration. No one wanted a five-hundred-pound steel rail dropped on a dignitary's toe during the celebration, and the Chinese could be counted on not to do that.

On the given signal, when all the dignitaries were in place, seven little men in blue pajamas scampered forward with the last rail, fully aware that a bone-breaking brawl could break out any second. That's when a Salt Lake City photographer yelled "Shoot!" to his assistant holding the rack with the flash powder. With their limited understanding of the King's English, the Chinese only understood one definition for the word "shoot," and that didn't have anything to do with taking pictures. The pigtailed men dropped the rail and raced for the safety of their camp. The entire assembly roared with laughter. Some of the tension that had been building for the fight between the two camps was relieved, at least temporarily.

The second item of humor was just as unexpected as the first. It occurred after everything was in place except for the final gold spike.

Leland Stanford, a former grocery wholesaler from Sacramento, now a director of the Central Pacific Railroad, was selected to drive the final spike. He was a short beaver of a man with a bushy dark brown beard. With the sledgehammer in hand, he had to wait a long time for the spike to receive the proper wiring. The transcontinental telegraph had been finished eight years earlier, and the wires were being attached to the golden spike so that when it was struck by Leland Stanford's hammer, the impact would be heard from coast to coast.

Motioning for the dignitaries to back away and give him room, Mr. Stanford swung the heavy hammer in a sweeping arc above his head and down with all his strength. Everyone present was getting ready for a big cheer. Instead there was loud laughter as the hammer missed its mark and made a dull thud on the pine tie. Stanford was undaunted by the failure and loud jeering from men who had pounded spikes every two feet across an entire continent—twenty-eight to thirty spikes per rail, four hundred rails per mile for nearly three thousand miles. These men were so familiar with pounding spikes that they could do it blindfolded if necessary, and they could drive a spike all the way home with only three blows of the hammer, most of the time.

Stanford swung the hammer down again, this time driving the golden spike several inches into the soft wood, sending a simultaneous message to San Francisco and New York. The transcontinental railroad was finished, and in half the estimated time.

While the reporters in the audience had noble thoughts of a young nation being sewn together with steel threads, Stanford undoubtedly was figuring his profits. The U.S. Government had given the railroad companies ten square miles of land divided in alternate sections on either side of the right-of-way for each mile of track laid. When it was all over, the Central Pacific and Union Pacific railroads received deeds for 116 million acres of land—ground that suddenly had value because of railroad access. In addition, the companies received low interest government loans to finance the construction. The money was allocated at a rate of sixteen thousand dollars per mile on flat ground, thirty-two thousand dollars per mile on hilly or semi-rough ground, and forty-eight thousand dollars per mile in the mountains.

At the time of the Promontory celebration, Leland Stanford could only guess what his share of this two-year project would be. If he guessed he would make millions, he was right.

While the reporters were entertaining great notions and Leland Stanford was counting his money, Sam Storm and Lance Claw were anticipating a glorious fist fight with the Central Pacific crew members.

Chapter 1

"You can swill that buffalo juice down your rotten guts until hell freezes over, and nobody'll give a damn," roared John Casement, known to the men working on the Central and Union Pacific railroads as Blackjack. If anyone deserved the most credit for the transcontinental railroad being finished May 10, 1869, in half the predicted time, it was Blackjack. He was a relentless, intense, slave driver of a man. He wore a Russian military cap, a jet-black beard, knee-high cowhide boots, and carried a bullwhip, which he knew how to use. The Irish called him boss; the Chinese, bossyman. The men jumped whenever Blackjack barked a command. More iron rails were laid under his foremanship than anyone else's during the entire transcontinental project. Blackjack demanded and got obedience, cooperation, and hard work from everyone under his control, especially the Irish and Chinese, who seemed to be in mortal fear of the fiery foreman.

"But there won't be no drunken brawl, not here at Promontory Summit, not as long as I'm the boss," Blackjack continued in his gruff, forceful voice. "None at all. No fights. Now get that through your dumb, thick skulls!" He was standing in the open doorway of the galley wagon where the working men ate in shifts, forty at a time, as the railroad construction moved forward. The men were wolfing down their final meal before collecting their last gold coins.

The galley wagon contained one long table that reached the full length of the rail car, no walk-around room at either end. When a man on the side away from the door finished eating, he merely stepped up onto his bench, then onto the table as he crossed over to the door—always careful not to place his foot in someone's food. The fare was simple, boiled beef heaped in wooden buckets, one nailed permanently to the plank table every four feet. Between the buckets there were platters piled high with two-inch-thick slices of heavy brown bread, fresh baked that same day. Any leftovers were thrown out to the scavenger bands of ragtag Indians who followed the construction crews. Each man had a tin cup that he filled and refilled with water by dipping it into wooden barrels located in each corner of the galley wagon. Forty tin plates, twenty on each side of the table, were nailed to the table in perfect rows. Once a day they were swabbed clean with a mop. Some of the men used their own forks to eat their food, and those without utensils simply wrapped two slices of bread around a big chunk of meat and ate with their hands. For flavoring, there was salt, but no pepper. And as a special treat for the last meal—at the conclusion of the golden spike ceremony—there were big slabs of butter for the bread.

"And to help you remember—the more stubborn members of this motley crew—there will be no one-way rail passes for any man caught fighting at Promontory, from this moment forward," continued Blackjack. At the conclusion of the transcontinental railway each worker had been promised, in addition to his regular wages, a one-way ticket to the destination of his choice, anywhere between Omaha and San Francisco. With tickets on the new rail system selling for eight cents a mile, the free ticket was a substantial benefit, except perhaps for the Mormon crews who would return to Salt Lake City and the vicinity.

"There will be no fighting. Is the message clear?"

The galley wagon was quiet except for the muffled chewing of the men—like cattle at a manger—and the occasional clank of a fork against a tin plate. While some of the bolder members of the crew were looking directly at Blackjack, most were looking down at their food or empty plates. Blackjack wasn't the kind of man one looked in the face, not if one wanted to stay alive and healthy. He didn't carry that bullwhip for looks only. He used it, frequently.

"Why can't we fight?"

All eyes shot to the west end of the galley wagon to see who dared question the foreman. It was the curly-headed half-breed, Lance Claw. The question was loud and clear, not timid or hesitant in the least. In fact, there was even a tone of defiance in the young half-breed's voice as he maintained eye contact with the surprised foreman. The half-breed's eyes were clear and calm, even beautiful, like those of a woman. But there was nothing feminine in the young man's bearing or body. His bronze skin stretched tightly over high cheekbones and a strong jaw. Beneath his threadbare shirt there was the unmistakable rippling of steel-hard muscles—except for the smooth breast pocket housing a well-worn deck of playing cards. Though he was only twenty-five summers old, his knuckles and face contained the scars of many fights. The silence was heavy as the bold young half-breed and the intense foreman stared at each other. The half-breed was the first to speak, but he didn't look away.

"I mean, with the railroad finished, the work over, what's it to you if some of the men want to beat on each other?"

The foreman wasn't prepared for such a simple question. He wasn't accustomed to discussing orders with subordinates. His face began to redden as the silence continued. The young half-breed did not look away. He was waiting fearlessly for his answer. The foreman didn't like that.

The silence changed. The muffled chewing stopped. There was some murmuring among the men. The boldness of the half-breed had found fertile ground and was spreading. The foreman didn't like that. He felt his iron control over the men slipping. Blackjack began to realize for the first time that the railroad really was finished, and that his rule over the men would soon be finished, too. Tomorrow he would no longer be the boss of a hundred men, but one of them in the ranks of the unemployed.

Blackjack was the first to look away, down at his leather boot as he raised it to the bench. He dropped his bullwhip on the table beside the boot, then looked up at the men, all of whom were now looking at him.

"My last order is to stop any brawling. Something to do with all the reporters sniffing around and the whole country looking at us, thinking we're the men who worked together to pull a country together, after a civil war that tore its guts out. To them we're heroes, not a bunch of drunken brawlers. My last order is to keep 'em think'n that, to stop any brawl'n."

He looked back down at his boot, amazed, as were the rest of the men, at his eloquence. He looked up again.

"We've worked damn hard together, and a lot of you grunts have felt more than one nip from this here sidekick." He picked up his bullwhip and looked kindly at it. "Probably a few of you would like a chance to return the favor. Don't blame you. But there can't be a brawl." He looked up again, a sudden idea giving light to a normally dark countenance.

"They didn't want brawl'n, but they didn't say noth'n about a regular fight." Blackjack smiled, a phenomenon most of the men had never seen.

"I'll fight any man in camp, at sundown. Everybody can come and watch. Maybe you'll see old Blackjack take a lick or two, but don't count on it." He was growling again, his confidence back. "I intend to tear apart the man who dares stand up to me. Who'll it be?"

Blackjack was back in control. He had unwittingly, but successfully, made the transition from railroad foreman to king of the mountain. While every man in the galley wagon fully intended to watch Blackjack's last battle, all were content to be spectators only, and were entertaining no thoughts of accepting the challenge. Except two. Lance Claw, the half-breed who had asked the question earlier, and his blond companion, a kid of about twenty years, Sam Storm. Both young men were looking into Blackjack's face, seriously considering his challenge. While the half-breed had the stoic look of his Indian ancestors, young Storm was smiling.

Storm was always smiling, or so it seemed. Even when he was the first in camp to lick the Irishman, he did it with a smile on his face. The blue-eyed young man loved competition—horse races, dog fights, wrestling matches, and fist fights. Competition made him happy, and when he was happy, he smiled.

Both young men had felt Blackjack's whip. Both had yearned for a chance to make it right. Both now had that chance. But not without substantial risk.

The two young men looked at each other. Storm was the first to speak, still smiling, and loud enough for everyone in the galley wagon to hear, especially Blackjack.

"I'll fight the buffalo chip."

Blackjack cut off the cheering of the workers by slapping his coiled bullwhip soundly on the table.

"Don't forget to bring your bullwhip, Storm," he bellowed. "I fully intend to use mine." He turned and stomped out of the galley wagon.

Chapter 2

"You're crazy to fight ol' Blackjack with bullwhips," said Lance Claw as he and Sam Storm jumped to the ground from the galley wagon. The May sun was low in the deep blue desert sky. They were walking toward one of the bunk cars where their gear was stored.

"You heard how he nipped that German's ears off out in Nebraska," continued the half-breed.

"Both of 'em, they say," replied young Storm, a smile on his tanned face. "Man's got to be pretty good to do that."

"They say the big Frankfurter dropped to his knees and bawled like a baby, trying to squeeze the bloody flappers back in place. But they never took. Lost 'em both."

"Insist on a regular fight, without the bullwhips," persisted Claw. "You won't get much court'n done without any ears."

"I'll wear my hat. Pulled down over my ears."

"What about your eyes and your neck and your face and your back? Do you even know how to use a bullwhip? I never seen one in your hand." Claw never seemed to be at a loss for words.

"Used one a little on the ranch. With the stock. But I don't figure to lick him with a bullwhip."

"How?" replied Claw, more than a little curiosity in his voice.

"While Blackjack's been boss'n everybody around, I've been lift'n iron rails. Figure, I'll be stronger. Quicker, for sure. He's got the edge on experience, but I figure I can last longer—if he doesn't get me early."

"But how you gonna keep his whip from tear'n you up?"

"Get in close, I figure, where it won't do him any good, then pound that soft belly of his." Storm playfully reached around his companion's neck with one arm, then jabbed him in the stomach with the other, pretending to be in serious combat.

"Wanna wear my leather jacket? Leggings, too?" asked Claw, finally giving up any hope of stopping the bullwhip fight.

"Good idea," responded Storm as they climbed into the bunk car. "Maybe we can find a leather neckerchief, too. No use offering Blackjack any more bare skin than necessary."

The two friends were alone in the bunk car, the other men already assembling at the clearing where the fight was to take place.

"This stuff ain't armor," reminded Claw as he helped Storm into the leather clothing. "Take away some of the sting, but that whip'll still take your breath away, and still leave some nasty welts."

Sam was adjusting the leather neckerchief when he heard someone calling.

"Samuel! You in there?"

It was a familiar male voice, and the fact that it called him "Samuel" instead of "Sam" or "Storm" left no mistaking that it was his brother Patrick, undoubtedly come to talk him out of the bullwhip fight. With an annoyed expression on his face, Sam headed for the doorway, but not before picking up the bullwhip he had arranged to borrow from a bunkmate.

As Sam stepped into the daylight, he was surprised to see that his brother was not alone. In fact, Pat was riding in a fancy carriage, complete with a flat canvas cover fringed with tassels. A cream puff of a man with plump cheeks was holding the reins to the sleek bay geldings, obviously pampered with stalls and horse blankets. Otherwise they would have looked gaunt and shaggy, like range horses look in the spring. Sam had seen the man before, a dry goods broker from Salt Lake. His name was Brutus Young. He had been selling supplies to the railroads, and had been working closely with Pat over the last few months.

But Sam didn't give more than a darting glance at the carriage, the plump driver, the sleek horses, or even his brother. He was staring at the young woman seated between the two men, undoubtedly the most beautiful woman young Storm had ever seen.

She wasn't like the typical farm girls Sam knew in his native valley at the foot of the majestic Mt. Timpanogos—the ones with the red hands, sunburned noses, broad shoulders, and constant giggles. Nor was she like the delicate Salt Lake City girls—the thin, white-skinned ones, afraid to look a man in the eye—the kind of women who never wore anything other than full-length dresses and rode horses sidesaddle when riding was necessary, otherwise enjoying the comfort of covered carriages.

This girl looked different, in many ways. Though she was wearing the finest starched dress made from imported blue and white satin, her long black hair hung freely about her shoulders like that of an Indian. It was apparent she had not wasted any time at a hairdresser. The skin on her bare shoulders was not red and rough like the farm girls, nor was it white and pampered like the Salt Lake City girls. The skin on her strong and shapely shoulders was smooth and healthy with a mild suntan—almost olive in complexion. There was a glossiness to her skin like that of a well-muscled cow pony on a hot summer afternoon. Without asking, Sam figured she was not the sidesaddle type, but the kind of woman who could straddle a half-wild horse and give a man a hard race across the open prairie. The fact that she was dressed in the finest satin dress Sam had ever seen only enhanced the mystery of this magnificent young woman.

And when Sam stared at her she didn't look away, her dark eyes never blinking, giving the appearance of wisdom beyond her years.

For the first time in his life, Sam Storm found a woman more interesting than a fight. In fact, for a moment, all thoughts of the upcoming battle with Blackjack vanished from the young man's head. And when they returned, there was a feeling of regret that the fight might interfere with a chance to get better acquainted with this woman. Sam was temporarily bewildered, having never felt anything like this before in his short twenty years.

"Why don't you stop staring at Kathryn and tell us what you are doing in those leather rags?" demanded Pat, attempting to embarrass his brother. Sam could feel the color rising through his neck to his cheeks, and that made him angry.

"Dress'n up to fight Blackjack," he responded, ignoring the comment about staring at the girl, but still looking at her, refusing to be intimidated.

"You're really going to do it?" said Pat, his words more a statement of incredulity than a question.

"Yep," said Sam. He then changed the subject by asking, "Aren't you going to introduce us to the young lady?"

Pat quickly apologized for the oversight, then introduced his brother and Lance Claw to Brutus Young and Kathryn Cannon. Brutus quickly added for Sam's benefit that he and Kathryn were engaged to be married. Sam was undaunted.

"I'm flattered that you came to watch me fight, Miss Cannon . . . or can I call you Kathryn?" asked Sam, not taking his eyes from those of the young woman who seemed to be getting annoyed and a little embarrassed at the young man's intense attention.

"I came here for the golden spike ceremony, not to watch you or anyone else fight—" began Kathryn before she was interrupted by Pat.

"We're just stopping to let you know I'm going into Salt Lake with Brutus and Kathryn. Be attending the Golden Spike Ball tomorrow night, then heading back east to school. Just wanted to say good-bye to my little brother."

"Besides," interjected Brutus Young, "a lady like Kathryn wouldn't want to watch two men whip each other like wild brutes of the forest."

Lance Claw, who had been silent up until now, began to laugh, something to do with Young's "brute of the forest" comparison. Sam didn't try to figure out why his friend was laughing. He knew better. Claw's sense of humor frequently left white men and red men wondering what was funny.

"I'll bet Kathryn would love to watch the fight," said Sam, again looking intently at the young woman. "More exciting than a dog fight. Guarantee it."

Brutus started to object, but Kathryn put a hand on his arm, signaling him to be silent.

"Maybe I should stay," she said, looking over at Brutus. "Being a practicing nurse, my services might be needed at the conclusion of the fight." Then she looked at Sam. "I think I would really enjoy pouring iodine in this man's wounds."

"Think I'd like that too, ma'am," Sam responded quickly, and he meant every word. The thought of being stretched out on the ground, head on Kathryn's lap as she dressed his wounds, was the most exciting thought he had had all day. He made a mental note that should he have an opportunity to end the fight quickly, he would pass it up in an effort to make sure he received at least several good wounds before the fight was over—wounds for this young woman to nurse.

"The men are wait'n," said Lance, bringing Sam back to the present. "Time we be head'n over to the clearing."

Chapter 3

"What's that shoot'n?" asked Brutus Young as he guided his team behind a group of men walking to the clearing where Blackjack and Sam Storm were going to square off with bullwhips.

"Blackjack warming up his bullwhip," responded Patrick.

"Bullwhips can't crack that loud," said Kathryn, hesitation in her voice. "Or can they?"

"Blackjack's can," said Patrick. "He practices at five o'clock every morning as he walks beside the bunk cars rousting out the men. Loud as a gun, and just as dangerous. With that old bullwhip he can flick wasps off the molasses barrel, put out cigars, and if he's in a fightin' mood, take a man's ear off. Hate to see what he could do if he really got mad."

"Looks like we'll find out soon enough," said Brutus. "Hope your brother Sam'll put up a good fight. Glad it's him instead of me."

"Sam's crazy," said Kathryn. "Why would a sane man fight someone like Blackjack, a man that good with a bullwhip?"

"Don't know," said Patrick, looking away thoughtfully toward the Great Salt Lake. "Determined, spoiled, dumb—not sure what it is. Just always seemed to get what he wanted. Wasn't always easy, but he always seemed to come out on top.

"When he was fifteen he disappeared into the desert one morning. Said he was going looking for wild horses. Nobody took him seriously. Wild horses hadn't been seen in the area for years. When he didn't come home that night, we began to worry. Two days later we went looking for him. Searched almost a week. No sign at all. About a week after the search was called off, when we were talking about holding a funeral for Samuel, he comes galloping into the yard with five of the orneriest mustangs you ever saw. Not much more than skin and bones, they were kickin' and bitin' each other. Their tails were draggin' on the ground."

Brutus paid little attention to the narrative about Sam Storm as he pushed his team through the groups of men. Brutus didn't want to be late for the fight.

On the other hand, Kathryn listened intently to the story about the young man with the clear, blue eyes whom she had just met. It seemed incredible that a fifteen-year-old would venture into the stark desert—Indian country—and not only survive, but return with five wild horses. She didn't know any grown men, or at least she didn't think she did, who would undertake that bold an adventure.

"When everybody started getting after him for not telling where he was going," continued Patrick, "Samuel said, 'But I did. Said I was going after wild horses. Everybody knows there's none around here. Took awhile to find 'em. Then I had to catch them. Wasn't easy bringing 'em home, either.'

"The next morning he started breaking them. One was a young stud. Bucked Samuel off five or six times, but the boy just kept getting back on until the animal was too weary to buck. Samuel is good with horses. Always gets his way. Persistent, but not mean. Don't know how many times he's been kicked or bucked off. Always goes back for more. I think he's fearless."

"Has he a chance with this Blackjack?" asked Kathryn, finding herself more fascinated with Samuel than she would care to admit. She reminded herself that she was engaged to Brutus Young.

"Don't know," said Patrick. "Blackjack's no fool. Didn't get to be foreman of the entire track-laying crew for being soft. And I don't think he would be fightin' Samuel if he didn't think he could win. Blackjack's no kid. Not the kind of man to get in a fight if he wasn't pretty sure of coming out on top."

"Is Samuel good with a bullwhip?" inquired Kathryn, beginning to worry about the young man she had just met.

"Knows how to use one, but he's not *really* good, not like Blackjack," said Patrick. "But knowing Samuel, he's probably got a strategy, something up his sleeve, I hope."

Kathryn didn't respond, wondering if she really wanted to see the battle that was about to take place. She had been trained as a nurse and had worked almost a year in the Deseret Hospital in Salt Lake City as a nurse's aide. Still, she had no stomach for pain and injury. And the steady crack of Blackjack's whip in the approaching clearing reminded her that the black-bearded foreman of the Union Pacific Railroad was about to dish out a generous portion of pain and injury to a bold, blue-eyed young man she had just met—a boyish but fearless man to whom she felt an unusual attraction.

Chapter 4

Blackjack had been demonstrating his whip-cracking talents for some time when Sam Storm finally stepped inside the circle of men, opposite the big foreman. The Union Pacific workers were gathered on one side of the circle, the Central Pacific men on the other. There were gasps of surprise and hoots of delight from the Union Pacific men over Storm's costume—the wide-brimmed leather hat pulled down over his ears, buckskin leggings, buffalo hide shirt, and a leather bandanna covering his nose, mouth, and neck front. Even his hands were covered with cowhide gloves. The only exposed skin on his entire body was a narrow strip across his eyes. The hat and shirt were too large, giving a shaggy, comical appearance to the young man. Some of the Central Pacific workers offered crude jests about the awkward appearance of the young fighter.

Storm ignored the jests. The creases at the corners of his blue eyes indicated he was still grinning. To the youthful Sam Storm, life was a game. The thrill of battle far outweighed the fear of pain, insult, or injury.

Blackjack bent over and began to laugh, a deep belly laugh. Storm's appearance had caught him by surprise. The seriousness of the approaching fight had somehow been shattered by the ridiculous appearance of the costume. Blackjack's humor began to spread through the crowd as the Union Pacific men began to laugh with him, while the Central Pacific men continued to jeer.

But the laughing and jeering stopped more quickly than it had begun when without warning Blackjack's arm shot forward, a quick twist of the wrist uncoiling the black bullwhip in a fraction of a second. Before young Storm could react, the snakelike end of the whip had wrapped around his hip and laid a searing welt across the seat of his trousers—the only place where the leather leggings did not cover. Instinctively, the young man grabbed for the whip end, but his fingers closed on nothing but air. The tip had already been jerked away as Blackjack prepared for a second strike, laughing as he envisioned how the welt across Storm's backside would give the boy more than a little discomfort if he attempted to ride a horse in the near future.

Storm didn't wait for the whip to strike again. Dropping his own whip to the ground, he lunged toward Blackjack. His strategy was simple and obvious. Get in close where the bullwhip would be ineffective. Storm knew better than to try and outwhip Blackjack at twenty paces.

The youth had barely covered half the distance when Blackjack's whip shot forward again, this time wrapping around the young man's ankles, sending him headlong into the thick dust, just short of his target, just a few feet away from the loudest of the jeering Central Pacific men.

Again Storm instinctively reached for the whip end. Again the wily snake was withdrawn before the young man could grab it. Beneath the bandanna it was difficult for anyone to notice that the grin had finally vanished from Storm's face.

As he reached forward to get his balance and continue the charge, the whip laid another welt across his backside. This time Storm ignored the whip and lunged forward with all the speed he could muster, finally getting close enough to make the whip ineffective.

Just as Storm was cocking back his fist to finish off the older man, one of Blackjack's cowhide boots smashed into his stomach—the effect like running full speed into an oak tree in the middle of the night. As the air rushed from his lungs, Storm grabbed desperately for the boot, this time succeeding.

Both men went to the ground in a churning cloud of dust as each tried to get the best of the other. Storm managed to deal several solid blows to the body of the older man before the two fighters finally ground to a halt, each holding what he thought was a deadly grip on the other. As the dust settled, each man trying to tighten his grip, Blackjack began to laugh again.

"What's so damn funny?" hissed Storm through his clenched teeth.

"Just seems kind of crazy," replied Blackjack after a brief pause to tighten his grip on Storm's arm, "You and me killing each other just to put on a free show for all this Central Pacific trash. Seems funny. Makes me laugh. Makes me feel stupid, too."

Beneath the bandanna, Storm's grin returned.

"You be havin' second thoughts about callin' off the big row between the two crews?" he asked softly, so the nearby Central Pacific workers could not hear.

"Aye. So be my feelings. What say we git up and square off like we was going to fight with our fists, then start knockin' the grins off those pig faces?"

"Bet we'd git plenty of help once we got things started. Send 'em crawling back to California. Let go o' me."

The two dust-covered men released their holds on each other and rolled in opposite directions, simultaneously springing to their feet, fists ready to go at each other a second time. Storm pulled the bandanna from his face to make breathing easier.

Storm began dancing about, boxer style, seemingly looking for an opening, as the two men worked toward the edge of the clearing, close to the nucleus of the jeering Central Pacific workers. Blackjack struck the first blow, a sweeping right hook seemingly aimed at Storm's head. The young man ducked, allowing the fist to continue its journey into the face of the closest railroad worker. Storm followed up with a blow to the belly of the next man. Hundreds of spectators suddenly became participants as the circle of men closed upon itself—hundreds of burly railroad workers wrestling, boxing, sweating, bleeding.

At a distance, in the safety of his carriage, Brutus Young was shouting and cheering, enjoying every moment of the brawl, not caring which side was winning. Next to him, the young woman Kathryn was standing, leaning out to one side to avoid the carriage canopy. One hand was over her mouth, a distressed look on her beautiful face, as she strained to keep track of the brave young man wearing the buffalo shirt and buckskin leggings.

Chapter 5

The next morning, a change of plans left Patrick O'Riley behind to finish some bookwork at the company store while Sam Storm and Lance Claw headed for Salt Lake City with Brutus Young. Kathryn had departed for the city the night before with some of the railroad dignitaries.

Everyone of any importance was going to Salt Lake City to attend the Golden Spike Ball. It was to be held at the Social Hall, where Brigham Young and Leland Stanford were to be the guests of honor. The Golden Spike Ball was billed as the social event of the decade. Business and political leaders from across the country and in the area were invited.

Sam and Lance didn't have invitations to the ball, but Brutus did, and he made the most out of this added bit of prestige.

"Every important man in the territory will be there," boasted Brutus as his buggy bounced along the dusty wagon path. "Won't be many younger than me. What are you guys doing tonight?"

"Don't know," responded Sam with little enthusiasm. "Maybe we can make a dollar or two holding teams for guests at the ball."

"Great idea!" exclaimed Brutus, always enthusiastic over a new money-making idea.

"I ain't in any mood to stand around holding horses all evening," said Lance, looking down at his bandaged right fist. Sam's right hand was bandaged, too. Both had bruises on their faces. Sam was sitting on a folded-over sheep skin, the welts from Blackjack's whip across his backside causing more than a little discomfort. The brawl had lasted nearly an hour, and no man in camp had remained unscathed, except Brutus, who had stayed in the safety of his carriage.

"Yep, you fellows are lucky to be ridin' with me," said Brutus, changing the subject.

"Why's that?" asked Lance, offering the expected response when it became obvious after an awkward silence that Sam didn't want to be engaged in further conversation with Brutus, at least not for the moment. Sam had his mind on other things, namely a young woman who would be going to the Golden Spike Ball with someone else.

"I'm going to be one of the wealthiest men in the whole territory," bragged Brutus.

"How's that?" asked Lance, content to let Brutus talk all he wanted.

"I'm a dry goods broker."

"What's a dry goods broker?" asked the half-breed.

"You don't know what a dry goods broker is?" asked Brutus, not able to resist the temptation to put down someone who didn't know something that he knew. But Lance wasn't intimidated. He didn't care, not that much.

"No. What's a dry goods broker?"

"I sell nonfood items to stores."

"How's that going to make you one of the richest men in the territory?"

"Ever hear of ZCMI?"

"Yeah," said Lance. "The big church-owned store that's replacing all the little stores throughout the territory. Mormons'll only buy from ZCMI, nobody else."

"Yeah, and do you know who the head buyer is for ZCMI?"

"Nope."

"My uncle." Brutus sat back proudly, his thumbs stretching out his suspenders. "He'll buy all kinds of stuff from me, and I'll make 10 percent on every single item, sometimes more. Going to St. Louie to buy stuff next week. Ever been to St. Louie?"

"Nope," responded Lance.

"In ten years I'll be so filthy rich you guys will be proud to know me," continued Brutus, his enthusiasm growing with Lance's mild encouragement. "You'll tell your kids how you once rode to Salt Lake in a carriage with Brutus Young."

In his excitement, Brutus had let the horses slow to a walk. Storm was the first to notice.

"Think we'll make it in time for the dance?"

"If we hurry," responded Brutus, clucking his tongue to signal the horses to speed up. "Got one stop to make on the way." He slapped the reins over the horses' rumps to make them go even faster.

"What if you're late?" asked Sam, suddenly taking an interest in the conversation.

"Kathryn'll just have to wait, I suppose. We'll be late for the dance."

"I'll bet she wouldn't like that," said Storm.

"Like it or not, she won't say nothing."

"Why's that?" Storm was very interested now that the conversation had turned to Kathryn.

"I'm a good catch, you know," said Brutus proudly. "She wouldn't blow a good thing. She's lucky to be engaged to me." Storm bit his tongue, resisting the urge to say something sarcastic.

Lance was the next to sneak. "How do you figure to be such a good catch?" The half-breed's voice sounded innocent enough, but he looked out across the prairie so the dry goods broker wouldn't notice the smirk on his face.

"I'm going to be rich, and I'm not a polygamist," said Brutus with confidence. "If she wasn't engaged to me, the polygamists would be lined up clear to the front gate asking old man Cannon for his daughter's hand as a fifth or sixth wife. Being engaged to me saves her from all that."

"When do you figure on marrying her?" asked Storm.

"In the fall sometime," said Brutus. "Once I get my new business underway."

"Fall!" exclaimed Lance. "If I was engaged to a woman like that, I'd forget business and git married tomorrow."

"Civilized people don't mate like animals," responded Brutus, a condescending tone in his voice. "It takes time for civilized people to develop lasting relationships."

"Glad I ain't civilized," responded Lance, a wide grin on his face. "How about you, Sam? You civilized like Brutus here?"

"Where is it you have to stop?" Sam asked Brutus, ignoring Lance's question, but suddenly very curious about Brutus's plans for the rest of the day.

"See a man about buying some brooms," said Brutus quickly, glad someone had changed the subject.

"For ZCMI?" asked Sam.

"Yeah, an old man and his retarded son. Live a couple of miles up a roadless canyon. They do good work and sell cheap. I'll make a bundle if I can get them on contract to sell everything to me."

Storm didn't respond, but not from boredom or lack of interest. Brutus's words had triggered an unthinkable idea in the young man's head, one that wouldn't go away.

With Storm suddenly quiet, Brutus attempted to resume his conversation with the half-breed.

"You've lived among the Indians?"

"Raised by them mostly. They're my people, them and the blacks."

"With the coming of the railroad," explained Brutus, "there'll be a lot more tourists. Seems every one of them wants Indian souvenirs—bows, arrows, moccasins, feathers, robes, necklaces, even scalps. Especially scalps. Every tourist wants to bring home a scalp. Who could supply me with that kind of truck?"

"Depends on how much you're paying," responded Lance coolly.

"Oh, I'd pay plenty all right, and so would ZCMI and the tourists."

Lance and Brutus discussed the various prices that could be charged for Indian trinkets, especially scalps, until Brutus pulled the wagon to a halt at the mouth of a rugged, roadless canyon heading east into the Wasatch Mountains.

"Broom maker lives up there, mile or two. Want to come with me? We'll have to hurry."

"Yeah," said Lance, starting to get out of the wagon.

"No, thanks," said Sam. "We'll wait here."

A surprised look on his face, Lance glanced at Sam.

"What's wrong?" asked Brutus, also noticing the unusual nature of the request.

Sam looked down at his feet, slowly placing both hands over the back of his trousers. "Hurts like blazes. Thought maybe Lance would stay behind and help change the dressing. Can't do it by myself."

"Be back in about half an hour," laughed Brutus as he trotted up the trail by himself. "Don't wander, or I'll leave you. Can't be late for the ball."

When Brutus was out of sight, Sam looked at Lance and said, "Do you think she would go with me?"

"What?" asked Lance, not comprehending.

"To the ball. Kathryn. With me."

"I don't understand."

"If I pulled up to her house in this carriage and said Brutus sent me because he got tied up on business and couldn't come himself, but didn't want her to miss the dance. Think she would go with me?"

Lance began to laugh. "I think she would. But we might go to jail tomorrow for horse stealin'."

"We'll worry about that tomorrow," laughed Sam as he slapped the horses' rumps with the reins.

As the carriage pulled back onto the Salt Lake road, Brutus Young was still hurrying toward the broom maker's cabin, confident in his ability to sew up the Utah Territory broom business.

Chapter 6

Leaving Brutus behind at the broom maker's had been an easy thing for Sam to do. In fact, it had seemed like the natural thing to do. The thought that Brutus might turn his name over to the authorities as a horse and carriage thief didn't bother Sam. As he saw it, he was just borrowing the carriage, would take good care of it, and would see that it was returned to its rightful owner after the dance. Sam had no criminal intent but was merely involved in a romantic rivalry. Kathryn Cannon had already promised to marry Brutus, so the young dry goods broker obviously had the advantage, but Sam Storm wasn't about to be discouraged by something as insignificant as an engagement promise.

While hijacking a team of horses and a carriage had been easy for Sam, approaching Kathryn's front door was not. Sam was dressed appropriately for the Golden Spike Ball, having found a dark suit in Brutus's suitcase, conveniently located in the back of the carriage. Sam was even seated in the backseat, his friend Lance Claw playing driver. Lance's bay saddle horse was trotting behind the carriage.

Sam looked the part of a gentleman. But having been raised on a farm in a rough-and-tumble frontier community, he still felt out of place on the Avenues, the area east of Temple Square where Salt Lake City's new rich were building luxurious homes. The first few years in the valley, in the late forties, the Mormon pioneers had barely scratched out a living. Once gold was discovered in California, however, and the Oregon Territory was opened for settlement, with tens of thousands of Americans migrating to the far West, the Salt Lake Valley became a bustling trade center. Those who controlled the trade made fortunes, and Kathryn's father, Willard Cannon, was one of them.

Kathryn's mother had died just two years after arriving in the Valley, shortly after the birth of Kathryn's younger brother, Willard Jr., when Kathryn was three years old. Willard had remarried quickly, not one wife, but two. Kathryn and Willard Jr. were raised by the two stepmothers, who perhaps weren't as loving as their natural mother might have been, but who were certainly not cruel or abusive. In compliance with her father's wishes, Kathryn attended the best private schools and the nursing academy, socializing in the most exclusive circles as well. She had had every desirable educational and social opportunity available to a young woman in Salt Lake City in the 1860s. Willard Jr., on the other hand, had been thin and sickly since birth and seldom left the Cannon home.

But there was one thing that bothered Willard Cannon as his daughter began to mature into a beautiful woman. While Willard had taken two wives for himself and fully endorsed the Church's stand on plural marriage, he was quietly but firmly opposed to the apple of his eye becoming the third or fourth wife of an older man. The older men controlled the money, had the highest positions in the Church, drove the nicest carriages, and owned the best homes. In fact, the older, well-established businessmen were about the only ones who could support more than one wife. But he didn't want his Kathryn married off to an old polygamist.

Still, as his beautiful daughter reached puberty and began to look like a mature woman in the beautiful dresses her father purchased for her at no small cost, a number of polygamists began to call at the Cannon household with increasing frequency. Willard wasn't so concerned with his peers, the businessmen. He could protect his daughter from their advances. But he did fear the Church leaders. How could he say no to one of his stake leaders, or perhaps even a General Authority, who might want his daughter's hand in marriage? If he believed they were inspired men, if he believed plural marriage was a true principle revealed through the Prophet Joseph, then he couldn't stand in the way of his daughter entering the principle. He stayed awake nights, worrying about his daughter's future. He didn't really object to any of the teachings of the Church. He just wanted his first child to be happy.

While many of the plural marriages seemed to be happy ones, many were not, particularly for the second, third, or fourth wives. If the first wife was past her prime when a new wife joined the family, the first wife frequently became jealous of the younger, prettier wife, and she could make life miserable for that new wife. Sometimes Willard even had nightmares of his daughter becoming the thirteenth wife of a certain Church leader Willard didn't like.

But those nightmares ended the night Kathryn danced into the parlor announcing her engagement to Brutus Young. Now she was off limits to the polygamists. Brutus had rescued Willard's daughter from a potential hell, and Willard from his nightmares—and for this Willard was eternally grateful. He loved Brutus with all his heart.

To make matters even better, Brutus was a regular church attender and appeared to be embarking on a prosperous career as a dry goods broker. Willard couldn't be happier at how things were turning out for his daughter. That's why he had a look of both surprise and disappointment on his face when he opened the door and found Sam Storm standing there, announcing that he had come to take Kathryn to the Golden Spike Ball.

"But what happened to Brutus?" asked the surprised father.

"Got tied up in a big business deal," responded Sam, looking down at his feet. "Up by Brigham City. A big broom contract. Something to do with ZCMI, I think." He was pleased at how well his lie came out.

"Why did he send you?" asked Mr. Cannon.

"Didn't want Kathryn to miss the dance, I suppose." Sam was looking past Mr. Cannon now, into the house.

"Come in," said Cannon with obvious reluctance in his voice. He sensed that something was wrong, but he couldn't put his finger on it. He did notice that the young man was using Brutus's carriage and probably didn't have one of his own.

As they entered the parlor, Sam responded politely to the usual questions about his family, upbringing, and professional plans. Mr. Cannon showed open disappointment in the young man's lack of plans for a future career. Having just ended his job as a common laborer on the railroad, Sam was now a drifter with a little money in his pocket and no plans for the future. Maybe he'd get a job at the temple construction site, or maybe he'd just return to the family farm in American Fork. Cannon wasn't impressed with Storm, who was beginning to have second thoughts about his plans to take Kathryn Cannon to the Golden Spike Ball.

Sam sat in the parlor for what seemed an eternity listening to Willard Cannon's praise of Brutus Young—a young man who had a good business head, clearly defined career plans, and all the right social contacts. Yes, Brutus was going to be very successful and make Kathryn very happy.

When Kathryn entered the room, she was more beautiful than Sam had remembered her. Her black hair hung in loose curls about her tanned shoulders. Her fine olive skin contrasted perfectly with her white satin dress and yellow shawl. Her walnut eyes sparkled, and there was a light flush of surprise in her cheeks at discovering the young fighter, instead of Brutus, waiting to take her to the dance.

As Sam stood to greet Kathryn, he felt the adrenaline surging into his veins. He was pleased that she greeted him with a warm smile and remembered his name. Sam was suddenly very glad he had left Brutus behind at the broom maker's cabin. The tedious questions of Kathryn's father were no longer important or even distracting. Sam sensed the need to take control of the situation, to go on the offensive and get out of the house as quickly as possible. There were no odds in standing around answering a lot of questions that would force him to tell more lies.

"Brutus sends his deepest apologies," he began, taking Kathryn by the hand. "The biggest business deal of his blossoming career was hanging in the balance and he just couldn't get away, but knowing how much this ball means to you . . ." Sam continued talking in an effort to prevent anybody else from saying anything as he led Kathryn to the door, hoping to get her outside before her father fouled things up. Sam was pleased that Kathryn offered no resistance, nor did she attempt to say anything except a brief farewell to her father, saying she would see him later at the dance.

As they passed through the doorway, Sam nodded a polite good-bye to Mr. Cannon before pulling the door shut between them and escorting Kathryn quickly to the waiting carriage.

Chapter 7

"What really happened to Brutus?" asked Kathryn, after letting Sam help her into the carriage.

"Don't you believe he sent me to take you to the ball?" responded Sam, grinning. Lance was clucking the horses into a fast trot.

"No," answered Kathryn, thoughtfully. "Brutus wouldn't have missed this ball for anything."

"Are we talking about the same Brutus?" asked Sam. "He's all business. I'll bet the only thing he wanted for his sixteenth birthday was a bound set of ledgers."

The comment about the ledgers caught Kathryn by surprise. She laughed, then said, "You're right about Brutus having his mind on business much of the time. But that's exactly why he wouldn't miss the ball."

"How's that?" asked Sam.

"With this ZCMI thing coming together, the central purchasing and all, and so many General Authorities of the Church attending the ball tonight—he wouldn't miss making all those business contacts for anything."

"Then why did you come with me?" asked Sam. "If you don't believe Brutus sent me."

Kathryn thought a minute, then replied, "I don't know." She looked at Sam. "Tell me what happened to Brutus. This is his carriage. Where is he?"

Since Kathryn hadn't been fooled by his lie, Sam decided to try the truth. He explained how he and Lance had hijacked the carriage while Brutus was hiking up the canyon to see the old man about the brooms.

"But where is Brutus now? It's getting dark." There seemed to be genuine concern in Kathryn's voice.

"Bet he's limping down the road carrying an armload of brooms, with blisters all over his feet," responded Lance, unable to stay out of the conversation any longer. Sam and Lance started laughing over images of poor Brutus hobbling under a load of brooms, unwilling to risk losing his inventory by leaving it behind. Kathryn wasn't laughing.

"Take me home!" she barked as soon as the two young men ceased laughing. "At once!"

Lance made no effort to stop or turn the horses. Sam looked at Kathryn, unsure how he should handle her request. "But the dance—," he began.

"I have no intention of going with you," she replied sharply. "Not after what you did to Brutus. Take me home this instant . . . or I'll scream!"

Lance pulled the horses to a stop. He had no intention of having a kidnapping charge added to the crime of carriage theft. Sam didn't say or do anything for a minute, still trying to figure out how to handle the situation and convince Kathryn to go to the ball with him.

"Are you going to take me home, or am I going to walk?" asked Kathryn as she stood up to get out of the carriage.

"I'll take you home," said Sam, not wanting her to leave. He gently took hold of her hand to restrain her.

"But I'm not taking you home," said Lance, turning and handing the reins to Sam. He jumped to the ground and walked to the rear of the carriage to untie his saddle horse.

"I'm headin' to the dance, and if you two can work things out, I'll see you there," Lance shouted over his shoulder as he galloped off down the street.

Sam crawled into the front seat where he could better handle the horses. Kathryn remained in the rear seat.

"I'm not going anywhere unless you get up here with me," said Sam, his voice firm. Reluctantly she climbed into the front seat, seating herself at the very outside edge, as far from Sam as possible. He pulled the horses' heads to the left to head them back toward Kathryn's house, and clucked for them to get moving.

There was silence for a few minutes. Kathryn was the first to speak.

"I can't understand how you could do such a thing to Brutus," she offered, continuing to look straight ahead.

"I wanted to take you to the dance," responded Sam in his simple straightforward manner. More silence.

"Why?"

"I don't think I know you, or me, well enough to give a good answer to that question," replied Sam, thoughtfully. "I can only say that I wanted to take you to the ball bad enough that I was willing to leave a man stranded in the mountains and steal his carriage. First time I've ever done anything like that."

"I hope it's the last."

"If I promise never to do it again, will you change your mind about coming to the ball with me?"

The fact that Kathryn didn't answer immediately gave Sam hope that perhaps she was considering changing her mind. As he waited for her response he noticed the sound of approaching horses behind the carriage. He didn't look back, not wanting to distract Kathryn from the thought process that might lead her to changing her mind. The hoofbeats grew louder. Sam slowed the team a little so the riders would pass. Instead, they stayed even with the carriage after reaching the rear wheels.

"I want to go home," said Kathryn quietly enough so the riders could not hear.

Sam was about to protest when one of the approaching riders made a comment to one of his companions, loud enough for Sam and Kathryn to hear.

"Brutus Young's carriage all right. No doubt about it."

Sam and Kathryn looked at the three riders—overgrown stable boys, unshaven and soiled, mounted bareback on shaggy horses.

"Must be friends of Brutus," whispered Kathryn, "but I don't know any of them."

"Who's the plowboy driving it?" one of the stable boys asked his companions.

"Stranger to these parts, probably a rust eater from the railroad," responded one of the others.

"Those are Brutus's horses, too."

"And Brutus's girl."

"We'd like to be left alone, if you don't mind," said Sam.

"Isn't it interesting that they're headed away from the ball?" said one of the strangers, ignoring Sam's request.

"Probably headed up to the foothills to be all by theirselves, lookin' at the stars, and doing some other stuff."

Sam pulled the team to a stop.

"Look," he said, his voice firm. "If you guys are looking for trouble, you've come to the right place." Sam handed the reins to Kathryn and took his coat off. "Get off those horses," he continued. "I'll fight all of you. Right now. Here in the street. Let's get to it."

"But there are three of them," whispered Kathryn, trying to hand the reins back to Sam.

"And there's one of me," responded Sam. "I think that's more than enough." Sam started to get out of the carriage.

"You're a foolish boy," scolded Kathryn, "thinking you can solve every problem that comes along with your fists."

"Hold the preaching," answered Sam, suddenly halting his exit from the carriage with one foot on a wheel spoke and another on the floor of the carriage as a new idea came to mind.

"Look," he said to Kathryn. "I don't have anything better to do tonight, now that you're not going to the ball with me. Of course, if you change your mind, I certainly would avoid getting bruised and dirty. The decision is yours."

Kathryn looked up into Sam's eyes and smiled. At last she was giving in, thought Sam. He sat back down on the carriage seat.

"I hope they kill you," she said, still smiling. "I am not going to that dance with you."

Sam looked over at one of the strangers, who was thoroughly enjoying the conversation between him and Kathryn. "One at a time, or all at once?" asked Sam.

"Doesn't look to me like this feller needs two beatings in one evening," said the rider, and they all laughed, except Sam, who suspected they were merely trying to avoid a fight with a tiger. Kathryn handed the reins back to Sam, grateful that a fight had been avoided.

As the three riders moved ahead to take their mischief elsewhere, Sam's face was still flushed with anger—but he wasn't so upset that he didn't notice how two of the riders conveniently guided their mounts beside the heads of each of his buggy horses. As the riders simultaneously reached out to take hold of the bridles of the buggy horses, Sam knew instantly what they were up to. The trick was as old as horses and wagons. Sam had been on the guilty end of this prank a few times himself. The riders were about to slip the bridles from the heads of the buggy horses. If they succeeded, the result would be an uncontrollable runaway.

Sam knew exactly what to do and did not hesitate.

"Hang on!" he shouted to Kathryn as he slapped the reins down on the horses' rumps with all the force he could muster. A little unexpected movement on the part of the team would have prevented the riders from removing the bridles, but Sam had more than that in mind. There was a saddle horse directly ahead of each front wheel. If the team lunged ahead quickly enough, getting a front wheel between the hind legs of each of the saddle horses, their riders would be in big trouble as their horses fought to get free of the wheel. Sam had caught would-be bridle snatchers twice before in this manner, and both times their mounts had gone over on their backs. Sam had never caught two horses at one time before, but he figured the results would be the same. They were.

Both saddle horses ended up on their backs, their cursing riders rolling through the dirt. The buggy team broke into a dead run, and though Sam could probably have brought them under control, he didn't try. He had another trick or two up his sleeve.

While the driver of a lurching carriage has reins to help maintain balance, the passenger beside him has no such luxury and must grab on to whatever is handy to avoid being bounced out. Such was the case with Kathryn. As the buggy lurched forward, she had no choice, short of bailing out, but to slip her arm around Sam's and hang on tightly, just as he wanted her to do.

His first goal accomplished, with Kathryn close beside him and hanging on tightly, Sam focused on his second objective. Keeping the reins tight to give the appearance of trying to stop the team and avoiding other teams and riders on the streets at the same time, he managed two ninety-degree turns on two of the wider streets, getting the team headed back toward the center of town.

By the time the team was back to a walk, the carriage was in heavy traffic—other carriages carrying well-dressed passengers heading in the same direction.

"How about that?" said Sam, as Kathryn removed her arm from his and scooted back to the far side of the seat. "These crazy runaways brought us to the Social Hall. Might as well stay for the Golden Spike Ball."

Unnerved by the runaway, Kathryn offered no objection as Sam guided the team onto Social Hall Lane.

Chapter 8

The Social Hall was packed with bearded middle-aged men in black suits and women of all ages in long, flowing dresses. Long tables were stacked high with sliced turkey, beef, pickles, ham, rolls of all kinds, and wooden kegs of red and white wine from Santa Clara. Wine was not yet a prohibited drink in Mormon society, and the best wine from Santa Clara was used for the Sunday sacrament throughout the Mormon colonies.

Neither Sam nor Kathryn had ever attended an event with so many dignitaries. Virtually every Mormon Church leader not on a foreign mission was in attendance. The executives of the Central and Union Pacific Railroads nearly matched the Church leaders in numbers, though the railroad leaders had fewer female companions. Some of the Church leaders had five or six wives with them. It would be another ten years before polygamists would be forced into hiding.

Sam recognized some of the railroad dignitaries from the golden spike ceremony the day before. He also noticed a few of the General Authorities he had seen at Church conferences in Utah Valley. The vast majority of people, however, were complete strangers. But that didn't bother Sam. He hadn't come to the ball to socialize with friends. There was only one thing on his mind, and that was getting better acquainted with Kathryn Cannon.

The live band consisted of a dozen or so fiddlers and an equal number of brass instruments. The dance floor was crowded, mostly square dances and waltzes. But Sam wasn't in the mood for dancing, not yet. Sam knew that once Brutus reached town, there would be trouble, and it might be difficult to see Kathryn again, especially considering the preference her father had for Brutus.

"Why are you engaged to Brutus?" asked Sam as he and Kathryn moved in a line along one of the food tables making turkey sandwiches.

"That's a personal matter and none of your business," responded Kathryn. Though she had reversed her decision about coming to the dance with Sam, she wasn't about to spill her deepest personal feelings to someone who was all but a stranger to her.

"Do you love him?" persisted Sam, realizing he was risking upsetting her.

"Of course I do," responded Kathryn.

"How much?"

"About as much as I am coming to hate you," she snapped back.

"Do you think he loves you?" continued Sam.

"Yes, he does."

"More than his business?"

"Look, I don't have to stand here and be interrogated by you," responded Kathryn. "Brutus is a good man, a hard worker, an active member of the Church, and it appears he is going to be very successful in business. A lot of girls have an eye on Brutus Young."

"One more question," continued Sam, ignoring her response. "If Brutus had to choose between you and his business, if he could have only one, but not both, do you think he would pick you over his business?"

Kathryn set her plate on the table, obviously making an effort to stay calm without making a scene in front of so many prominent strangers.

"Good-bye, Mr. Storm. I am going to the other end of the hall to join my father. I hope you will have the good manners not to follow me."

Sam took advantage of her reluctance to draw attention. "And I'll punch the first man you dance with."

Kathryn looked up at Sam. She was fighting mad now. "You know I could have you thrown out."

"Not without a fight that would disrupt this whole event."

"Someday you will learn there are better ways to solve problems than with your fists. If I dance with you several times, will you then allow me to go to my parents?"

"As you wish," Sam replied. He took her by the hand and led her onto the dance floor, beginning to wonder why he had gone to so much trouble to spend an evening with Kathryn Cannon. But as he turned her to him, looking into her beautiful face, holding her right hand in his left and placing his right hand on her waist, he knew there was no place on earth he would rather be than with this Kathryn Cannon. He didn't understand his feelings. He only knew his entire outlook on life changed when he looked into this woman's eyes, touched her hand, smelled her perfume. Nothing else was important, only to be close to Kathryn Cannon.

So complete was Sam's concentration on the woman in front of him that at first he didn't notice the firm hand on his shoulder. Not until the hand jerked him around, forcing him to release his hold on Kathryn's waist.

One moment Sam was looking into the eyes of a beautiful woman, the next into the angry face of her furious fiancé, Brutus Young. Before Sam could say or do anything, two strong men grabbed him by the arms.

"This is the thief who stole my carriage," shouted Brutus, his voice shaking with anger.

"You loaned it to me, friend," responded Sam, trying to sound calm, yet earnest.

Brutus only became more angry. "Loan, hell. You stole it and I'll see you behind bars if it's the last thing I do." He was shouting.

Judging from the way the two men were holding him, Sam figured he could kick his way out, but with Kathryn at his side, he hesitated. He had already embarrassed her enough, and in a brawl she could possibly be harmed. He couldn't risk that. He decided to let the two men drag him away. But first he had a question for Brutus.

"How did you get here so fast?"

Brutus didn't have to answer the question, but he did so willingly. "An old family friend of yours from Missouri."

"What?" asked Sam.

"A feller named Dick Boggs. Brought me right to the Social Hall when I told him who stole my carriage."

Dick Boggs. The hair stood up on Sam's neck. He had never met his father's old enemy. But he knew enough about the old man to know his presence meant danger for the Storms. He would have to warn his father, right away.

It wasn't until the two men started dragging him toward the door that Sam spotted Lance Claw pushing through the crowd. Before Sam could say anything to explain his situation, Lance slugged the man holding onto Sam's right arm. It was a solid blow, directly on the jaw, and the man melted, relaxing his hold. The other man let go too, preparing to defend himself. But there were no additional blows forthcoming. Sam was trotting after Lance, who was headed for a side door. Before preventive measures could be attempted, the two young men slipped outside.

As they raced across the cobblestone courtyard where many of the nicer carriages were tethered, Sam noticed a broken-down cart with an old man on the seat. With a wooden leg, a shredded ear, and a black patch over one eye, there was no mistaking the identity of Dick Boggs. Sam slowed down for a better look, a first look at his father's old enemy.

"Come on, get the lead out," shouted Lance. The two young men disappeared into the night.

Chapter 9

The sun was already down when Sam appeared on Kathryn Cannon's doorstep the evening following the Golden Spike Ball. He still didn't know for sure if the authorities were looking for him in connection with the theft or borrowing of the carriage belonging to Brutus Young. Brutus had seemed angry enough to file charges, but Sam didn't know if the young businessman had followed through on his threat.

Sam had spent the day relaxing in a cottonwood grove beside City Creek, where he and Lance had set up a temporary camp, avoiding the busy streets where the law might be looking for them. Lance had left early that morning to visit friends and hadn't returned.

Sam had left the grove once during the day to locate a wagon headed for Utah Valley, one that could deliver a message to his father, a warning that Dick Boggs was in Salt Lake. In the note Sam wrote that he didn't know why Boggs had come to Salt Lake, how long he was going to stay, or where he was headed.

Sam thought a lot about Kathryn during the day—too much, he thought. She didn't like him and was engaged to another man. He kept telling himself that he would be better off forgetting her completely. There were lots of other women around. But memories of Kathryn would not leave him—her flowing black hair, her smooth olive skin, quick smile, the dark lively eyes, the perfume, the firmness and warmth of her hand in his. By the time evening arrived Sam was ready to throw caution to the wind and pay her one last visit, though he figured the chances were slim that he would be able to reach her. But he had to try.

Sam was still wondering how he would get inside if Kathryn's father greeted him at the door when fifteen-year-old Willard Jr. opened the door and invited him in.

Willard Jr. was pale and thin and walked with a trace of a limp. He had a handful of matches in one hand, having been making the rounds lighting the oil lamps for the evening.

Sam immediately felt sorry for the boy who, for health reasons, couldn't enjoy normal exercise, sunshine, and a boy's appetite.

"Are you the fellow who stole Brutus's carriage?" were the boy's first words. His voice was hesitant and breaking, still trying to make the transition from a boy's voice to a man's.

"I borrowed it and returned it without a scratch," smiled Sam, not feeling threatened by the boy's accusation.

"My pa doesn't like you."

"I can understand that," responded Sam, the smile gone. "That's why it might be best if he doesn't know I'm here. Why don't you go get your sister and tell her I would like to talk to her for a minute?"

The boy looked into Sam's face, wondering whether or not to trust this stranger. Sam smiled again, giving the boy time to make up his mind.

Before the boy had reached a decision, however, the silence was shattered by the booming voice of Willard Sr. as he stepped into the doorway leading from the dining room.

"Who invited you into this house?"

"I thought—" began Willard Jr. in a timid voice, but his father didn't wait for him to finish.

"After all the trouble you caused yesterday and last night, I'm surprised you have the nerve to come to this house! It amazes me you're not in jail. You should be, you know. I have a mind to call the sheriff—"

"Sir," began Sam, trying to sound polite. "It appears I'm going to be leaving town—"

"Good!" bellowed the old man.

"And I would like to see your daughter for a few minutes before I leave. To say good-bye."

"And what gives you the right to see my daughter?" demanded Willard Sr.

"The right?" questioned Sam.

"You're a common laborer on the railroad. A carriage thief. Do you have a profession? A trade? Do you own property? A home?"

"You sound like a merchant trying to sell a daughter like a piece of meat to the highest bidder!" exploded Sam, regretting his outburst before it was finished.

"Get out of this house, this minute!" ordered the old man.

Sam didn't move, then continued in a determined voice. "I came to see your daughter. Please tell her I would like to speak to her."

The silence was heavy, neither man willing to back down to the other. Sam ached to slug the old man, but he was not a bully. Willard Sr. was fat and soft from comfortable, sedentary living. An old man, no match for young Storm. There would be no pushing, shoving, or slugging. Still, Sam did not respond to the old man's order to leave.

"Willard," said the old man to the boy, keeping his eyes on Sam. "Get the sheriff."

The boy looked at his father, then at Sam, and began to back out of the room.

"That won't be necessary," said Sam, looking at his feet. "I won't make any more trouble." He turned and took a step toward the door, beginning to believe he had been whipped and would not see Kathryn after all.

But as Sam's eye caught sight of the newly lit lamp on a little table by the door, an idea came into his mind. For a young man accustomed to solving confrontations with his fists, Sam became intrigued with the possibility of winning this confrontation without his fists. He wasn't sure what stimulated the idea, possibly the understanding that he was hard and strong and his opponent soft and pampered. Maybe there was a way to win without brute force. He would try. For a young man accustomed to hard work on the railroad and frequent fist fights, pain was not a major concern.

Sam stopped beside the table and removed the glass cover from the oil lamp. He turned to face the old man, at the same time placing the palm of his hand immediately over the exposed lamp flame.

"What are you doing?" demanded Willard Sr.

Sam looked calmly into the old man's eyes, waiting a few long seconds before responding. The boy's eyes were wide like saucers, his mouth open.

"I will hold my hand in this flame," began Sam, "as long as you will let me talk with your daughter."

"You're crazy!"

"I will hold it in the flame a full minute, if you will give me that much time with Kathryn."

"Stop it!"

Sam didn't move. He was surprised that his hand was so steady as the flesh began to hiss and the smell of burning hair and skin began to fill the room.

"I want to see your daughter, Mr. Cannon. Just for a few minutes. To say good-bye." The silence that followed was disturbed only by the sound of sizzling flesh.

Mr. Cannon was the first to speak, but with difficulty. He was clearly shaken by what was happening in his parlor. "Okay, but only a minute. I'll fetch her."

Sam removed his hand from the flame and replaced the glass cover. The old man left the room.

"Will you get me a cloth with some cold water on it?" Sam asked the boy.

Willard Jr. disappeared into the kitchen and returned a moment later with a wet dishtowel. As Sam was wrapping it around his hand, Kathryn appeared in the doorway from the dining room.

It was apparent from her bright, breezy entry that her father had not told her about Sam putting his hand in the flame. Sam almost forgot about it himself, so taken back was he by her appearance.

Kathryn was wearing a white doeskin dress, an Indian dress, beautifully decorated with blue and white beads and porcupine quills. The soft, pliable deer skins draped comfortably over her young body made her look more of a woman than Sam remembered her looking in civilized dresses. Her long black hair and olive skin looked richer against the soft leather. The blue and white beads seemed to enhance the sparkle in her dark eyes.

"Do you like it?" Kathryn asked with a smile.

Sam nodded.

She stopped showing off her dress, her expression becoming serious, sensing that something was amiss in the parlor.

"What's that burning smell? What happened to your hand?"

"You should have seen it!" exclaimed Willard Jr., who was still in the room. "He just shoved his—"

"Just burned my hand," interrupted Sam, cutting the boy short. "A little accident with the lamp. Nothing serious."

Kathryn seemed to accept the explanation. Not wanting to talk about his hand, Sam turned the discussion back to the dress.

"The dress is beautiful," he said. He wanted to add, "And so are you," but he couldn't quite get the words out. Instead he asked, "Is it Blackfoot?"

"I don't know."

"Blackfoot squaws decorate mostly with blue and white beads."

"How did you know that?" she asked.

"My father knows a lot about Indians. Lived with the Utes for a while when he was my age, before the pioneers came to the Valley."

"Your father must be an interesting man."

"Where did you get the dress?" asked Sam, changing the subject. Time was too valuable to be spent on family history.

"Brutus gave it to me. After the dance last night."

Sam was sorry he had asked the question.

"And he gave me a pair of real Indian moccasins," added Willard Jr., who apparently had no intention of leaving the room.

"It was thoughtful of you to drop in to say good-bye," said Kathryn. "I'm surprised my father allowed me to see you."

"I'll always remember last night," she continued, a gleam in her eye in anticipation of having some fun with Sam. "Especially throwing those two rowdies from their horses, and the runaway. It was so exciting. Someday I'll love telling my children about the reckless young adventurer from the railroad who tried to steal me away from their father."

Sam didn't like her any less for the cruel statement. At least he thought it was cruel. But it did stir his fighting spirit.

"I think those kids would get a lot more enjoyment," began Sam, smiling again, "hearing how their adventuresome father rescued their mother just in time from an unhappy marriage with a boring dry goods broker."

Kathryn was searching for an appropriate comeback when the conversation was interrupted by a knock on the front door.

Willard Jr. rushed to the door and welcomed Brutus Young into the parlor. Under the young businessman's arm was an oversized art board covered with a paper overlay.

Sam looked down at his bandaged hand, wondering what else was going to go wrong.

Kathryn was the first to speak to Brutus.

"Sam stopped by to say good-bye. He's leaving town."

Brutus marched right up to Sam and grabbed his good hand.

"Glad to catch you, old boy," he said in a loud but sincere voice. "Wanted to let you know there's no hard feelings about yesterday. Didn't press charges. Like to forget the whole thing."

"You're awful quick to forgive a fellow who hijacked your carriage and tried to steal your fiancée," responded Sam.

"If it hadn't been for you I wouldn't have run into Boggs. You know, your pa's old enemy from Missouri. I was hustling down the trail with an armload of brooms when he picked me up. Coming down from the Montana gold field, he was . . ."

For the first time, Brutus noticed that Kathryn was wearing the white doeskin dress. He looked at her.

"Do you like it?" he asked. She nodded, appreciating the fact that her fiancé was finally giving her some attention. But it didn't last long. Brutus looked over at Willard Jr. and asked if the moccasins fit.

"Just right," answered Willard Jr., quickly explaining why he wasn't wearing them. "Got them wet this afternoon. They're hanging up to dry."

"Boggs had a whole wagonload of Indian truck," Brutus said to Sam, "the kind of stuff I told you and your half-breed friend I wanted to buy—dresses, shirts, moccasins, bows, arrows, buffalo robes, leggings. Even some scalps, cradle boards, and teepee covers. Boggs was bringing it down to sell, and I bought it all, the whole wagonload. With the railroad finished, the new tourists will pay almost anything for authentic Indian truck."

Sam didn't hear the last sentence. Something was wrong with the mix of Indian trade items in the wagon. While Indians sometimes traded teepee covers among themselves, he had never heard of an Indian selling a teepee cover to a white man. He didn't know why.

"Sold half the stuff today," continued Brutus enthusiastically, "at a profit you wouldn't believe, and Boggs is already on his way back for another load. Says there's plenty more up north."

"I love the dress," said Kathryn, hoping to get Brutus away from business matters.

"I have something else for you," said Brutus with a big smile, handing her the art board he had been holding under his arm. Carefully, she removed the paper cover, exposing a beautiful color rendering of a three-story brick home, complete with gables, shutters, pillars, and all the other extras popular on luxurious homes in the 1860s.

"I don't recognize it," said Kathryn.

"That's because it isn't built yet," announced Brutus proudly. "Construction starts next week. When we are married in the fall, it will be yours."

Kathryn threw her arms around the grinning Brutus.

"Been thinking about it a long time," added the happy businessman. "But didn't decide on it for sure until today. I was scared of the debt, but with this new source of Indian trinkets, the broom contract, the ZCMI consolidation, I just decided to go for it."

Kathryn tightened her hold on her fiancé. "Oh, Brutus. You're so kind, so thoughtful, so generous . . ."

Sam slipped out the front door without saying good-bye. The pain in his hand didn't hurt so much as the feeling of loss over a woman who had never been his in the first place. As he searched for answers, the words her father had spoken earlier in the evening echoed as painful memories in his mind. "You're a common laborer on the railroad . . . Do you have a profession? A trade? Do you own property? A home?"

He couldn't forget the teepee covers, either. Something wasn't right.

Chapter 10

Lance and Sam were seated on the ground, their backs against the trunk of a big cottonwood tree beside City Creek. Together they were browsing through the latest copy of the *Deseret News,* the official Mormon newspaper in Salt Lake City.

"Gotta make a lot of money, fast," said Sam as he stared at the paper.

"You and everybody else," replied Lance.

"You should have seen her melt in his arms when he showed her a drawing of the house he was going to build for her."

"She's no fool," said Lance. "Molly tells her girls they can marry more money in five minutes than they can earn in a lifetime."

"Who's Molly?"

"Good friend, a smart lady. I'll take you to meet her sometime. She has a good head for money."

"That's what I need, lots of money," said Sam. "I'll bet Brutus's house will cost ten thousand dollars!"

"That's a big house," said Lance. "Bet old Brutus plans on havin' lots of kids."

Sam knew he was being teased but didn't take the bait.

"I'm going to build a bigger house, one that'll cost about twenty thousand dollars."

"You'll have to go to bank or train robbing to get that kind of money," said Lance in jest, but when he saw the look of serious contemplation on Sam's face, the half-breed quickly splashed cold water on the idea.

"Even if you were successful at it, you wouldn't be able to stop anywhere long enough to build a house, not with Porter Rockwell on your tail," Lance continued.

Porter Rockwell always got his man. If there was a single reason for the relatively low crime rate in Utah Territory, the credit went to Porter Rockwell, a legend in his own time. Nobody knew the exact number of men he had killed, except maybe Port himself, and he wasn't telling. But those in the know figured that close to 150 men had departed to the next life with the aid of Port's bullets.

"Maybe you could get the banks to just give you the money," suggested Lance, smiling.

"What do you mean?" asked Sam, a questioning look on his face.

"You might try walking into a bank and telling the president that you are going to hold your hand over his lamp flame until he gives you his money."

Sam ignored Lance's attempt at humor. He didn't see anything funny about the painfully scorched flesh on the palm of his hand. Seeing Sam wasn't in any mood to be teased about his hand, Lance quickly changed the subject.

"They're hiring at the Provo woolen mills," said the Indian. "Paying $1.50 a day. Take thirty years to earn your twenty thousand dollars, if you live at home and don't spend any along the way.

"You might want to consider the silk business," continued Lance. "Brigham Young himself shipped in one hundred thousand mulberry trees. If old Brig is going to raise silkworms, there's got to be a lot of money in it."

"But I can't wait five or ten years to find out," responded Sam.

Suddenly Sam pulled the paper away from Lance.

"Here," he said, looking at a small advertisement. " 'The Royal Canadian Mounted Police want to buy good, well-broke gelding saddle horses over fourteen hands tall. Will pay eighty to one hundred dollars a head, delivered to Fort Macleod, Alberta Territory, by August 30 this year.' "

Lance whistled. "You can buy half the horses in this valley for less than fifty dollars a head. Some for fifteen or twenty dollars."

"Suppose a guy could get two hundred horses through," speculated Sam. "If he cleared seventy-five dollars a head, he could make fifteen thousand dollars!"

"If he didn't lose the horses to the Blackfeet, along with his scalp," cautioned Lance.

"They wouldn't be paying that much money if there wasn't some risk involved. I'd take my chances with the Blackfeet for fifteen thousand dollars."

"Where will you get the twenty-five dollars a head to buy two hundred horses?" asked Lance. "That's five thousand dollars, plus food, wranglers—a whole outfit."

Sam reached into his pocket and pulled out a handful of bills and coins. Carefully he counted his money. He looked at Lance and smiled.

"I've got $87.60, hardly enough to outfit a single rider. Maybe it can't be done."

The two young men were quiet for a few minutes, both intrigued with the possibility of driving a herd of horses to Canada. Sam was counting dollars. Lance was taken up with the excitement of a new adventure. Lance was the first to break the silence.

"I know where you can buy horses for less than a dollar each."

"Three-legged bone bags, I'll bet . . ."

"No. Good horses, but there's a trick to it. I'll bet Molly would finance our outfit, too."

"Wait a minute," said Sam. "One thing at a time. Where do you get horses for a dollar?"

"How much do you know about Injuns and firewater?"

"That it's against the law to sell it to them."

"Did you know that most bucks, after they've had a swallow or two, will trade a horse for a quart bottle of firewater?"

"But it's against the law, like robbing banks."

"Not exactly. It's against the law for a white man to sell spirits to Injuns. But I don't know of any law against an Injun selling it to his own people. I'm an Injun. I'll do the selling."

Sam put the paper down. Lance was serious. This horse idea might have some merit after all.

"What exactly is firewater, anyway?" asked Sam. "I mean, how do you make it?"

Using the palms of his hands, Lance smoothed out a patch of dirt to use as a figuring board. Then he picked up a sharp stick to write with.

"Let's see," he said. "You can buy Valley Tan, the straight stuff, for five dollars a gallon here in Salt Lake." He scratched the figure $5 in the dirt. "Too powerful for Injuns, so you water it down four to one."

"That gets the cost down to $1.25 a gallon," figured Sam. Lance scratched the figure $1.25 in the dirt.

"Or about thirty-one cents a quart!" added Sam. "And you say you can trade one quart for one horse?"

"There are some other expenses," continued Lance. "Injuns like to taste their firewater. You got to add some chili powder and brown sugar."

"That couldn't add more than a few cents a bottle, bring the cost to maybe thirty-five cents a quart."

"The bottles cost a nickel each."

"That brings it to forty cents a quart."

"Then you got to figure on giving some of it away."

"What do you mean?"

"You don't know nuthin' about Injuns. You just can't ride into a village and offer the chief a bottle of firewater for his prize buffalo horse."

"How do you do it then?" asked Sam.

"You ride in like you was just passing through, but you give them a few bottles to pass around because you like them and they let you camp with them. Soon as they get loosened up a little they start asking for more. You tell them you can't do it. They keep asking. Finally you say you need some more horses and the trading starts. You might have to give two or three bottles for the first horse, but it goes down from there. The more drink they get in 'em, the easier it is to trade. Then you git out as soon as the trading's done, even if it's in the middle of the night. Got to git as far away as you can before they sober up."

"I wonder if that's how Dick Boggs got all that Indian stuff?" said Sam.

"Could be. Maybe we'll run into him."

"What about the teepees?" continued Sam.

"What teepees?"

"Boggs sold Brutus a bunch of teepees, along with the other stuff. Something's not right about that, but I don't know what."

"I'll tell you what's not right," said Lance. "Injuns don't trade their teepees to white men. It takes fourteen or fifteen buffalo hides to make a teepee, and two or three weeks of sewing, plus all the scraping to get the hair off. I've never seen a white man yet who understood the value of a teepee and would pay a fair price. Squaws won't let their men trade off the teepees, not even for firewater, and I never seen a man want to, anyway. Winters get mighty cold in the mountains."

"Then where'd Boggs get the teepee covers?"

"Not by trading firewater. Maybe he stole them."

"Sounds like trading firewater is the same as stealing," said Sam, not wanting to throw cold water on what appeared to be a brilliant money-making endeavor, but finding his conscience nagging him.

"Might seem like stealing, but when you're sitting around the fire with the Injuns just beggin' you to trade, you feel like you're doing them a big favor."

"How do you know all this?" asked Sam, looking directly at Lance.

"You know I was raised with the Gosiutes. They were always trading horses for firewater, faster than my pa Ike could steal 'em back. When I go home, I always take a few bottles with me to trade for horses. That's how I keep my pockets full when I'm not working."

"Doesn't it bother you? Don't you feel like you're taking advantage of your people?"

"No. A man's lucky to keep a horse a year anyway, there's so much horse stealing going on. The Blackfeet steal from the Shoshones. The Shoshones steal from the Gosiutes. The Gosiutes steal from the Comanches. The Comanches steal from the Apaches. And there are lots of exceptions. Everybody steals horses from everybody else. I figure a buck is better off getting a bottle of firewater out of a horse than just having it stolen and getting nothing. I don't worry about it, and if you want that new house you shouldn't either."

"What do you figure it would cost to get this thing going?"

"I figure we need about one hundred dollars for the firewater, somewhere between two hundred and two hundred fifty bottles. Another two hundred dollars will get us supplies and three packhorses, two for the firewater and one for supplies. Another hundred dollars will probably cover any wranglers we need to hire later on once the herd becomes too big for the two of us to handle."

"I didn't know you knew so much about finance," commented Sam.

"A half-breed has to look out for himself. Nobody else will."

"Now, who's this Molly you think will finance our trip?"

"Her name's Molly Skinner. Kind of famous in these parts. Some mountains named after her. One in Skull Valley, another near the Spanish Fork River. But I won't take you to meet her unless you promise never to tell your pa."

"Why's that?" asked Sam.

"Your pa wouldn't like it. She runs what he would call a house of ill repute."

"She's a friend of yours?"

"Sure. We got a lot in common. People don't like us. Me, because I'm a half-breed. Her, because of what she does. Anyway, she's helped me out with money a few times in a pinch. And I've always paid her back with interest. She's my friend."

Sam stood up and brushed off his trousers.

"Let's saddle up and visit Molly Skinner. If she agrees to back us, we should be on the trail in two or three days."

Chapter 11

The thing that surprised Sam most about Molly Skinner's place were the shelves of law books along one of the walls—not just a few books, but dozens of big, thick volumes bound in green, brown, and black leather. They made up as impressive a collection as one would expect to find in any law office. But this was not a law office, and had it not been early afternoon with the sun shining brightly outside, Sam probably would not have entered Molly's place.

He wasn't afraid, not Sam. It was a matter of conscience, his childhood training among the Mormons. He had been taught that places like Molly's were evil and to be avoided. And though he was an adult now, twenty years old, he knew his parents, Dan and Caroline, would be hurt if they knew he was in such a place. He had not come for the regular services, however, but to secure a business loan. Besides, no one in his family or church would ever know he had been here.

Even more surprising to Sam than the law books was Molly's appearance. She didn't look cheap and gaudy like the tent-dwelling women who followed the railroad camps. There was a clean, well-scrubbed look about her. Her greeting was warm and disarming, her handshake firm and businesslike.

Molly was perhaps forty years old. Except for her lower-than-normal neckline and a little extra makeup, she could have passed for the well-dressed first wife of a prominent citizen. Sam was impressed, but wary.

"I'm curious about the law books," he said as Molly motioned for him and Lance to be seated on a red velvet sofa.

"Lot of people would like to shut me down, especially your President Young. A woman in my business has to know her rights and be able to lay it out, chapter and verse, before the judges."

"Wouldn't it be easier to just hire a lawyer?" asked Sam.

"If I hired a lawyer every time one of my girls found herself behind bars, I'd soon be broke. A lot cheaper, and quicker, just to handle the legal matters myself."

"Do you have a degree? Are you licensed?"

"Completed a correspondence course, but can't take the bar."

"Why not?" asked Sam.

Molly looked into Sam's eyes, wondering if the young man was really so naive, or if he was playing games with her. She thought of responding with something sarcastic, like how she had banged her head on a rock when thrown from a horse. She concluded, however, that he was probably sincere in asking his question, and decided to give him a straight answer.

"There are a lot of men in this territory who don't think women should be allowed to practice law, especially women in my profession." She smiled. "But you just wait and see. I'll make it." Then, changing the subject, she asked, "Would the two of you like something refreshing to drink?"

"Sure," said Lance brightly.

Molly rang a little bell, and a moment later a young red-haired woman in a purple silk dress glided into the room carrying a tray with a crystal pitcher and three glasses. Molly introduced the young woman as Betty, and Sam blushed when Betty winked at him. Much to his relief, she left the room after pouring the drinks.

Sam looked curiously at his drink. It didn't look good at all, like someone had mixed half a cup of shredded raw onions in a glass of water. But suspecting his eyes were probably deceiving him, he raised the glass to his lips for a sip. To his surprise, the drink was both tart and sweet at the same time, with more flavor than a cherry pie.

"What is this?" asked Sam, removing the drink from his lips.

"Do you like it?"

"Delicious!"

"Fresh lemonade. The first train from Sacramento brought in a load of lemons. I suppose you'll see a lot of lemonade, and orange juice, in Salt Lake now that the trains are running."

Sam had had an orange once, a Christmas gift, but the taste of lemon was new. He didn't say anything else until he had finished off his second glass. By that time, Lance had started explaining the purpose of their visit.

Molly listened patiently until Lance finished explaining how he and Sam intended to trade firewater for horses, then sell the animals to the Royal Canadian Mounted Police.

"Why don't you just sneak into their camps at night and steal the horses?" she asked when Lance was finished.

"Too dangerous," said the half-breed without hesitating. "Want to hang onto my scalp. An Indian that's traded you a horse for a bottle of firewater probably won't come after you." It was obvious the half-breed was only concerned with the practical side of the endeavor. If he had a conscience, it wasn't showing.

"And what do you think of all this?" Molly asked, looking at Sam. "A good Mormon boy like you should have some concerns about breaking the laws against selling firewater to the Indians. Don't you even feel a little bit uncomfortable taking advantage of those poor heathens?"

Rather than answer her question, Sam took the offensive. He was upset by her question, angry. Maybe his conscience was bothering him more than he would like to admit.

"You're a fine one to be giving lectures on what is right and wrong. You sound more like a preacher than a . . ."

"I'd like you to know I run a legitimate business," responded Molly, angry too. "I provide a generous amount of service for a fair price. Nobody leaves here feeling cheated. And I pay my bills, on time. People may disagree morally with what I do, but everybody agrees that I run my business in an honest, responsible way—and that is more than I can say about this scheme of yours to separate the Indians from their horses."

"Look," said Lance, attempting to make peace. "Molly, you've made it clear you don't like what we're about to do." She nodded.

"And Sam," Lance continued, "it appears you don't have a very high opinion of what my good friend Molly does for a living." Sam nodded.

"We could probably argue all day and never come to an agreement on who's right and who's wrong, if there is a right and a wrong to these questions. I don't see any sense in arguing problems that can't be solved, not today anyway."

"As I see it," Lance continued with more deliberation, "the most important question is the one Molly must answer." He turned to Molly, then asked, "Do you know what that question is?"

"What?" she asked.

"Will you loan us the three hundred dollars to finance this undertaking?"

Molly smiled. "Lance, I really don't know if there is any hope for you, as a person, as a member of the human race."

"Will you?" persisted the half-breed.

"My mind says no, but my heart says yes."

"Then you'll do it?" said Lance enthusiastically.

Molly left the room for a minute and returned with 15 twenty-dollar gold pieces in her palm.

As she handed them to Lance, Sam asked, "What kind of return do you want?"

"Return?" she paused. "I don't want any return."

"You're getting old," laughed Lance. "How does one hundred percent sound?"

"It doesn't matter," she said, a sad look coming over her face.

"Why?" asked Sam.

First she looked at Lance, then at Sam. "I already told you this loan comes from the heart. And my heart tells me something else."

"What's that?" laughed Lance, not seeming to notice Molly's soberness.

She looked into the half-breed's cheerful face. "It's hard to be concerned with interest rates when I don't think I'll ever see you again."

"Don't be silly," said Lance. "We'll be back in three months with 100 percent return for you." Molly didn't respond, except by asking the two young men if they would like some more lemonade.

"Wait a minute," said Sam, as he held his glass out for a refill. "If you don't think Lance is coming back, how come you're loaning him the money?"

Molly looked at Sam a long time, as if deliberating how much to tell him. Her voice was cold when she finally spoke.

"You want to know why I would loan money to a man I never expect to see again?"

"Yes."

"Anyone doing what you two are doing to the Indians couldn't understand, even if I told you. Would you like to leave now?"

The two young men stood up. Sam finished off the last of the lemonade in his glass as Lance slipped the gold coins into his right front pocket.

"See you in about ninety days," said Lance cheerfully. He gave Molly a brief and enthusiastic hug before following Sam through the doorway into the sunny street. Molly didn't respond as she closed the door.

Chapter 12

"That's Boggs, all right," said Sam, his voice quiet and low so the sound wouldn't carry beyond Lance's ear. With a wooden leg and a patch over one eye, Dick Boggs was a man easily recognized at a distance. The two young men were lying on the ground beneath the thick, green branches of a cedar tree on the crest of a brushy hill. Their saddles and packhorses were tethered about a half mile back, well out of sight in a deep gully.

Before them on a grassy plain of the Snake River Valley were twenty-six Shoshone lodges and Boggs's wagon, surrounded by hundreds of grazing horses. Beyond the horses the mighty Snake River, still brown with runoff from the Yellowstone country, wound lazily through the lush meadows. It was late afternoon with the sun shining brightly through the deep blue of the spring sky.

"Wish I knew what he was doing there," said Lance. "Doesn't seem to be trading. He's taken some bundles out of the wagon, but hasn't put nothin' back in."

"I still think we ought to wait until he leaves before we go in," said Sam.

"He doesn't look to be in any big hurry to leave."

"I'd wait a week before I'd enter the same Indian camp as Boggs," said Sam. "The man's a snake and reeks of death and danger, even this far away."

"First time I ever heard you sound scared," said Lance, looking away from the distant teepees and into his friend's face.

Sam didn't look away from the teepees. "Just cautious," he said, feeling a little embarrassed that his half-breed friend had detected the fear. He bit his lower lip, determined not to let his worry show again.

"Do you want me to shoot him?"

"What?" asked Sam, turning to look at his friend.

"After he leaves the Shoshones. When he's sitting beside his fire at night. I'll just walk up in the dark and put a bullet in him. He'll never know what hit him."

"You would do that?" asked Sam.

"You said he was a snake. You're afraid of him. He can't be trusted. What good is he alive?"

"But you don't just go out and shoot a man because he's poison."

"Why not? This ain't the city anymore. No law out here 'cept what a man can hold in his hand." Lance drew a black revolver from its holster. "In this country a man like Boggs can cause a lot of grief—until someone puts him in the ground." Lance checked the cylinder to make sure it was full.

Sam stared at his friend. They had known each other a long time and had fought side by side in numerous railroad camps. Both were heavily armed for the dangerous trip to Canada. But the subject of killing had never been discussed before. Sam was stunned by Lance's matter-of-fact willingness to gun down Boggs. Maybe he didn't know Lance as well as he thought he did. For the first time he realized that the trip to Canada might really involve killing. He wondered why he hadn't thought of that before. But it was too late to turn back now. He would do everything he could to prevent any killing.

"Let him go," said Sam. "We'll both shoot Boggs when he gives us good reason to, but not before. All right?"

"The only problem I see with that," responded Lance, thoughtfully, "is by the time a man like Boggs gives you a good reason to kill him, sometimes it's too late to do it."

"I guess we'll just have to take that chance," said Sam.

Lance shrugged his shoulders and looked back toward the teepees, unable to understand what he thought was the mushy thinking of his white companion.

Chapter 13

As Dick Boggs drove his wagon out of the Shoshone camp early the next morning, heading west, Sam wondered about Lance's proposition to kill the old man. Lance had made it sound so easy, so matter-of-fact, like chopping down a tree. Boggs certainly had it coming with all the trouble he had caused the Mormons back in Missouri, and whatever he was up to now in trading Indian souvenirs to Brutus Young, something wasn't right. Still, to just gun Boggs down like a pesky skunk didn't sit easy with Sam.

Boggs was not yet out of sight when Sam and Lance returned to their tethered horses to saddle up.

"Remember, we're not sneaking drink givers," said Lance, as he and Sam rode toward the Shoshone village.

"What?" asked Sam, not understanding.

"Sneaking drink givers. That's what Injuns call white men who sell them firewater."

"Name seems to fit us pretty good."

"Could get us killed, too."

"How's that?"

"If they decide to scalp us and take our firewater, they won't have soldier boys coming after them. Sneaking drink givers are outside the protection of white law, and the Injuns know it."

"Then what . . ." Sam started to ask.

"Besides, some of the old chiefs are beginning to see what the firewater is doing to their people. They don't take kindly to sneaking drink givers. Wouldn't want one of the old men telling the young bucks to lift our topknots."

"Topknots?" asked Sam.

"Scalps, hair on our heads."

"Then how do we trade them whiskey without them knowing we're whiskey traders?" asked Sam, sarcasm in his voice. He was irritated that this business about how the Indians felt about whiskey traders hadn't been explained to him earlier—instead of the moment they were riding into a large Shoshone village with three packhorses loaded down with firewater.

"Just keep your mouth shut, like a wide-eyed bacon eater, and I'll take care of everything," suggested Lance with a smile, thoroughly enjoying his companion's uncertainty.

"And what's a bacon eater?"

Lance smiled. "A greenhorn."

Sam remembered when the tables were turned back in the railroad camps. Lance, the half-breed off the prairie, was like a frightened animal, unsure of himself in a white man's world, counting on his friend Sam to help him in situations he didn't understand. Now Sam was the one who didn't understand. Lance was enjoying the turnabout.

The teepees formed a loose *V* on the grassy plain. Lance led the way, his horse holding its head high, its ears forward as it entered the open end of the *V*. Sam followed, leading the packhorses.

Lance held his right hand high, the fist closed except for the first two forefingers, which were extended and touching, the sign of friendship among the tribes of the plains.

Children of all ages and sizes scampered from teepees and the open prairie to greet the visitors, quickly forming a noisy procession behind the packhorses. The older children wore leather breechcloths or dresses. The smaller children were naked. The women remained crouched in the doorways to their teepees or stood just outside their teepees, watching the approaching men. The Shoshone men walked toward the apex of the *V*, the same place where Lance and Sam were headed, apparently the dwelling place of the chief or head man.

The chief, a big heavy man, emerged from his teepee just as Lance pulled his horse to a stop. The chief was not distinguishable by any special headdress or clothing but by his authoritative manner. He was the first and only man to approach Lance and Sam. Lance's arm was still held to the square, the two fingers extended to signify friendship.

Lance continued to hold his hand in the air as the chief looked him over. No words were spoken.

After what seemed a long time to Sam, the chief slowly extended his left hand, palm up. He placed his right fist over the extended palm.

Lance's previously stern face broke into a friendly smile at the chief's test of friendship. Sam didn't know what was going on. The closed fist on the open palm was the sign for tobacco.

Lance reached back into his saddle bag and tossed a black plug of chewing tobacco to the now smiling chief.

After securing the twist in his belt, the chief slapped one palm forward against the other in the direction of the lone mountain to the north, asking the travelers if they were heading north.

Lance pointed his forefinger straight up then toward the distant mountain, answering yes to the chief's question. Then Lance made a curling downward motion with his fingers in front of his mouth, telling the chief he was hungry, obviously fishing for an invitation to stop and eat.

The chief made the same curling motion with his fingers in front of his mouth, then held both fists on top of his head, forefingers curling upward and inward to indicate he had buffalo meat for his visitors.

While dismounting, Lance tossed some blue and red beads to the children and women. Sam dismounted too, paying careful attention to the sign language as Lance explained to the chief that he and his companion were headed to the Montana gold fields with a load of supplies for the miners—that they didn't have anything of real value to trade to their red friends.

Sam was trying so hard to follow the sign language that he didn't notice the little boy pulling on his shirt.

"The kid wants to give you something," said Lance.

Sam looked down at the naked little boy who had a toy bow in one hand and a two-foot length of buffalo intestine in the other. The intestine was dirty, except for the end the boy had been chewing on. The boy held the intestine out to Sam.

"Heard me tell the chief we were hungry," said Lance quickly. "Wants to share his breakfast with you. Better take a bite or two before they think I was lying about us being hungry."

"You're the one that said we were hungry," responded Sam.

"Maybe the story would be more believable if *you* helped the kid with his breakfast."

"Take a bite, fast," hissed Lance.

Sam figured he had no choice in the matter. He was not really sure if the situation was serious or if his friend was just playing a trick on him. He assured himself that he would not forget the incident so that at a later, safer time he could get revenge. Sam reached out and accepted the dirty intestine from the boy. Holding his breath to avoid any possible smell the thing might have, Sam enthusiastically bit off a big chunk from the clean end and gulped it down. With a smile of gratitude he handed the remainder back to the boy, who with a squeal of delight ran back to his teepee to spread the news of sharing his breakfast with the white man.

Lance and Sam followed the chief and two of his companions into the chief's teepee. While the red men began gnawing on the twist of tobacco, Lance and Sam helped themselves to a rack of buffalo ribs that had been simmering near the fire. Slicing between the two end ribs with his knife, Lance removed an entire rib, almost three feet long, and handed it to Sam. Then he cut another for himself.

By the time Lance and Sam had cleaned off their first rib, the plug of tobacco was completely consumed and the chief was packing his pipe for an after-breakfast smoke.

During breakfast Sam and Lance learned the chief was called Curly Bear. The stone bowl of his pipe was shaped in the form of a bear's head, and triangle designs were carved the length of the long wooden stem.

While the men were passing the pipe around, Lance excused himself for a moment to get something from his packhorse. He returned a moment later with a quart bottle of firewater. The Indians beamed, except the chief.

Using sign language, Lance went to great length to explain that the firewater was for the miners in Virginia City, but since the Shoshones were friends with the miners, he was sure the white gold hunters wouldn't mind sharing with their red brothers. Lance held the bottle out to the chief while the other Indians looked covetously at its tan contents.

Curly Bear hesitated. Lance suggested that the white men in Virginia City might be offended if the great Shoshone chief refused their little gift. One little bottle of firewater never caused any trouble.

Seemingly persuaded by Lance's arguments, Curly Bear finally accepted the bottle, quickly removed the cork with his teeth, and commenced to guzzle. Nearly a third of the bottle was gone before he removed it from his mouth and handed it to the next Indian, who didn't swallow quite as much to make sure every other man in the teepee received his fair amount.

No sooner had the last drop disappeared than the Indians, including Curly Bear, began to ask for more. Very emphatically, Lance swept his hand across his body, the palm forward then rotating inward, an emphatic refusal to produce more liquor.

The Indians persisted in begging for more firewater, but Lance's answer was always an emphatic no as he began consuming his second three-foot buffalo rib.

Sam sensed that the Indians were getting angry at Lance's apparent indifference to their pleas for more firewater. Lance was so busy chewing on his buffalo rib that it was like he really didn't care what the Indians wanted. Sam hoped Lance was doing the right thing.

It wasn't until Lance had finished his rib and wiped his hands clean on his buckskins that he began talking to the chief again, still in sign language. He said the miners in Virginia City needed more horses and probably wouldn't be too upset if he traded some of their whiskey for a good horse or two.

Immediately the chief sent one of his companions to fetch a horse. The men stepped outside the teepee to do the bartering. When the brave returned with a bay gelding, Lance quickly checked its teeth and hooves, then asked the chief how many bottles of firewater he would take for it.

The chief chatted with his friends for a moment, then held up five fingers, indicating five bottles. Lance walked around the horse again, slowly, taking a closer look. The Indians were restless, annoyed by Lance's apparent reluctance to trade. Before Lance finished his second inspection of the horse, several of the braves were urging their chief to lower his asking price to four bottles.

Without any further attempts at communication, Lance walked over to his packhorse and removed not five, but seven bottles and handed them to the surprised chief. Lance then explained in sign language that he didn't want to cheat his friend, the great Shoshone chief, by giving him only five bottles for such a fine horse. Lance said he wished he could give the chief even more, but since the whiskey belonged to the miners in Virginia City, he wasn't privileged to do so.

The Indians cheered at their good fortune and began uncorking the bottles. Lance and Sam stepped aside to discuss the situation.

"Why'd you give him seven when he only asked for five?" demanded Sam.

"Drunken Injuns can get awful mean if they don't like you," explained Lance. "Those two extra bottles will buy us plenty of good-will, enough to get us through a lot of trading."

"Things will get pretty wild around here in a little while," explained Lance. "Fights, horse races, arguments, singing, dancing, the works. Help me unload a couple of boxes of bottles, then take the animals out a few hundred yards. Let the horses graze, but don't unsaddle them. I'll have kids bring you the horses I trade for. Be ready to leave as soon as you see me coming."

Sam did as he was told, finding it easier and easier to go along with Lance's wishes. So far, things were working out just fine—as long as Lance didn't continue paying seven bottles for each horse. At that rate they wouldn't be able to get a very large herd.

But Sam wasn't disappointed. He waited all afternoon with the horses, and every once in a while an Indian child would lead out a new animal. From all the noise coming from the camp, it sounded like the Indians were enjoying their firewater.

It wasn't until the sun was just about to touch the western hills that Sam spotted Lance staggering unsteadily toward him, carrying an almost empty crate containing the remainder of the untraded whiskey bottles.

While securing the leftover firewater to the packhorse, Sam did some quick figuring. They had traded off forty-three bottles to get twenty-one horses. Not a bad day's work. He just wished Lance was in better condition to help him with the horses. The half-breed had shared too many drinks with his Indian friends and had a hard time even getting onto the back of his saddle horse.

Knowing he wouldn't get any help from Lance with the herd-ing, Sam tied the new horses head to tail in a long single file line. By the time darkness settled on the Snake River Valley, Sam and Lance had put several miles between themselves and the loud celebrating still going on in the Shoshone camp.

Chapter 14

The sparkling blue waters of the Snake River were a welcome sight to Sam and Lance after spending the greater part of a hot afternoon working their way through a brushy lava bed they should have gone around. But working through it hadn't looked so bad, and they'd figured they would save time by going straight ahead. They were wrong.

The rocks became bigger and bigger, the crevices deeper and deeper. The only thing that kept them from turning back was the hope that they were almost through, that the hardest part was over. But the lava bed seemed to continue forever. One of the horses severely cut a hind foot on a piece of black obsidian and was limping badly, making progress slower than normal for the rest. Another caught its leg in a crevice and thrashed about, breaking the tail of the horse in front of it, the one it was tied to. The animal with the broken tail was put to the end of the line, where its tail would no longer be needed to lead another horse. Then as Sam was attempting to help the horse that had its leg caught, he nearly stepped on the tail of a three-foot rattler trying to get out of the way. Sam and Lance killed this snake and two others as the two men found their way through the rocks.

To make matters even worse, the black lava rocks were like a thousand furnaces, absorbing the already hot afternoon sunshine. Both men and horses were sweating profusely. There was not the slightest hint of an afternoon breeze to cool the travelers or to harass an increasing number of green-headed deer flies seeking the blood of both man and beast.

So when the weary party finally emerged from the rocks at the edge of a grassy plain stretching away to the sparkling blue waters of the meandering Snake River, the horses—all except the lame one that had been released from the string to find its own way the best it could—trotted to the river with no efforts from Sam and Lance to stop them.

After untying the horses from each other to make it easier for them to drink and graze, Sam and Lance slipped out of their sweaty buckskins and dove into the refreshing waters, swimming for a tiny white sandbar in the middle of the river.

They had no worries about the weary horses going anywhere, not after the rugged journey through the rocks. It would be several hours before even the most ambitious of the horses had any thoughts of wandering.

After crawling out of the icy water, the two young men stretched out on their bellies in the warm white sand. The deer flies had stayed behind with the horses, making Lance and Sam's comfort complete as they began to nap in the late afternoon sunshine. Despite the problems of the lava rock crossing, including one horse gone lame and one with a broken tail, Lance and Sam's horse-trading adventure was beginning successfully with twenty-one horses in their outfit. They were already discussing getting an additional wrangler as soon as the herd reached thirty animals, a number they would reach easily at the next Indian village, or so they thought.

Lance was the first to awaken. He heard a horse whinny and looked up to see why. Immediately the young half-breed was on his feet, shouting something in Indian across the rushing waters of the Snake. A second later Sam was on his feet too, shouting in English at the half dozen mounted Indians who had just rounded up Lance and Sam's horses. Four other Indians were dismounted at the shore and had almost finished lashing Lance and Sam's saddles, guns, firewater, and other supplies onto three other horses.

Upon hearing the shouting from the river island, one of the Indians helping with the saddles and supplies, a fat fellow with a black loincloth and a big head, notched an arrow onto his bow string and let it fly in the direction of the island. The arrow thunked harmlessly into the wet sand at the water's edge to remind Lance and Sam that they would be foolish if they attempted to interfere with the theft of their goods and animals.

By the time the Indians next to the shore had loaded the goods on packhorses and had mounted to leave, the other Indians herding Lance and Sam's horses were nearly out of sight around the north end of the lava rocks.

Just when it looked like the last of the Indians were going to leave, the fat Indian with the black loincloth dismounted and hurried to the water's edge, where he picked up Lance and Sam's buckskins and moccasins and rolled them in a bundle, which he quickly tied to the back of his saddle. As he mounted his pony, he shouted something indistinguishable across the rushing waters to the two naked young men now beside themselves with frustration over what was happening, and their inability to do anything about it.

As soon as the Indians were out of sight, Sam and Lance dove into the icy water and began swimming toward shore. The sun was down, but the evening was still warm.

Upon reaching shore their worst hopes were realized. Everything was gone—their horses, food, weapons, trade goods, and even the very clothing from their backs. They had nothing, or at least they thought they had nothing until Sam spotted the lame horse up by the lava rocks. Unable to travel with the other horses, it had been left behind by the Indians. The horse was a gentle chestnut gelding, almost chocolate in color.

"Were they Shoshones?" asked Sam, still angry and wanting to know who his enemies were.

"Don't think so," responded Lance thoughtfully. "Their horses were big and fleshy, many spotted. My guess would be Nez Perces, maybe Flatheads or Bannocks."

"Will they come back for us, knowing we're unarmed?" asked Sam.

"Don't think so. They got twenty-one horses and nearly a hundred bottles of firewater. With a take like that, they'll probably be in a big hurry to get home, unless they get sidetracked with the firewater."

"Wish we had eaten before taking a swim. I'm sure hungry," said Sam, changing the subject.

"Me too," agreed Lance. "If we had just taken our rifles with us to the island." Then with bitter determination he added, "I'll never let my rifle get out of reach again, not in wild country, never again." Sam nodded. They had learned a bitter lesson the hard way, with the full consequences yet to come. They were hungry without food, naked without clothing, barefooted without horses, and unarmed in Indian country.

"What should we do?" asked Sam.

"I'm hungry," said Lance. "Maybe we ought to get something to eat, then something to wear, then something to fight and kill with. Then we can decide where we're going to go."

Sam was amazed at the matter-of-fact tone in Lance's voice. He reminded himself that Lance had been raised with the Gosiutes, a tribe accustomed to living off the land, frequently without horses, formidable weapons, and even adequate shelter. Lance had been raised among a primitive people who knew how to survive in this wild land. Though Lance's people seldom achieved comfortable living, they seldom starved or froze to death, either.

When Lance started walking up the hill toward the lava rocks, Sam followed, trusting his half-breed friend to know what to do. He remembered the rattlesnakes they had killed earlier in the afternoon.

"I hope you have something better in mind than finding those snakes," said Sam.

"You don't like snake meat?" asked Lance, turning to smile at his friend.

"Not after they've been lying dead in the sun all afternoon with the guts still in 'em," replied Sam.

"You get hungry enough, even snake tastes good," added Lance, turning to resume his journey up the hill. "But I got something better in mind for tonight."

Chapter 15

"I don't think we should kill him," said Sam.

Lance bent over and picked up the front hoof of the chestnut gelding, the one that had been left behind by the Indians because it was lame.

"See that black," said Lance, holding the hoof out so Sam could see the soft inside of the hoof. "That's the butt end of an obsidian chip. No telling how deep it goes into the frog. Even if we could dig it out, this animal would be lame for months."

"A good horse like this ought to have a chance to heal up. If he doesn't, then maybe we could kill him."

Lance looked away, obviously annoyed by what he thought was stupidity on the part of his white companion. Then turning back, he said, "Look at yourself, and me. Bare naked. No weapons. No horses. No food. How far do you think you can walk without moccasins?"

Sam knew Lance was right. But there was something about his half-breed companion's nonchalant willingness to kill that still bothered him. Growing up on the ranch there had been several occasions when it was necessary to destroy a horse, but Sam had never had the stomach for it, and had always managed to shift such unpleasant duties to his father.

"How are you going to do it?" asked Sam. "You don't even have a knife."

"Wait here," said Lance, disappearing into the lava rocks.

Sam sat down on the grass and watched the lame horse graze.

A few minutes later, Lance returned, a large dusty rock in each hand.

Dropping to the ground, cross-legged, beside Sam, Lance began to carefully tap the two rocks together. After several taps the outside edge of one of the rocks fell away, revealing a smooth, black obsidian surface. Lance continued tapping until he had fashioned two fist-sized shards with at least one razor-sharp edge on each.

"Take a good hold of that lame hoof," ordered Lance.

The half-breed could tell by the questioning look on Sam's face that an explanation was needed.

"You don't expect me to just walk and slit his throat while he's just standing there, do you?"

Sam didn't respond.

"If I tried that," explained Lance, "he might get away, and even with a bad foot, it might take days to find him. As soon as he figures out we want to kill him, he'll be able to travel a lot better on that lame foot. Got to get him on the ground. Grab that foot."

As soon as Sam had a firm hold on the lame hoof, Lance grabbed the hind leg directly behind Sam and pushed with all his might. The horse resisted but was no match for the determined young men.

As the horse rolled onto its side, Lance leaped onto the neck, catching the nose in the crook of his elbow and forcing it up.

Sam handed Lance two of the razor-sharp shards and turned away. He heard the gurgling from the windpipe accompanied by the thrashing of hooves. Then all was quiet as the last of the red blood oozed onto the green grass.

Using one of the shards as a cutting tool, Sam went to work fashioning a bow drill as he had been taught by his father. He was glad to have something to do to keep his mind from dwelling on the slaughter of the poor horse. A bow drill was needed quickly. It was almost dark, and the warmth of a fire would be welcome during the chill of the night. They were hungry, and cooked meat was preferable to raw flesh. Lance cut Sam a string for his bow from the hide of the horse's belly.

By the time the stars came out, the young men were roasting chunks of meat over a blazing fire. When they had eaten their fill they finished skinning the horse by the light of the fire. During much of the night and throughout the following day they worked feverishly with hide, obsidian, and some plant fibers, fashioning moccasins, loincloths, sleeveless vests, and bags with drawstrings for carrying the long strips of jerked meat that were drying over the fire.

Using the tip of a deer horn found near the lava rocks, Lance picked away at the obsidian shards, fashioning a stone knife and two spear heads. With hot pine pitch and wet sinew, he secured a handle to the knife and shafts to the spears.

"Want to head back to Salt Lake?" asked Lance as he finished securing the second spear head to a shaft. The sun was going down behind the western hills, a little over twenty-four hours since their horses and supplies had been stolen.

"And tell Molly we lost her investment money, and let Kathryn's father see how my first business endeavor failed?" responded Sam, obviously discouraged with their bad luck.

"You got any better ideas?"

"You thought any about following them Injuns and getting our horses back?"

"You're crazy."

"No, wait a minute," persisted Sam, his voice becoming enthusiastic. "Do you think those Injuns think we're coming after them?"

"After leaving us naked on a sandbar without moccasins, weapons, or horses? No, I don't think they're worried about us coming after them, not at all."

"Then maybe that's what we ought to do. If they're not expecting us, maybe we can catch them by surprise, like they did us, and get our horses back."

"You ever seen a man skinned alive? That's what those northern tribes do if they catch you stealin' their horses."

"I don't figure on getting caught," responded Sam boldly. "Besides, we might end up with an even bigger herd and turn this adventure into a successful business trip after all."

"Promise me one thing, then."

"What's that?" asked Sam.

"That you'll stop being so civilized about killing."

"I'm sorry about the horse. You were right about putting him down."

"Someday we might run into an Injun or two that need fast scalping, and there might not be time for you to stop and say your prayers and start feeling sorry for them; that is, if you want to keep your own scalp."

"I won't let you down again, Lance. That's a promise."

Sam stood up and looked in the direction the Indians had departed with the stolen horses.

"Trail should be easy to follow. Hasn't been any rain to wash the tracks away."

Lance looked down at the dirt. "Hope I get a chance to see the look on that fat Indian's face—the one with the black loincloth and the big head—when he sees us galloping away with his horses."

"We'll leave an hour or so before dawn," said Sam. Lance nodded his agreement.

Chapter 16

"There's our horses," whispered Sam.

"And about two hundred more," said Lance.

The two young men were stretched out on their bellies on a rocky ledge overlooking a lush green valley near the forks of the Salmon River. They had followed the trail of stolen horses for four days. From the meandering of the trail and the frequent stops for grazing, it had soon become obvious to Sam and Lance that the horse thieves did not expect to be followed—not by two naked boys who had no weapons, transportation, food, or clothing.

Fresh-skinned horsehide didn't make the most comfortable clothing. The horsehide was slippery and soggy against the skin. And when mixed with the perspiration of a forced march, it soon became smelly. Frequently the young men removed all but their moccasins to give their skin and their new clothing a chance to dry in the warm summer air. The moccasins had to be restitched daily as they stretched under vigorous wear. Still, Sam and Lance stayed doggedly on the trail of the horse thieves, encouraged by the knowledge the horse thieves didn't think they were being followed. For food, Sam and Lance carried plenty of partially dried horse jerky. For weapons they carried crude spears with obsidian heads.

"We're in Shoshone country, at the very edge maybe," guessed Lance. "But I still think they are Nez Perces. Heard they sometimes come this way to and from the buffalo country on the plains. See all the rifles? Nez Perces have a lot of rifles. Lots of horses, too. Big ones. They trade with settlers along the Oregon Trail."

The big horse herd was grazing quietly in a long meadow shaped like a *V*, with the river on one side and rock ledges on the other. The teepees were stretched in a line across the open end of the *V* to prevent the horses from wandering onto the open prairie.

"How can we get our horses back?" asked Sam.

"Only one way. Steal them, and maybe some more while we're at it," said Lance.

"How do you suggest we do it?"

"The Injun way would be to sneak in among the horses during the night, mount up at first light, then try to stampede off as many as possible. Such raids are common. That's why many of the fastest horses are picketed by the teepees. Those horses can't be driven off, and if there's a raid, they can be mounted quickly to defend the village or to prevent large numbers of the horses from being driven off."

"How many could we reasonably hope to get away with?"

"Maybe fifteen or twenty, but we'd lose most of them if the Injuns chased us," said Lance.

"Would they chase us?"

"Sure. Wouldn't you chase somebody who stole your horses?"

Sam nodded. He and Lance were doing just that.

"Then let's do something different," suggested Sam. "Something an Indian would never think of doing, something that will catch them totally by surprise, something that has never been done before.

"I don't want fifteen or twenty horses, anyway. The Indians stole more than that from us. I want a hundred horses, at least. And I don't want the Indians chasing us."

"That's a big order," said Lance. "Injuns have been stealing horses from each other for about a hundred years. They've perfected the art of horse stealing. And then Sam Storm comes along and thinks he can do better than all the Injuns put together, on his first raid. I'm listening. How you going to do it?"

"I don't know," said Sam thoughtfully, not in the least offended by the sarcasm in his friend's voice. "But I'll bet if we think about it for a while we can come up with something."

Lance looked with incredulity, then respect, at his determined companion. Maybe this unusual white man could come up with a better way to steal horses. Maybe not. Maybe he would get the both of them killed. Considering their circumstances, that certainly seemed the more probable outcome.

Chapter 17

From their rocky ledge, Sam and Lance watched the Indian camp throughout the day, occasionally chewing on half-dried strips of horse meat but speaking very little.

They observed the terrain—the meandering Salmon River with the scattered clumps of willow and cottonwood along its banks. The horse herd of more than a hundred animals. The row of teepees across the lower end of the meadow, a barrier to keep the horses from wandering from the meadow. The cook fires. The willow racks heavy with drying meat strips. The Indians with their women and children. The dogs. Two hides staked out on the ground for scraping.

But most interesting of all were the two naked Indians tied with ropes from their necks to a big wooden stake. From a distance it was impossible to make out distinct features. Other than the black hair and bronze skins, the only other recognizable feature was the distinct chubbiness of the two Indians.

"Too fat to be slaves," said Lance. "Slaves don't get enough to eat. Probably captives, and new ones at that. Notice how they gather handfuls of dirt to defend themselves when other Indians come near. And how they appear to be spitting back when spit upon. Still got a lot of fight in them."

"Any idea what tribe they belong to?" asked Sam.

"If the ones that stole our horses are Nez Perces, then the captives are likely Blackfoot, or maybe Gros Ventres. Nez Perces are always wandering into Blackfoot or Gros Ventre country to hunt buffalo. Of course, they don't mind picking up a few extra horses or captives when they get the chance."

"What'll they do with them?" asked Sam.

"Probably torture or kill them when they get in the mood," said Lance, his tone of voice matter-of-fact. "Maybe just keep them as slaves, or sell them. I don't know."

"Do you care?" asked Sam, disturbed once more by his companion's apparent lack of concern.

"I don't care about them," said Lance coolly, "as much as I care what happens to those horses. You got any ideas yet?"

Sam looked at his half-breed companion and shrugged his shoulders, wondering if Lance was really as cold as he seemed. Someday he would find out, probably. In the meantime he had to concern himself with the horses.

"Tell me again," began Sam, "how we would go about trying to steal those horses if we were Injuns."

"We'd sneak into the meadow during the night," began Lance easily. "Crawl around among the horses, getting them used to us and picking the ones we wanted to ride—the ones that looked fastest and strongest. We'd get ropes or bridles on these as quietly as possible. If a horse didn't want to let you catch him, you couldn't chase him around. You'd just have to pick another."

Lance continued, "Once you got your bridle on the one you wanted, you'd move him slowly, while he was still grazing, to the position you wanted to be in at dawn when we made a break for it, trying to drive other horses in front of us."

"How do you know when it's time to mount up and go for it?" asked Sam.

"As soon as it's light enough to see, and hopefully while the Injuns are still asleep and not ready for you."

"And those Injuns come after you as soon as they find out what you're doing?"

"Yeah," answered the half-breed. "Unless you cut free the four or five tethered horses, the ones they tie by their teepees for these emergencies, and can do it without the Injuns hearing you."

"What are the chances of doing that?" asked Sam.

"Not good," said Lance. "There's dogs in the camp. Strangers would have a hard time getting past them."

"How many horses could we hope to steal without cutting the tethered horses free?"

"Just the ones we were riding," continued Lance. "Couldn't be slowed down by herding anything. If we cut the tethered horses free, the ones near the teepees, so the Injuns couldn't follow us right away, we might get away with twenty or thirty animals."

"Just what they stole from us. That's not good enough," said Sam.

Lance shook his head.

"Look," he said. "Injuns been stealing horses for a hundred years, and it seems they got things pretty much figured out. If you think you have a better way, let's hear it."

"Looks like we have two problems," said Sam thoughtfully. "First, we got to do something with the tethered horses so they can't follow us, at least not right away. Second, we've got to get some help with the herding so we won't have to leave most of the animals behind."

Lance nodded his agreement, then asked, "How?"

"Listen up," said Sam, smiling brightly. "I think I have a plan that just maybe our grandkids will be bragging about a hundred years from now—if it works."

Lance didn't say anything but watched closely as Sam smoothed the dust between them with his palm and began to sketch the layout of the valley below.

Chapter 18

The night was almost gone, but the stars had not yet begun to fade away when Lance and Sam finished lashing the cottonwood logs together to create a floating pole fortress. With the helpful light of a three-quarter moon, they had been working quietly through most of the night.

The two huge cottonwood logs at the base were nearly two feet in diameter and almost totally submerged in water by the time the fortress was finished. The logs were lashed together with green willows, the largest on the bottom and decreasing in size to the top of the floating fortress, which consisted mostly of sticks and brush.

The fortress was at the edge of a thick cottonwood grove about a mile upstream from the Indian camp, at the top of the meadow where the Indian horse herd had been grazing. During the night, Lance and Sam had crawled among the grazing horses and caught two of the animals and led them back to the cottonwood grove. The horses were tethered near the floating fortress.

As Sam quietly piled on the last big armload of brush, Lance climbed on one of the ponies.

"Don't let her go," he cautioned, "until the stars in the east begin to fade." He dug his heels into the pony's sides and disappeared into the night, in the direction of the Indian camp.

Sam crouched beside a cottonwood tree, facing the rugged Bitterroot Mountains to the east, waiting restlessly for the stars to fade in the gray dawn. He thought of his father, Dan Storm, who had come to this wild country before the first pioneers with Lance's father—the big black man, the escaped slave called Ike. He thought of his mother, Caroline, how kind and loving she had been to him as a child, and how she probably worried about him now. And his father's second wife, Sarah. She had been a second mother and would be worrying too. He thought of his brothers and sisters and the good times they had had on their American Fork farm.

Sam wondered if he would ever see them again. The crude obsidian knife in his belt would offer little protection if things didn't work out in the next few hours. He remembered Kathryn Cannon, the beautiful young woman from Salt Lake who was the motivation for him and Lance undertaking this horse-gathering adventure. Sam wished she could see him now, getting ready to risk his life for her. He hoped Brutus Young wasn't trying to hurry his marriage to Kathryn before Sam could get back with his newly acquired fortune. There wasn't much time, and Sam still didn't have anything but the clothes on his back. But there were enough horses in the nearby meadow to make him a wealthy man by most people's standards, if Sam could only get the horses to Canada and sell them to the people preparing to start a new police force called the Royal Canadian Mounted Police.

There was no doubt in Sam's mind as to what would happen to him if he were caught by the Nez Perces. Horse thieves received no mercy. A quick death would be fortunate. The Indians would prefer torturing him, if they got the chance.

Sam forced himself to think about Kathryn, to remember all he could about her—the long black hair, the smooth olive complexion, the large dark eyes, deep and clear and warm. These thoughts gave him courage for the work ahead.

At the first hint of gray over the Bitterroot Mountains, Sam dropped to his knees on the sandy beach and assembled his fire-building tools—bow, drill, spindle, baseboard, and tinder bundle. It was too dark to see the gentle curling of smoke as he vigorously worked the bow back and forth, but the spark was bright as he carefully dropped it into the tinder and began to puff on it. The spark grew brighter and brighter and Sam blew harder and harder until the tinder suddenly burst into flames. Quickly he crawled to the top of the floating fortress and carefully placed the flaming bundle inside the sticks and brush.

As soon as Sam was sure the fire was not going to go out, he jumped down from the fortress. Using a long pole, he pushed the fortress away from shore and into the main current of the Salmon River. He ran to the tethered pony, then turned and watched the spreading flames as the Salmon River carried the blazing fortress toward the row of teepees at the far end of the meadow. He hoped Lance was ready. To the east the stars were beginning to fade away before the gray dawn.

Chapter 19

Although the sky was beginning to turn gray, the meadow in the shadow of the mountains was still dark as Sam began to herd the Indian ponies together. He moved them slowly, so as not to attract the attention of the sleeping Indians at the far end of the meadow. Sam penetrated the far corners of the meadow and then several clumps of trees, not wanting to leave a single horse behind. The fire on the floating fortress, now about halfway to the line of teepees, was bonfire size and growing. The sleeping Indians had not seen it yet.

Sam and Lance had a simple plan. They figured that when the Indians and their dogs saw the blazing fortress, they would run over to the river bank to see what was happening and watch the flaming raft as it floated by. As soon as the Indians were on the bank engrossed by the blazing raft, Lance would emerge from hiding and untie all but three of the ponies tethered near the teepees. Then he would cut free the two naked captives tethered to the big post, the ones they had observed from the distant cliffs the day before. Lance and the two captives would then take the three remaining horses and join Sam in driving the main herd through the line of unguarded teepees.

The idea to free the two captives had come from Lance, but not out of compassion as much as practicality. Four riders could handle the big horse herd much better than two. Lance figured the two captives would be more than willing to help their liberators make off with the Nez Perce horses.

From his hiding place beneath a clump of serviceberry bushes,

Lance watched the approaching fortress as the flames grew brighter and brighter. He heard the occasional whinny of a horse from the meadow where Sam was quietly rounding up the herd, or so he hoped. That was the plan.

After the raft had covered three-fourths of the distance to the line of teepees, Lance's biggest worry was that maybe the Indians were sleeping so soundly they wouldn't see the fire and the whole plan would be spoiled. Still, there was nothing to do but wait. The two captives were near the teepees farthest from the river. That was good. Lance would cut free the horses closest to the river first, saving the three farthest from the river for him and the captives to use for their escape.

The floating fortress was almost in line with the row of teepees when the first Indian shout was heard. Almost the entire raft was on fire by this time, lighting up the camp. Lance crouched closer to the ground as the Indians began piling out of their teepees, the dogs barking wildly.

The first part of the plan worked perfectly, as every Indian in sight ran to the river's edge to watch in amazement as the blazing fortress floated by. Several young braves even dove into the cold water and began swimming toward the fire.

Lance moved quietly but quickly from one tethered horse to another, gently removing the halters and lead ropes, leaving the animals free to wander off on their own. He didn't want to attract the attention of the Indians on the shore with horses galloping off into the night, at least not yet.

After freeing all but the last three animals, Lance worked his way to the post where the two captives had been tied the afternoon before. As he crept around the teepee nearest the big post, the firelight from the river shed enough light on the two forms crouched near the post to let Lance know that he and Sam had made at least one false assumption in forming their plan.

From the distant cliffs Sam and Lance had assumed the two captives were warriors from another tribe. The fact that the captives had a lot of fight in them and were throwing dirt and rocks at their captors only confirmed this opinion. But in the light of the flaming fortress, Lance didn't find two captured braves—but two women, dirty and naked, except for a wide leather belt on the bigger one. Both had long black hair, dirty and matted, partially covering their faces. There were cuts, scratches, and bruises on their arms, legs, and faces. They had been treated badly, roughly, by their captors, the usual fare for prisoners of war.

At first the two women didn't see Lance watching them from the shadows of the nearby teepee. Lance hesitated. Women could be more of a burden than a help in driving the horses over the mountains. Frequently Indian women were poor riders. Sitting atop a horse pulling a travois was one thing, but galloping across the plains after stampeding buffalo was a skill reserved for men. While some Indian women learned to ride well, most did not.

Lance was about to retreat when he had another idea. Perhaps the women were Blackfoot Indians. As soon as he and Sam crossed the Bitterroot Mountains they would be in Blackfoot country. Maybe the women could show them some shortcuts, would know where the safest trails were. But even more important, the two women might help clear the way for safe passage through almost five hundred miles of Blackfoot country. Holding his hand over his mouth to indicate silence, Lance stepped out of the teepee's shadow into the firelight so the two crouching women could see him.

Chapter 20

At first the two captive women were afraid of the approaching half-breed with the obsidian knife in his hand. They retreated to the ends of their tethers, scooping up handfuls of dirt to throw into the face of the approaching man who was signaling for them to be silent. It wasn't until he cut their tethers that they realized he had come to help them.

Had Lance motioned for the women to follow him to the nearby horses to make their escape, they would have done so, and probably made a safe exit. The Nez Perces and their dogs were still gathered along the river bank and totally engrossed in the flaming raft.

But Lance suddenly decided to change the plan. The vacated teepees contained items he and Sam would need for their trek to Canada—especially guns, ammunition, steel knives, and rawhide ropes. And the women needed clothing. Crossing the mountains, the nights would be cold. Maybe even the days, if there were storms.

With the two women close at his heels, Lance entered the nearest teepee. To his delight, he found a repeater rifle with almost two boxes of cartridges. Unable to find any women's clothing, the two women slipped into buckskin shirts and leggings. Lance uncovered two skinning knives and handed them to the women in a gesture of friendship to assure them that he was indeed their friend and could be trusted.

As they emerged from the teepee, Lance pushed the women in the direction of the two nearest horses, handing one the repeating rifle while he hurried to the next teepee with hopes of finding another of those valuable guns.

Unfortunately for Lance, the next teepee was not unoccupied. An old woman with a crippled foot had found the pain of walking more compelling than the curiosity of the flaming raft and had remained behind in her bed. Lance didn't see her as he entered the teepee, but became abruptly aware of her presence when he heard her terrified scream.

Lance ducked outside and raced for the last horse. The two women were already mounted, ready to make their escape.

Had the old woman's scream been the first sign of something amiss, Lance would have probably made a safe getaway. But a minute earlier several braves had noticed two of the tethered horses wandering off and were hurrying back to camp to check the rest. After hearing the old woman's scream, they spotted Lance racing from her teepee. They caught him just as he was untying the last horse, a bay gelding. The two women galloped off into the gray dawn as Lance was wrestled to the ground. The bay gelding galloped off to join his friends in the long meadow.

When Sam saw that several of the Nez Perce braves were leaving the river bank and hurrying back to the camp, he knew the time for being careful, contemplative, and quiet had passed. In the light of the burning fortress he could see that two riders were already mounted, possibly Lance and one of the captives, or more likely both of the captives who were waiting for Lance to find a third horse. Hopefully Lance wouldn't take long. In a matter of seconds, the entire tribe would know a horse raid was in process.

While digging his heels into the ribs of his restless pony, Sam reached out and slapped the nearest horse on the rump with a length of rawhide, then another. As these horses started running, others joined in. It was easy to get them going in the crisp coolness of the gray dawn, a time of day when horses are inclined to kick up their heels to warm their chilled muscles.

It was easier to see now, with the last of the stars almost gone. Sam raced from side to side behind the stampeding horses, carefully eyeing each willow clump or cottonwood grove to make sure none were left behind.

By the time the entire herd of well over a hundred horses was at a full gallop, Sam could see what appeared to be dozens of Indians racing to the line of teepees to head off the stampede. Soon they would be waving blankets and flaming torches and firing rifles in an effort to head back the horses. Sam whooped and hollered in an effort to make the horses run even faster. He hoped Lance and the two captives would soon be joining him to help push the herd through the line of teepees and now-screaming Indians.

The lead horses were already beginning to slow their pace before the waving blankets and torches when Sam spotted the two riders approaching from his right. At first he wasn't sure if they were friend or foe. They were definitely Indian, both with long black hair and wearing buckskin leggings and shirts. One was carrying a repeater rifle.

Waving his arm, Sam motioned for the two riders to move closer to the galloping horses and help him drive them through the line of teepees. When they obeyed, Sam felt a lot better, assured the two riders were the captive Indians who had come to join in the raid. In fact, the bigger of the two Indians aimed the repeater rifle into the air and fired several rounds, the sound of which put new life into the stampeding horses.

The Nez Perces were too late in setting up their line of defense. That, combined with the distraction of several of the braves capturing one of the horse thieves, made their defense line incomplete, allowing the stampeding horses to head for the open places and race through. The entire herd and the three riders had passed by before the holes could be plugged up. The entire herd, including every one of the animals that had been tethered by the teepees for just such emergencies, was gone. There was howling and cursing as the Nez Perces realized how they had been tricked with the burning fortress. The new captive would pay dearly for the loss of an entire herd. After they had finished with him, runners would be sent out to follow the trail of the departed herd, looking for strays. Once some of them were captured, a war party could then be organized to go after the horse thieves in an effort to recover the main herd.

It wasn't until the weary horses had slowed to a walk, and the first rays of morning sunshine were shooting over the snow-covered peaks of the Bitterroot Mountains, that Sam realized his two companions were female.

The horses, slowing to a walk, allowed the two women to move in close to Sam, who was between them now. With the horses walking, there was less chance of strays heading off to either side.

"Friend got catched," said the big one, grinning beneath her stringy hair. Her face was still filthy, but her teeth were clean, white, and straight. She handed the repeater rifle to Sam, a sign of trust and friendship.

Sam just stared at her for a minute, his face expressionless. Then he started laughing, and he wasn't sure why. But there was something funny at finding these two fellow horse thieves to be women—two riders who had joined him while the raid was in process and had handled their horses so well. In their loose buckskin shirts and leggings, it had never occurred to him they might be women, but they were, and somehow that was funny. The women laughed with Sam, and they didn't know why either, except that it seemed the sociable thing to do, to laugh with this blond white man who was not much more than a boy.

"Did they shoot him—my friend?" asked Sam when they were through laughing.

"My friend, the one who set you free, did they kill him?" he asked again, when he could see they were having trouble understanding.

"No," responded the chubby one. "Tie up." She repeated herself by crossing her wrists, a sign language term for being tied up.

Sam understood. He pulled his horse to a halt. All the laughter was gone. His friend, Lance, was captive in an Indian camp that had just lost all of its horses. Perhaps the torture had begun already. The burning sticks, the sharp knives cutting away pieces of flesh, skinning palms of hands and bottoms of feet, emasculation, and other tortures, the common fare of captured horse thieves. One thing was for sure. The torture would not end quickly. Lance would not be permitted the luxury of a quick death. The torture could last for days, perhaps a week.

Sam looked at one of the women, then the other. He didn't even know their names, or what tribe they were from, though he suspected they were Blackfoot by their seeming willingness, even eagerness, to drive the horse herd over the mountains into Blackfoot country.

"Me help friend," said Sam with slow deliberation, pointing back the way they had come. "You drive horses over mountains. We find you."

The women seemed to understand, but they shook their heads in protest, not wanting their new friend to go back. Sam ignored their protests. Jerking his weary horse's head around, he dug his heels into its ribs and headed back down the trail toward the Nez Perce camp.

Chapter 21

It was midmorning when Sam tied his pony, a sorrel mare, in a gully thick with cedar trees. With rifle in hand, and taking advantage of the natural cover, he moved quickly to the edge of a rock overhang where he could see the Nez Perce camp.

Sam quickly scanned the camp and meadow. Not a single horse was in sight. Of course there was a chance that one or two riders were out on the trail of the stolen herd. The horse raid was a fantastic success—except for the capture of Lance Claw.

The Indians were gathered at the center of the camp. There was lots of yelling and arguing. A group of warriors at the center of the group were applying war paint, checking quivers and pouches of supplies, obviously preparing for a journey, probably a forced march, on foot, after their stolen horses. Sam felt a sickening feeling in the pit of his stomach. He needed to be with the two women driving the horses over the mountains. The angry warriors wouldn't have any trouble following the trail. The horse herd would have to be pushed hard to stay out of reach of the pursuing warriors.

Then Sam saw Lance, his hands and feet bound with rawhide, on his side in the dust, not far from the main group of Indians. The real torture had not begun, though several Indian boys were throwing rocks and shooting arrows from their toy bows at the half-breed horse thief. Lance endured the toy arrows and stones without reaction, apparently conserving his energy for the real torture that would soon follow, probably immediately following the departure of the war party.

Sam decided the best time to make his move would be as soon as the war party was out of sight and hearing. If he was successful, there would still be time to beat them to the horse herd, which he hoped was now on its way over the mountain pass.

The only problem was how to get Lance out of there. Only a portion of the warriors were leaving to follow the horse herd, only the best runners. Just as many were remaining behind, and they would be armed with bows and arrows, some with rifles.

Still uncertain as to how he might set Lance free, Sam returned to his horse, untied it, and led it down a draw thick with chokecherry and willow bushes. He wanted to get the horse as close as possible to the Indian camp, hoping he and Lance would need it for a fast escape. Beyond the draw to the east there was open ground where Sam and Lance could quickly outdistance any pursuers, if Sam could just figure a way to get his friend back to the horse.

Sam had covered about half the distance to the camp and had just tethered the horse with a slip knot behind a thick clump of serviceberry bushes when the war party, a total of nine runners, departed on the trail of the lost horses. Sam decided to wait until the Indians were out of sight before he moved any further. He was grateful for the repeating rifle in his hand, though he was not sure how he might use it in freeing his friend.

The runners were not yet out of sight when Sam heard some unusual noise not coming directly from the Indian camp—like the laughter and shouting of children, combined with the sound of sticks knocking against tree trunks. Cautiously, Sam moved toward the new sounds. The laughter grew louder.

Then combined with the laughter was a scream of terror, then another. Then more laughter. More banging of sticks. Sam continued, with caution, not at all sure what he might find.

When he finally spotted the children, four of them, between six and ten years of age, he understood why the screams of terror were mixed with laughter. Two of the children, a boy and a girl, were tied to a big cottonwood tree with a long rawhide rope. They screamed in mock horror as the other children, both boys, pretended to beat and torture them. They were playing "torture the prisoners." Sam wondered how the cruelties of adults could become the seemingly innocent play of children.

One of the boys carefully picked up a stick from the ground as if it were on fire and held it close to the girl's eyes. She screamed as if her eyes were being burned out. The rest of the children laughed with delight.

The other boy, wooden knife in hand, pretended to cut away a square of skin from the chest of the little boy tied beside the girl. He screamed and kicked, pretending to be in terrible pain.

Sam guessed the play of the children had been triggered by the anticipation of a real torturing to take place later that day, with Lance Claw as the victim. Then he thought of another game the children might like to play. Yes. One that might help win the release of Lance Claw. Sam dropped to his knees and began to crawl toward the unsuspecting children.

A few minutes later Sam jumped out of the bushes and grabbed one arm of each of the boys who had been doing the torturing. He didn't have to worry about the boy and girl tied tightly to the tree. They weren't going anywhere.

He wrestled the boys to the ground and sat on one while he proceeded to tie the other's hands behind his back with the end of the rawhide rope. They were far enough from camp that he figured the screams wouldn't attract any unusual attention, especially not after all the noise the children had already made in their play.

Cutting off strips of rawhide rope, Sam tied each child's hands behind his back. Then, with the remaining rope, he fashioned four slip-knot loops in a row into which he pushed the children's heads. With the children firmly in tow, he headed back to his horse.

A minute later Sam was mounted on the horse and driving his four howling captives toward the Nez Perce camp. The rifle and reins were in one hand, the end of the children's tether in the other.

Sam felt uneasy about what he was doing. He wasn't so much afraid of getting caught or shot—he had been in worse situations. What bothered him was the deception he was about to play on the Indians. His success would depend on how convincing his deception would be.

If the Indians were to trade hostages with him, Lance for the children, they had to be convinced Sam would harm the children if they didn't cooperate. But Sam didn't want to hurt the children, even if the Indians refused to give up Lance. If the Indians suspected his true feelings, he and Lance would be in real trouble. He had to convince the Indians their children would die, possibly be dragged to death by the rope about their necks, if the parents didn't set Lance free.

As soon as the captive children marched into the open, in plain view of the Indians in the village, Sam fired his rifle into the ground behind the closest child. His purpose was twofold. First, to frighten the children and perhaps get some of them crying, and second, to attract the attention of the entire village. He wanted all the women to see the frightened children. Hopefully the women would put additional pressure on their men to allow the exchange in order to save their children. He had already tied the end of the tether around his horse's neck to make it obvious to the Indians that if they succeeded in shooting Sam, his panicked horse, linked to their children's necks with the rawhide rope, would inflict serious harm.

The Indians were talking excitedly, some of the women wailing, but all of them remained within the bounds of the camp as Sam pulled his horse to a halt less than a hundred yards from the nearest teepee. He didn't figure he would have to explain to the Nez Perces what he wanted. They should be able to figure that out for themselves, possibly with some help from Lance, who knew a little Nez Perce. From all the shouting, Sam guessed the Indians hadn't expected to see him so soon. They were obviously upset to see themselves tricked a second time by this white man in less than a twenty-four-hour period.

Lance, his feet cut free, was brought to the front of the group of braves facing Sam. Sam waved for Lance to come to him, but the Indians were still unsure as to what they should do and refused to let the prisoner go.

Sam acted quickly, reminding himself that his friend's life was in the balance. He yanked the mare's head to one side, forcing her to turn quickly, jerking the children from their feet. Then he pulled the mare back, dragging the howling children a short distance through the sagebrush.

Even at a distance, it was easy to see the confusion in the Indian camp. The chief and some of the warriors were apparently reluctant to let the hostage go, while the mothers of the four children were begging and pleading for the safety of their little ones.

Sam guessed that if the tables were turned and Lance were in his shoes, the half-breed would probably kill one of the children just to let the Indians know he meant business. Sam did the next best thing. He fired the rifle into the dirt again as he jerked the children off their feet a second time, leaving the Indians to wonder if one of their children had been shot. The grief-stricken mothers increased their wailing and pleas for the safety of their children.

It seemed to Sam that a lot of time was passing with nothing happening. He kept looking about for any sign of Nez Perce warriors trying to get behind him. He could see nothing out of the ordinary. He wished he knew what the Indians were saying to each other. He wished he knew what Lance was thinking, saying, hearing.

All of the children were crying now as Sam allowed the dusty little urchins to get back on their feet. There were red marks on their necks where they had been jerked about by the stiff rawhide, but no signs of serious injury. It was repulsive to Sam to see the children afraid for their lives. He longed to assure them they were safe, that he wouldn't harm them, that he intended to let them go. He thought of his own brothers and sisters and how he would feel if anyone treated them as he was treating these Indian children. But he thought of Lance too, his good friend, who would be tortured in the most cruel manner if he were not freed in exchange for the safe return of the children. Sam yanked his horse back, jerking the children to the ground for the third time. He aimed his rifle at them and cocked back the hammer. Again the slow passage of time. If the Indians didn't do something soon, they would certainly begin to suspect the white man was bluffing.

After what seemed like an eternity, Lance, with his hands still tied behind his back, was allowed to walk toward Sam. Immediately, Sam urged the children to start walking forward. He didn't want any doubts in the minds of the Indians about his intentions of returning their children. He didn't want them to even suspect he might double-cross them, fearing they would forget the safety of the children and launch a sudden attack.

Lance was very dirty and a little bruised, but otherwise appeared unharmed as he reached the horse. Sam bent over and cut his friend's hands free. After briefly rubbing his sore wrists, Lance swung up behind Sam.

The Indians were watching to see if their children would be released unharmed. After looking about one last time to make sure the way was clear for a safe retreat, Sam untied the children's tether rope and let it fall to the ground. Then, spinning the mare around and digging his heels into her sides, Sam urged her into a full gallop in the direction of the brushy draw, Lance holding tightly to his waist.

Chapter 22

"If they hadn't let me go, would you have broke their little necks?" asked Lance after he and Sam had put several miles between them and the Nez Perce camp. They were still riding double on Sam's horse.

"No," said Sam simply. "I'd have let the kids go. I was bluffing. Even if they'd cut your arms off, I'd have let the kids go."

"The way you was shootin' that gun and jerking the kids around with the horse," said Lance, "I figured you was finally learning to get tough. The Injuns sure thought you was going to wipe them kids out."

"Good thing I fooled them," responded Sam before changing the subject. "What about them two women who helped drive the horses off?"

"The chunky one's called Leather Belly," explained Lance. "The other one is Kicking Woman. Both Blackfoot. Half sisters, daughters to Blackweasel, chief of a small band camped somewhere near the three forks of the Missouri River."

"No wonder you got caught," laughed Sam. "Did you ask them to tell you their life stories before leaving the Nez Perce camp?"

"You got it wrong," said Lance. "An old Nez Perce woman filled me in while my hands were tied. The Nez Perces like to talk to their prisoners before they kill 'em."

"How far will the Nez Perces follow us?" asked Sam.

"For a stretch, I'm sure, at least as far as the divide. But without horses, I don't think they'll go far into Blackfoot country. If we can keep ahead of them that far, I don't think we'll have to worry about the Nez Perces anymore, just the Blackfeet—and I don't know of any tribe that steals more horses or takes more scalps than the Blackfeet. Everybody hates them. Everybody is afraid of them. As enemies, they're mean and treacherous."

"The women, too?" asked Sam.

"The women too, except maybe those two up ahead with our horses. Remember, we saved them from the Nez Perces. Hopefully they'll be grateful."

"They seemed that way when I left them."

"Old Blackweasel would owe us a big favor if we brought his daughters home safely," continued Lance.

"What kind of favor?" asked Sam.

"Like maybe an escort to take us all the way to Fort Macleod," answered Lance.

"All we've got to do is find Blackweasel."

"And that isn't going to be easy," responded Lance. "Not with all the Injuns in between, each one wondering how he might get some of our horses."

It was almost dark when Sam and Lance found their horses grazing peacefully in an alpine meadow just east of the continental divide. A misty cloud of smoke from a campfire clung to the tops of some spruce and fir trees at the lower end of the meadow. After turning their weary horse out to graze with the others, Sam and Lance approached the campfire.

Leather Belly and Kicking Woman stood to meet the two men. The women had cleaned themselves in a nearby spring and looked much better. Even the knots had been pulled from their hair. Kicking Woman had braided her long black hair, while Leather Belly's hung straight and loose about her shoulders.

Kicking Woman was the first to speak. "Horses tired. Needed food," she explained, almost apologetically, as if she expected the men to scold her for taking such a long rest.

"You have food?" asked Lance, rubbing his palm over his stomach. By ignoring her comment about the horses, he showed he was not angry with her for stopping.

Leather Belly hurried to the fire, stick in hand, and began pushing several palm-sized ashcakes out of the ashes where they could cool on a flat rock. Apparently the women had found some flour in the teepee before leaving the Nez Perce camp. With nothing but horse meat and a few berries to eat for the past week, Sam and Lance quickly picked up the ashcakes in anticipation of a tasty meal. Both took big bites.

"Mine's got dirt in it," said Sam, his mouth full, still chewing.

"Squaws always put dirt in their ashcakes," said Lance.

"Why?"

"Don't know. They just do it."

Sam and Lance continued chewing the heavy biscuits. Even the dirt didn't prevent them from chewing and swallowing the nourishment their bodies needed. By the time the ashcakes were half eaten, Sam and Lance were seated in front of the fire, across from Leather Belly and Kicking Woman.

"I guess we'll be making an early start in the morning," offered Sam after a long silence of chewing.

"The moon will be up in about an hour," said Lance, looking to the east. "We'll leave then."

"We didn't get hardly any sleep at all last night," continued Sam. "We've got to get some sleep, sometime."

"Remember those Nez Perce runners who left the camp just before you rounded up the kids? It was just a few miles back that we got around them on the trail."

Sam nodded.

"They won't be sleeping tonight, so we can't either."

Lance held up four fingers, telling Leather Belly and Kicking Woman to catch that many horses. Then he stretched back on the ground and closed his eyes. A few minutes of sleep would be better than none at all. Sam did the same as the two women gathered their ropes and bridles and walked toward the grazing horses.

Chapter 23

By first dawn Lance and Sam found themselves in the thickest stand of lodgepole pines either had ever seen—tall, straight, mostly limbless trees as big around as a man's arm and as thick as hair on a dog's back.

It would have been bad enough with just the two of them and the two women, but with nearly a hundred horses, travel became almost impossible. They kept pushing forward with the hope the trees would begin to thin out, but the trees didn't, and eventually the party reached a point where it was as difficult to go forward as back the way they had come.

The horses were strung out single file, with Sam in front, Lance in the rear, and the two women in between. Being caught in the tangle of trees with nearly a hundred horses was bad enough, but what made the situation unbearable was the worry of Nez Perce runners catching up with them.

Just as the sun came up, the frustrated travelers finally reached a point where the lead horses refused to go any further. Not only were the trees so close together that the horses had to squeeze between them, but there was also a tangled mess of deadfalls blocking the way. Without ax or saw, the only way through was for the horses to scramble over the fallen trees. This they refused to do for Sam, even after repeated whippings with the end of a rope.

Sam was just starting to head back to the end of the line to discuss the situation with Lance when he ran into Leather Belly pushing to the front of the line to give him a hand. He had no idea what this chubby Indian girl had in mind, but when she asked for his knife he became curious to see what she was up to.

Leather Belly pushed her way through the tangle of pines until she found a young tree with more than the normal number of branches. Bending the tree over with one hand, she cut trough the trunk with the other, the pressure of the bend enabling her to cut quickly. Then she proceeded to slice off the branches about an inch away from the trunk, leaving a sharpened spike where each little branch had been. When she was finished, she wielded a five-foot pole covered with sharpened points.

She walked up to the first horse in the line, a sorrel Sam had been riding. It was standing in the exact spot where it had stopped, facing the tangle of fallen trees. The standing trees, both to the right and to the left, were too thick to allow the animal to turn in either direction.

Leather Belly raised her limber weapon above her head and slapped it down with all her might on the rump of the reluctant horse, several of the spikes penetrating the fleshy rump. The horse reared back on its hind legs, front feet pawing the air, still refusing to leap forward into the tangle of fallen trees.

The moment the front feet returned to the ground, Leather Belly again applied the cruel whip with all her might. This time the horse kicked back with its hind legs, but Leather Belly was safe to one side. When the poor animal ceased kicking, Leather Belly brought down her cruel whip for the third time on the now bloody rump. The horse had had enough. It leaped forward into the tangle of dead trees, lunging and thrashing forward until its feet finally found solid ground on the other side.

With a smile of relief, Sam led the next horse up to the tangle. Leather Belly only had to strike this horse once before it scrambled over the dead trees. Some of the horses went willingly over the tangle of fallen trees, not wanting to be struck even once by Leather Belly's wicked whip. Others required four or five hits before they finally lunged ahead.

Sam was amazed that none of the horses broke their legs or became hopelessly tangled in the fallen logs. He was also amazed at the matter-of-fact manner of this chubby Indian maiden. She was sending the horses through the tangle as if she had done it a dozen times before. Maybe she had. She certainly knew how to move horses through thick timber. He was glad the Indian women had joined up with him and Lance.

In less than an hour all the horses had passed over the fallen logs, and finally the forest began to thin out. In fact, as soon as Sam was back in the lead again he found a fairly decent downhill trail where his horse could maintain a fast trot. Now they would be able to make up for the time lost in the thick timber. They maintained the new pace for several hours, steadily increasing the distance between them and their Nez Perce pursuers.

It was almost midday when Sam was startled from a half doze by the barking of a dog. His horse stopped abruptly, a red dog standing directly ahead of it in a bend in the trail. For an instant Sam regretted that the only rifle was at the end of the line in Lance's hand.

At first Sam thought maybe it was a wild dog or wolf, but there was a leather collar on its neck. Sam scanned the woods and trail for any sign of its master. All was still. The rest of the horses behind him had stopped, too. There was a foreign smell in the air, like the stink of rotting flesh.

The dog barked again, refusing to budge from the trail to make way for the horses. The dog was thin and bony, and Sam guessed that it had not had a meal in at least several days. But he couldn't guess why it refused to leave the trail and eat the nearby flesh, or at least back down before the approaching horses. It occurred to Sam that the dog might be sick, might even have rabies.

Sam reached in his pouch and tossed one of the last pieces of horse jerky in the direction of the dog. It gulped down the meat with one swallow but growled threateningly when Sam attempted to move closer. The smell of rotting flesh was stronger than ever.

Sam dismounted, dropped to one knee, then retrieved another piece of horse jerky from his possibles bag. This time he didn't throw it to the dog, but just held it out as a sort of peace offering.

The dog hesitated. Sam didn't move. He just talked to the dog, sounding as warm and inviting as possible. The jerky was too much to resist—the dog began to inch forward. A few minutes later Sam was patting the big red dog on the head as it gulped down the last of his jerky. It appeared to be an Indian dog, with short pointed ears.

When the meat was gone, Sam walked slowly toward the rotten smell, the dog whining softly at his side. The big question in Sam's mind was why a dog would allow itself to starve when there was meat around.

As soon as he passed through the bend in the trail, Sam had the answer to his question. Stretched out on the soft pine needles, under a big ponderosa, was the dead body of an old man, an Indian. His body was swollen tightly inside his buckskins. Some flies were crawling over his face and hands. Beside him on the bed of pine needles were a primitive bow and a quiver full of arrows.

Sam dropped to his knees and caressed the head of the faithful dog that had maintained a lonely vigil at the side of its dead master.

Sam crawled forward and began covering the body with pine needles. Without a digging tool to bury the body, the least he could do was cover it to keep the flies away. The dog didn't object.

Sam was almost finished when he realized Leather Belly was at his side. She reached forward and took a knife from the Indian's belt and pulled the bow and quiver away from the body. Sam didn't like the idea of taking items from a dead man, but he also knew the knife and bow could be very useful. He forced himself to stop thinking about the right and wrong of the situation as he finished covering the old man with pine needles. Before mounting his horse, Sam slipped the quiver and bow over his shoulder. He allowed Leather Belly to keep the knife since he already had one himself.

Upon mounting his horse, Sam called to the dog to follow him. There was no reason stay to behind with a dead master. Besides, a watchdog would probably come in handy in the days and nights ahead.

As the horses started moving by, the dog remained beside its dead master, but after a minute or so it trotted down the trail to catch up with its new master, Sam Storm.

Chapter 24

Sam, Lance, and the two Blackfoot women pushed the horse herd hard throughout the entire night and most of the next day. They were heading north along the eastern foothills of the Bitterroot Mountains. To the east, on the open prairie, they spotted occasional herds of buffalo. In a few days they would be in the heart of buffalo country.

Sam was amazed at the endurance of the two women, how they could ride hour after hour without complaining and without resting. Like Sam and Lance, they too were interested in putting as much distance as possible between them and their former captors, the Nez Perces. Still, Sam was impressed with the ability of the two women to endure hardship.

The sun was almost down when Lance shot a deer, a two-point buck, near the mouth of a grassy canyon. Figuring both riders and horses were too weary to go any further anyway, the killing of the deer was a good reason to stop and make camp. Sam and Leather Belly drove the weary horses a little ways up the grassy canyon while Lance cleaned the deer and Kicking Woman began to set up camp right across the trail the horses would have to take if they tried to leave the canyon. No one expected the horses to try and go anywhere until they had had a long rest and their bellies were full of the sweet green grass.

Dark rain clouds had been gathering during the late afternoon. There had not been any rain, but the premature darkness accompanied by occasional lightning flickers gave sufficient warning of approaching rain. Kicking Woman started building a wickiup sufficiently big for all four of them. First she lashed the ends of three dead trees together, then raised them into a tripod. Then she began piling more dead trees, big strips of cottonwood bark, and brush onto the outside of the tripod. Just as it began to sprinkle, Sam and Leather Belly helped pile on the last of the brush and pine bows. A few minutes later, Lance returned with the deer and hung it in a nearby tree.

No one had the energy and patience to build a fire and wait for the deer meat to cook, not after nearly twenty-four hours of nonstop riding. After wearily gulping down the last of the horse jerky, the exhausted travelers curled up on a bed of fresh pine needles and fell into a deep sleep while the red dog, chewing on a deer shank, kept watch at the wickiup opening. Not enough of the drizzling rain got into the wickiup to wake anyone up.

It was the middle of the next day when Sam finally awakened and sat up. Leather Belly was seated near a smoky fire, tending a roasting deer leg. Kicking Woman was still sleeping on the far side of the wickiup. Lance was gone.

"Where's Lance?" asked Sam.

"Check horses," said Leather Belly, without looking up from turning over the roasting leg. When she finished, she looked over at Sam and smiled. "You hungry?"

Sam nodded. She sliced off a half-cooked chunk of the rich, red meat and handed it to him, then turned back to her cooking.

Sam watched Leather Belly as he gnawed hungrily on the chunk of meat. She didn't look as chubby as when he first saw her two days earlier. Had she lost weight during the long horseback ride, or was he getting used to her? He wondered how Kathryn Cannon would have behaved under similar circumstances. Probably all right. Still, Sam was amazed at the ability of these two Indian women to endure hardship without complaint. He didn't know how long they had been tied up captive in the Nez Perce camp. But that, followed by two days and a night of relentless riding, and the two women didn't look any worse because of the experience. Again Sam thought of Kathryn, definitely much more beautiful than either of the Indian women, and how interesting the journey might have been had she been along too.

Sam was chewing on his third chunk of venison when Lance burst into the wickiup, partially out of breath from running.

"Some of the horses crossed a saddle. Heading west up a big canyon to the north."

Sam placed his piece of meat on a flat rock by the fire and began to slip on his moccasins. Kicking Woman was sitting up now, awakened by Lance's arrival.

"Sam, maybe you'd better stay with the main herd," suggested Lance. "No telling how far they went, might be tomorrow before I can get them back. I'll take Kicking Woman with me. You and Leather Belly keep an eye on the main herd. We'll get back as soon as we can."

"Better take this," said Sam, tossing the rifle to Lance, at the same time wondering if his friend was developing romantic sentiments for this Kicking Woman. Even with her hair in disarray from a long sleep, and her buckskin shirt not yet settled to its normal place about her waist, she was not an unattractive sight. In fact, for the first time Sam noticed something very feminine and appealing about this woman, something Lance had apparently noticed a day or two earlier.

And Kicking Woman didn't seem to mind the extra duty she had just been given either. By the time Sam reached out to resume chewing on his piece of meat, she had slipped into her moccasins, picked up her own piece of meat, and was headed out the door to help Lance catch the horses they were going to ride.

"By the way," said Lance in parting. "Keep an eye out for bears. Lots of signs. Grizz, I think. Don't bring any more of that deer in the wickiup other than what you're going to eat right away. And don't get very far from the bow and arrows. You'll probably want to keep the fire going tonight."

Chapter 25

Sam didn't have to wander very far from the wickiup to realize he was indeed in bear country. There were overturned rocks, rotten logs ripped apart, piles of black droppings, and even claw marks on some of the bigger trees. Some of these marks were almost twice Sam's height, indicating at least one very large bear.

Sam remembered his father telling him about the Valley of Grizzlies in the Bitterroot Mountains, where his father had roped a huge grizzly nearly thirty years ago. From his father's descriptions, Sam suspected that the Valley of Grizzlies could be in the same general area, though probably at a higher elevation nearer the mountain peaks.

Sam wondered what would happen if he were attacked by a grizzly, if he would have the same courage his father had demonstrated many years ago. His father had had only a rope. At least Sam had a bow and some iron-tipped arrows, a dog, and even a woman to help maintain watch at night. Still, the thought of standing up to a grizzly was a sobering one.

By late afternoon the last of the rain clouds had vanished from the blue Montana sky. Sam and Leather Belly gathered a plentiful supply of firewood, enough to keep a bright fire burning throughout the night. The wood was stacked to the right and left of the doorway, just inside the wickiup.

As Sam cut more meat from the deer carcass, enough for their evening meal, he noticed the wind had changed and was carrying the smell of the deer meat up the grassy canyon. If there were any bears up there, he figured they would probably catch the scent of the deer before morning. Sam carried the carcass an additional fifty feet from the wickiup and raised it into the lower branches of a ponderosa pine tree. Sam raised the carcass high in the tree, high enough to keep it away from any hungry bears that might catch the scent during the night and come looking for the meat.

If a bear did get into the meat, the dog would probably chase it off. Sam was glad he had the dog, particularly to keep an eye on things at night. He hadn't picked out a name for it yet, but that would come, maybe after the dog proved its worth.

Leather Belly pushed a green cottonwood branch through the fresh piece of venison, resting the ends of the branch in forked sticks planted on opposite sides of the fire.

Near the fire on a framework of sticks was the deer's stomach, open at the top and stuffed full of half-melted back fat and bone marrow. Occasionally, with the help of willow tongs, Leather Belly would take a hot rock from the fire and drop it into the stomach, at the same time removing a cool rock that she returned to the fire. She was melting down the fat and marrow in preparation for making pemmican. During the afternoon she had gathered some wild raspberries and thimbleberries in the nearby creek bottom. Pemmican consisted of berries, meat, and melted fat. After a meat-only diet, the pemmican would be a welcome change.

The venison hadn't been roasting very many minutes over the glowing coals when Sam and Leather Belly began eating, slicing off partially cooked outer portions, exposing the red meat underneath. They ate the meat as it cooked, occasionally tossing a piece to the red dog resting patiently in the doorway of the wickiup, facing inward toward the cookfire.

"Buffalo better," said Leather Belly, her mouth full of the rich venison.

Sam nodded his agreement. Buffalo meat had a milder flavor and was generally juicier than venison, allowing one to consume more at a meal, though it was sometimes tougher. The buffalo fat and bone marrow didn't have the rich, gamy flavor common to venison. Buffalo was better, for sure, but until they were able to obtain a buffalo, the deer would do nicely. Sam sliced off another piece. It was almost dark outside.

"I wonder if Lance and Kicking Woman have caught up with

those horses yet," offered Sam. Leather Belly shrugged her shoulders to acknowledge his comment and admit her not knowing the answer, but she said nothing. In fact, she spoke very little, and though Sam noticed her silence, he didn't mind. Somehow he and this Indian woman were able to get along and communicate with very few words passing between them. And the silent times in between the infrequent words were not awkward.

When the venison was about half gone, the silence of the evening was shattered without warning by the half growl, half screech of an angry animal. A bear, probably a grizzly. Sam reached for the bow and arrows. Leather Belly piled an armload of cottonwood limbs onto the cookfire, disregarding the piece of meat that would soon be scorched. The dog leaped to his feet, spinning at the same time to face the blackness of the night.

The bear roared again, this time accompanied by the snapping of branches and the cracking of some large limbs. From the direction and intensity of the sound, Sam concluded it was after the deer carcass. And instantly he regretted having made the carcass so hard to get. It would have been better merely to have given the deer to the bear, hoping to appease the angry beast. Anything would have been preferable to having an angry grizzly nearby

The roaring and thrashing ended as quickly as it had begun. All was silent again, and Sam and Leather Belly were left to wonder what had happened.

"Guess he got the deer," whispered Sam over the crackling of the fire.

Leather Belly nodded, not taking her eyes away from the entrance to the wickiup.

Sam and Leather Belly would have been content to let the silence continue throughout the remainder of the night, but not the dog. He had been frightened by the initial roaring and thrashing, but the silence that followed was more than he could stand. He knew the bear was out there, but didn't know what it was doing. Maybe he suspected the bear had stolen his deer. Either way, before Sam or Leather Belly could stop him, the dog leaped through the doorway and disappeared into the blackness. Sam and Leather Belly didn't dare call after him, fearing they would attract the bear's attention to the wickiup with the roasting venison and steaming pemmican fat.

The outside silence was short-lived as the dog tried to drive the bear away from the deer. The bear roared his disapproval. The dog barked and snarled his challenge when it became obvious the bear didn't intend to leave.

The barking, snarling, and growling continued for what seemed several minutes. Sam and Leather Belly could only guess what was happening. Then from the sound of crashing brush it became clear that one of the animals was chasing the other, but it was impossible to tell which one was in the lead. It seemed that maybe the bear was in the lead because the noise of the battle seemed to be moving away from the wickiup.

Suddenly the dog yelped. The bear had turned and found his target. The dog yelped again and again.

The hair stood up on Sam's neck as he realized what was happening. The dog had been injured but not killed. The yelps were getting louder and nearer, as was the roar of the furious bear. The defeated dog was racing home, to what it thought to be the safety of the wickiup, the angry grizzly in hot pursuit. Sam scrambled to the back of the wickiup and notched an arrow on the string of his bow, preparing to defend himself and Leather Belly.

Chapter 26

With one arrow notched on the bow string, and another held in his left fist with the bow for a quick second shot, Sam watched the entrance to the wickiup. Though he had grown somewhat fond of the new dog, he hoped the bear would catch it or give up the chase before the dog entered the wickiup. Even if he had had a rifle, Sam didn't think he and Leather Belly would have had much of a chance once the grizzly got inside the wickiup, and as angry as it sounded from the growling and snarling, Sam didn't have any doubts but what it would follow the dog right into the wickiup. The blazing fire would probably keep a calm bear away, but not an angry one.

Then Sam noticed that Leather Belly had stationed herself beside the entrance at the front of the wickiup. She had an arm-length cottonwood limb in her hand, ready to strike the first thing to come through the entrance. Sam's first thought was that the Indian girl was very brave but very stupid. Stopping an angry grizzly with a cottonwood branch was like trying to stop the Snake River with a canoe paddle.

It wasn't until the red dog scrambled into the wickiup that Sam realized Leather Belly had not been waiting for the bear. She brought the limb down, a solid blow on the dog's shoulders, but the dog was moving too fast for the blow to be a solid one.

Realizing Leather Belly was trying to drive the dog back into the night so the bear could chase it elsewhere, Sam yelled at the dog, ordering it to get out, at the same time picking up a limb with his right hand to help drive it out.

But the dog didn't intend to leave, its shoulder already bloody from an angry sweep of one of the bear's front paws. With Leather Belly beating at its back, the dog scrambled behind the protective flames of the fire and rolled over on his back, firmly determined to take any blows these strange new masters might want to deliver rather than go back outside to face the approaching grizzly.

Realizing the clubs were not achieving the desired effect, Sam decided to pick up the dog and throw it outside, but just as he was starting to drop the bow and arrows, he realized the wickiup was beginning to shake. Sam forgot the dog and tightened his grip on the bow and arrows, ready to draw and fire at first sight of the beast.

Suddenly the bear's head thrust through the entrance into the firelight. The black upper lip was curled back in a snarl, the tiny ears flat back on the thick skull, the red eyes flashing an intense anger, the white fangs wet and shiny.

Before Sam could draw and shoot, the bear—momentarily blinded by the blazing fire—rose on its hind legs, lifting the entrance side of the wickiup on its powerful shoulders. The same motion pulled the back of the wickiup closer to the fire, pushing Sam forward, knocking him momentarily off balance.

But Sam recovered instantly, quickly drawing back the first arrow and letting it fly into the right side of the beast's chest. The arrow didn't go deep, however, apparently stopped by a stubborn rib bone. The grizzly swept the shaft away with his left paw as if it were an annoying insect.

Sam had just fired the second arrow when Leather Belly, without warning, stepped between him and the bear. With an upward thrust of her arms, she appeared to splash a container of water all over the front of the raging beast, nearly soaking the face and chest. It wasn't until the brave Indian girl bent over to grab a flaming limb from the fire that Sam realized she hadn't thrown water on the bear, but the melted back fat and bone marrow—hot grease.

As she thrust the flaming limb into the bear's face, the snarling beast swatted it away with a front paw, but not before the hot grease burst into flames, the bear's shaggy neck fur a thousand tiny candle-wicks refusing to be extinguished as the beast tried to rub the fire away. Soon the paws were flaming too, but by this time Leather Belly had scrambled out from under the partially raised wickiup, the red dog and Sam close behind, the bow still in his hand.

A moment later the screaming grizzly thrashed his way free of the flaming wickiup and raced for the dew-covered underbrush in the creek bottom, the red dog bravely nipping at his heels. The flames were soon extinguished, but from the sound of crashing underbrush, the bear didn't stop until long after the sound of the crashing brush was too far away to be heard over the wind in the pines.

Sam and Leather Belly pushed what was left of the wickiup into a crude circle and rekindled the fire in the middle. After they had finished and were making themselves comfortable to wait out the night, the thought of sleep only a distant possibility, the red dog, tail between its legs, approached the outside of the fire circle, whimpering timidly for permission to enter, obviously remembering the beating he had received the last time he had tried to approach the safety and warmth of the fire.

Sam called to the dog in the kindest tone he could muster. The dog took one step forward, then looked at Leather Belly, who had a stick in her hand. When she saw the animal hesitate, she tossed her stick into the fire, then held her arms out to the wary hound, a warm smile on her bronze face. Still cautious, the dog glided up to the fire, dropped to his belly, and began licking the bloody shoulder.

"We'll call him Flaming Bear Chaser," announced Sam.

Leather Belly didn't know the meaning of Chaser, but she grinned her agreement, then repeated after Sam, "Flaming Bear Chaser."

Chapter 27

The bear was dead when Sam, Leather Belly, and Flaming Bear Chaser found it the next morning. After crashing through the dense underbrush in the creek bottom, it had started to climb the hill on the other side; then, changing its mind, it had returned to the creek bottom further up the draw, where it had wallowed in the mud to soothe the seared skin around its face and neck. Apparently Sam's first arrow had penetrated a lung before the bear swept it away. The running had probably pumped the lung full of blood, causing the bear to drown in its own blood, Sam figured.

Upon finding the bear, Leather Belly took Sam's knife and waded into the mud, where she began cutting away the claws and several of the longest fangs. When Sam suggested she get some of the meat too, remembering how the bear had mutilated their deer carcass the night before, she gave him a look of disgust.

"Bear meat no good, not clean," she said as she waded to dry land, her muddy hands heaped with claws and fangs.

They walked over to the stream—to a sunny, grassy spot where they could sit with their feet in the water—and while Sam washed the mud and blood from the claws and fangs, Leather Belly rinsed off her hands and legs. Flaming Bear Chaser splashed back and forth in the shallow water, trying to catch the tiny wild trout.

The night had been long and tiring, and finding the morning sunshine warm and relaxing, Sam and Leather Belly stretched out on the green grass, soaking up the sunshine and watching two white puffy clouds move slowly across the deep blue mountain sky.

"Why do they call you Leather Belly?" asked Sam without looking at her.

"When little," she began in her broken English, "Father gave leather belt. Big gold buttons on it. Wore it everywhere. They call me Leather Belly."

"What were you called before that?" asked Sam.

"Huh?"

"Your name before they called you Leather Belly."

"Snow Child."

To Sam, the name Snow Child sounded much better, and he wondered why her parents would give their daughter an unfeminine name like Leather Belly. Maybe to them such a name didn't sound as bad as it did to a white man. Sam figured he still had a lot to learn about Indian ways, particularly those of the Blackfeet.

Turning toward Leather Belly and raising himself up on one elbow, Sam was about to speak when he noticed that she was sleeping, her long black hair spread fan-like on the green grass, her breast rising and falling with the steady breathing.

Sam didn't disturb Leather Belly's well-deserved rest. But he took advantage of her closed eyes to look at her more closely. The strong nose, the shapely eyebrows, her muscular arms and veined hands with callused palms and short broken fingernails—a woman accustomed to hard work. Yet her face was almost childlike, with no wrinkles in the fine bronze skin, slightly flushed beneath the high cheekbones.

Beneath the soft buckskin shirt her body no longer had the chubby look, at least not to Sam. She was not slender, just more muscular than most women, or so it seemed to Sam.

He thought back on his first impression of this woman, less than a week ago—a chubby, round-faced Indian child she had seemed to him. He had been so wrong. In a few short days she had become so much more. He remembered her standing in front of the raging grizzly, slinging the melted fat in its face. One step forward and a swipe of a mighty paw, and that bear could have ripped her head off. Yet she hadn't backed away until she had set the beast on fire. Her fast thinking and courage had probably saved her life, and Sam's too. Magnificent woman.

Leather Belly moved, turning on her side, toward Sam, pulling her knees closer to her chest. In moving, her buckskin shirt slipped just enough to reveal a patch of skin between her trousers and shirt, just above her navel. The skin was lighter in color, firm and smooth in contrast to the soft, rough buckskin of her shirt. Sam felt like touching, but dared not.

Then he thought of her name—Leather Belly. He hated that name. It didn't belong to this woman. He would change it, call her something else. If her parents could change her name from Snow Child to Leather Belly, then he would just change it again. But to what?

Sam thought of the experiences of the last few days, particularly the run-in with the bear. Her new name would have to have something to do with that—her courage, her quick thinking. It would have to be a name that would demand respect, a proud name, a strong name. A name that told a story, a name more like the woman sleeping in the grass beside him.

Sam thought a long time, considering many possibilities, feeling like a proud parent selecting a name for a new child. Finally, he reached out and put his hand on the woman's shoulder, shaking her.

"Wake up," he demanded. Her eyes opened.

"Grizzly Fire Woman."

"Huh?"

"Your new name. Grizzly Fire Woman. No more Leather Belly."

"Oh," she said. Then pulling her knees closer to her chest, she closed her eyes and went back to sleep.

Sam rolled over on his back, grinning.

"Grizzly Fire Woman," he repeated to himself with pride and satisfaction.

Chapter 28

"Him buffalo runner," said Grizzly Fire Woman, pointing to the lanky buckskin gelding.

"How do you know?" asked Sam.

"He look fast. Easy to catch. Trimmed feet. Injuns love good buffalo runners. Take good care. Him buffalo runner."

When Lance and Kicking Woman hadn't arrived by early afternoon, Sam and Grizzly Fire Woman decided to kill one of the buffalo on the open prairie beyond the mouth of the canyon. The deer carcass had been dragged out of the tree, mutilated and dragged through the dirt by the angry bear the night before, and Grizzly Fire Woman refused to eat any of the grizzly meat.

Their only weapon was the bow and arrows, but Grizzly Fire Woman assured Sam he wouldn't have any trouble getting a buffalo if mounted on a well-trained buffalo runner.

After selecting the horse, she proceeded to give Sam some pointers in the use of a bow and arrows from horseback. It soon became apparent to Sam that she could have made the kill herself, except that she was not strong enough to pull back the short, powerful bow.

Grizzly Fire Woman was not concerned about teaching Sam to be accurate with a bow and arrow. At five or six feet, anyone could hit a buffalo. She was concerned that Sam be able to notch the arrows on the bowstring without looking down. A rider could easily be unseated if his horse suddenly turned or jumped while the rider was looking down with his eyes focused on the arrow notch and bowstring. A buffalo chaser had to keep his eyes on the racing buffalo and the rapidly changing terrain, enabling him to anticipate and be ready for sudden leaps or changes in direction the horse would be making.

She also showed Sam how to keep the arrow from bouncing on the bow by holding his left forefinger across the shaft. But she cautioned him not to hold it too tight, because it would cause him to pull the string out of the notch when drawing back the arrow. Trying to heed all her instructions, Sam galloped the well-trained buckskin back and forth through the camp, shooting arrows into clumps of bear grass. It didn't take long until he felt like he wouldn't have any trouble placing one of the arrows into the side of a racing buffalo. With Grizzly Fire Woman accompanying him on one of the other horses, Sam turned his horse in the direction of the nearest herd of grazing buffalo.

Keeping out of sight of the grazing animals by following a dry gully, they were able to get within several hundred yards before Grizzly Fire Woman and Sam kicked their horses into a full gallop, racing out of the draw toward the startled buffalo.

The buckskin horse didn't need any coaxing or reining. He knew exactly what to do and raced ahead with all the speed he could muster. Sam dropped the rawhide rein and drew the first arrow from the quiver on his back.

By the time the arrow was notched and ready to fire, Sam's horse was racing beside the nearest buffalo, a fat cow. Grizzly Fire Woman was on the other side of the small herd waving and shouting to prevent the stampeding herd from turning away from Sam. Flaming Bear Chaser was following behind the herd, expressing his excitement with frequent barks.

The buckskin horse held its position five or six feet to the right and half a length behind the cow as Sam drew back the arrow and fired it into the side of the buffalo right behind the last rib. The shaft penetrated almost to the feathers, and as the beast leaped in surprise, the red blood began gushing from its mouth.

As the arrow struck the buffalo, the horse moved further away, awaiting the signal from Sam to move back in close to place a second arrow or to move ahead to another animal. Sam had no need for a second animal, so he notched a second arrow and leaned toward the wounded cow, the signal for the horse to move closer. The cow was beginning to slow down now, and after the second arrow sank into her side, she stopped completely, circled several times on wobbly legs, then fell to the ground. By the time Sam and Grizzly Fire Woman dismounted, the beast was dead.

Sam watched with interest as Grizzly Fire Woman rolled up her sleeves and went to work on the buffalo. She knew exactly what to do, having done it many times before. She avoided the mess and gore by skinning the beast without cutting it open. Sam rolled the animal from one side to the other so she could skin the back portions. When finished, she removed the two hindquarters at the hip sockets and tied them together with the sinews. These were laid over Sam's horse. The hide, back straps, and hump roasts were secured on her horse. The rest of the unopened carcass was left behind for the coyotes, magpies, and buzzards.

Lance and Kicking Woman were waiting in camp when Sam and Grizzly Fire Woman returned with the freshly killed meat. A fire was quickly kindled and, as everyone gulped down half-roasted chunks of hump roast, each took his or her turn recounting the adventures and happenings of the previous twenty-four hours.

Lance and Kicking Woman had recovered all but three of the lost horses and were proud to report the herd together again and ready for travel. Lance also expressed his concern about the length of the layover and the possibility of the trailing Nez Perces catching up with them. He suggested they begin driving the horses eastward into the heart of Blackfoot country as soon as they finished eating. Sam nodded his agreement, and Kicking Woman and Grizzly Fire Woman offered no objections.

Chapter 29

Upon reaching Virginia City two days east of the Bitterroot Mountains, Sam and Lance drove their horses along the white men's roads connecting Virginia City to Butte and Helena, then headed north into the heart of Blackfoot country. They sold horses in each of the mining towns, averaging, to their delight, about sixty dollars a head. Upon leaving Helena, their herd had been reduced to about forty animals and the herding was much easier. They had picked up an extra rifle, plenty of ammunition, four saddles, rope, and other needed supplies.

With the heavy gold in his belt, and with less than half of the horses remaining to be sold, Sam began to think more and more about the purpose of this crazy adventure. He remembered the beautiful Kathryn Cannon and the house he was going to build for her, provided he could convince her to break her engagement with Brutus Young.

But whenever Sam got to thinking very hard about his future plans, he found himself looking at Grizzly Fire Woman and remembering how her quick thinking and courage had probably saved him from the charging grizzly. He liked this young Indian woman who helped drive the horses day after day. Always willing to help, never complaining. Grizzly Fire Woman did not have the natural beauty of Kathryn, but after what he had been through with this Indian woman, he couldn't help but feel a strong attraction for her. But he was still determined to return to Salt Lake with the gold as soon as all the horses were sold.

After leaving the Helena mining camp and the last of the white men's roads, the two women led Sam and Lance unerringly to their father's camp on Two Medicine Creek, in the lush rolling foothills southeast of the mountains the Blackfeet called the backbone of the world.

There were tears in the old man's eyes as he embraced his two daughters. They had been stolen by the Nez Perces while he was away on a hunting trip, and when he returned the trail was too old to follow. Knowing they had probably been carried westward over the Rocky Mountains, he never expected to see them again.

Blackweasel was the classic Blackfoot warrior, though getting old, maybe fifty winters. The leathery skin on his face and hands was almost black from years of exposure to sun and wind. He had an aquiline nose, high cheekbones, a firm jaw, a broad forehead, and black, piercing eyes. The fire of life still burned strong in this proud old chief.

Blackweasel wore buckskin leggings, a red flannel loincloth, and a cotton shirt. Most of the members of his village wore combinations of authentic Indian clothing and trade goods obtained from the American and British trading posts.

There were nine lodges in the little camp, and as Blackweasel embraced his newly returned daughters, he was surrounded by half a dozen children of all ages and his three wives, all chattering happily at the return of Leather Belly and Kicking Woman. Blackweasel and his family all seemed pleased with the new name for his daughter, especially when Blackweasel heard the story of the grizzly attack and how his daughter had thrown the melted fat on the animal and set it on fire.

All the Indians in the camp were generally healthy and well fed on seemingly endless numbers of buffalo roaming the grassy prairies of the Blackfoot land.

Sam and Lance gave Chief Blackweasel his choice of any horse in their herd as a gesture of friendship. The next morning as they headed north for Fort Macleod, three Blackfoot warriors accompanied them, each with a payment of one horse for helping with the drive. Kicking Woman and Grizzly Fire Woman stayed behind with promises that Sam and Lance would return after selling the horses. Lance and Kicking Woman were off by themselves that morning, taking a long time saying good-bye.

Sam and Lance returned several weeks later, not as pleased as they thought they would have been over the sale of the horses. The government traders at Fort Macleod said they had sent out the announcement to the newspapers hoping people would bring them horses the following year. They hadn't anticipated so many horses coming in so quickly. They hadn't acquired sufficient stores of winter feed and therefore couldn't pay the advertised amount of ninety to one hundred a head. Sam and Lance only received an average of seventy-eight dollars a head, but still they were pleased when they headed south for the border with nearly eight thousand dollars in gold in their money belts.

As they were approaching Blackweasel's camp on Two Medicine Creek, Lance—who had been in a silent meditative mood during most of the journey to and from Fort Macleod—suddenly announced that he was not returning with Sam to Salt Lake City.

"What?" asked Sam, not sure he had heard his partner correctly.

"Not going back."

"Why not?"

"Going to marry Kicking Woman, live with Blackweasel and his band. Plenty of buffalo to feed all the kids we're going to have."

"What about the gold?" asked Sam, not sure whether to be happy or sad at losing his partner.

"You take my share. With a good woman, a rifle, a teepee, and a handful of good horses, I've got everything a man would want. Don't need the gold. You take it for your house."

"That's generous," said Sam, still taken back by his partner's sudden change in direction.

"Build a fancy mansion," said Lance, "and if things don't work out, come back and get old Blackweasel to give you Grizzly Fire Woman. Together we can take our families into one of those mountain valleys where the elk are so thick and tame they don't even run away when you shoot one. I'd take a life like that any day over living in a fancy house in a big city. If you change your mind, join me. I'll bet Grizzly Fire Woman would go along with something like that."

"I'll take the gold," said Sam, refusing to consider the prospects of settling down with Grizzly Fire Woman. He had other plans, and no matter how much he had come to like this Indian woman, he was not about to change directions.

"I'll build the house," continued Sam, "but if I ever sell it, half of what I get will be yours."

It was several mornings later when Sam said good-bye to Lance and his new bride, Kicking Woman. Then he led his horse over to Blackweasel's teepee, where Grizzly Fire Woman was standing by herself to one side, looking at her feet.

Sam didn't know what to say to her. No promises or intimacies of any kind had ever passed between them. Still, he felt bad, like he was deserting someone who meant a lot to him.

"You come back?" she asked, looking into his eyes for a moment, then back at her feet.

Sam wanted to lie, to tell her he would be back soon, when he had taken the gold to Salt Lake. But he knew differently. He would probably never return to these beautiful hills at the feet of the world's backbone.

"I don't know," said Sam, looking down at his feet too. "I don't know."

"You remember me?" she asked.

"I could never forget the woman who saved my life," he said, looking at her face.

She reached into the fold of her sleeve.

"For you," she said, as she uncoiled a beautiful bear-claw necklace. Ten claws, spaced about an inch apart with beaver fur covering the sinew string between each claw, hung on the necklace. The fur was smooth and soft, and each claw had been polished to a glossy black.

Sam leaned forward and let her slip the necklace over his head. But no sooner was the necklace in place than Sam began removing it. Sam could feel the emotion welling in his chest, and he longed to leap on the back of his horse and gallop away.

"But you are the one who really killed the bear. You wear it, Grizzly Fire Woman," he insisted.

"No," she said, reaching out to stop him with one hand, while with the other hand she loosened the leather lashings holding her dress close around her neck. When the lashings were sufficiently loose, Grizzly Fire Woman reached in and pulled out the front side of a bear claw and beaver necklace identical to the one she had given Sam. She had made it from the other ten claws.

"Me have one too," she smiled. "Both the same. We remember each other."

Sam let his necklace fall back into place around his shoulders, knowing it would be one of his prized possessions for the rest of his life. Then, without warning he grabbed Grizzly Fire Woman by the shoulders, pulled her close to him, and kissed her firmly on the mouth. Before she could respond, he let go of her, turned toward his horse, and swung into the saddle. He waved to everyone in the camp as he let the horse lunge into a full gallop, heading south toward the Helena mining camp. He was accompanied by two of the braves who had helped drive the horses to Fort Macleod.

Chapter 30

Sam could tell from a distance that something was wrong as he approached Curly Bear's camp on the Snake River. Upon leaving Blackweasel's village on Two Medicine Creek, Sam had headed south with his Indian escort to Helena, where he had joined an empty supply train returning to Salt Lake City.

Three days after entering the Snake River Valley, Sam spotted Curly Bear's lodges, or what remained of them, several miles to the west of the main wagon road. All the lodge covers had been removed from the poles to indicate the tribe had moved on. Sam thought it unusual in this mostly treeless country for traveling Indians to leave their lodgepoles behind. But some of the people had remained behind too. There was still smoke from a fire. Sam thought he could hear the distant howling of a dog. There were no horses grazing on the open prairie, but the gray sky was spotted with circling birds—magpies, hawks, buzzards, and a few golden eagles. Something was wrong. Sam decided to investigate.

"Be back in a little while, going to check out that Indian village," called Sam to the other men as he urged his pony into an easy gallop in the direction of the Shoshone camp. The red dog followed.

It was one of those unusually cold summer days, the sky black with clouds but very little rain. A brisk north wind was pushing the warm air further south. It was the kind of day when horses like to keep their backs to the wind.

Sam had covered about half the distance to the village when a sudden change in wind direction carried with it the stench of rotting flesh. He slowed his horse to a walk, noticing that though the wind was cold, his palms were clammy.

The stench seemed to be coming from a sandy draw just north of the camp and leading down to the Snake River. Sam turned his horse toward the draw. He noticed that the dog, which usually ran ahead of him, was staying close to his horse's heels.

As Sam pulled his horse to a stop at the edge of the sandy draw, the air was filled with screeching and the flapping of wings as dozens of startled magpies and buzzards left the ground for the safety of the skies.

Sam looked down on what appeared to be the site of a brutal massacre. The swollen, partially decayed bodies of more than twenty Indians—men, women, and children—cluttered the bottom of the draw. There was a black square on the top of every head, evidence the naked bodies had been scalped.

Sam dismounted and dropped to one knee, suddenly sick to his stomach. He leaned forward as his breakfast burst forth, splashing on the ground and running sideways in a wagon track.

The only thing he wanted to do was get on his horse and gallop away, never looking back, but a force from deep inside compelled him to look again at the ghastly sight. It was almost like a strange voice ordered him to look again because he hadn't seen what he thought he had seen. This was not the site of a massacre.

Sam looked again, this time walking partway into the draw.

Except for the black scabs on the tops of the heads, and the raw places where the birds had been feeding, there was no evidence of battle wounds—no protruding arrow shafts, no bullet holes, no knife wounds. Sam noticed signs of digging where the sides of the draw were steepest. This was not a battlefield, but a graveyard. But why hadn't the bodies been buried?

As he walked closer, Sam noticed black spots on most of the bodies. Scabs.

Sam stopped, then began to retreat. Pox. Smallpox. The dreaded disease that had destroyed entire tribes, the disease that was frequently fatal when contracted by white people but devastating to Indian tribes, sometimes killing up to 80 percent of those afflicted.

But why were the bodies naked? Why had they been scalped? And by whom? And why hadn't the bodies been buried? And if they had, why had they been dug up again and left to rot in the sun, the fodder of carrion?

So many questions, but Sam couldn't think. He knew only that he had to get away. He didn't think he would catch the disease himself, having contracted a mild case as a child. Still, he turned his back, picking up his horse's reins, walking slowly toward what was left of the Shoshone camp, the bare lodgepoles.

An old woman was crouched beside one of the smoky fires. Her buckskin dress was soiled and torn. Her matted gray hair was in disarray. Her wrinkled face and hands looked as if they hadn't been washed in many days. She did not look up as Sam approached. Even when he spoke to her, she continued to stare blankly into the smoky remains of her fire.

It wasn't until Sam placed his hand gently on the woman's shoulder that she looked up at him, and as she did so she opened her mouth and wailed, a mournful cry of grief, but there were no tears in her eyes—the last one having been spent long ago. Sam realized that what he had thought from a distance to be the howl of a dog had been the mourning cry of this pitiful woman—her family and tribe viciously ravaged by the dreaded smallpox, then scalped and stripped by a person or persons as despicable as Satan himself.

"Who took the teepee covers?" asked Sam when she stopped wailing.

She looked back at the smoking fire, ignoring Sam's question. He wasn't sure she understood his English.

"Who scalped the bodies?" he asked, simultaneously making a cutting motion across his scalp with his forefinger and pulling upward on his hair.

Again she did not respond. Sam stood up and walked away, checking out what was left of the village. He half-expected to find more bodies but didn't.

He wondered about the old woman and what would happen to her. He wondered what secrets were locked inside her mind and heart. Why had she been left behind by the survivors? What would she do? How could she survive in this camp of desolation?

Sam opened his saddle bags to see what food he might leave with her. Three pieces of buffalo jerky, some dried apples, and a little sack of flour—enough to keep a squaw nourished for a week or more.

Sam knelt down beside the woman and attempted to place the food in her hands. She let it fall to the ground in front of her.

"Damn it!" exclaimed Sam, suddenly getting angry. He stood up.

He was mad at his fellow white men for bringing smallpox to the Indians, who had no immunities against it. He was mad at those who had dug up and scalped the bodies of those who had died of the pox. He was even mad at God for allowing such a cruel thing to happen. And he was mad at himself for not arriving earlier, possibly in time to prevent the desecration of the bodies. But he was not mad at this poor woman who, in her grief, was unable to tell him what had happened. He wished he could help her bear her grief, but knew he could do nothing.

Sam leaped upon his horse, jerked its head around, and dug his heels into its sides. The horse lunged forward, toward the lumbering freight wagons several miles away. The dog followed close behind.

Sam hadn't gone more than fifty yards when he pulled the horse to a sudden halt. He looked back at the squaw realizing that if left alone she would probably soon be dead. And if she died, her secret would probably die with her. She certainly knew who had dug up and scalped her dead friends and family members.

Maybe after her grief had healed she would be able to tell Sam what had happened here. He wanted to know. He wasn't sure why, except that it just didn't seem right that a crime like that should go unpunished.

Sam galloped back to the woman and dismounted. Again she didn't look up. Sam didn't waste time talking to her. Taking a firm hold on one of her arms, he pulled her to her feet, then reaching behind one of her thighs with his free arm, he lifted her onto his horse. She didn't resist. Placing his foot in the stirrup he swung up behind his new ward.

As the horse galloped toward the freight wagons, Sam wondered what he would do with the old squaw when he reached Salt Lake City. He wondered if she would ever be able to talk about what had happened in the village. He wondered if she even knew enough English to be able to talk to him. But most of all he wondered what horrible sights this grieving woman had witnessed in recent weeks.

Maybe he would find out someday. Maybe he wouldn't. But at least he was saving this Shoshone squaw from what he figured to be certain death on the open prairie. There would be no more deaths in Curly Bear's village.

Chapter 31

After traveling with the old woman for three days, Sam found out she was called Snake Woman. She told him herself, in broken English. But when he tried to get her to talk more, to tell him who had scalped the bodies in her camp, she only turned away and resumed her mourning cry—vaguely resembling the lonely cry of a wolf in the night.

Upon reaching Salt Lake City, Sam headed straight for Molly Skinner's place. He hadn't forgotten how she had generously financed his and Lance's trading expedition, and he intended to pay in full the loan amount plus interest. But he had another reason for going straight to Molly's.

He couldn't have a wailing old squaw on his shirttail, not in Salt Lake City. Maybe Molly could take her in, have her do some housecleaning, perhaps. Once the old woman got over her mourning and was ready to talk about what had happened in her camp, Sam could decide what to do with her next. Perhaps he could take her to live with one of the other Shoshone bands, if he could find one that would take in an old woman. He had his doubts. Maybe he could invite her to be a housekeeper in the new home he was going to build.

Sam wasn't sure Molly would remember him, not without Lance along, but she did. In her usual friendly manner she invited Sam and Snake Woman into the parlor. It was midmorning and no guests were present.

Sam liked Molly. She didn't seem surprised to see him return. She received her gold pieces matter-of-factly, as if she had never had a doubt in the world about Sam and Lance paying her back. Sam just shook his head in amazement. He didn't tell her the Nez Perces had stolen all their horses and had nearly killed the two young adventurers when they stole the horses back. He didn't tell her about the grizzly attack and how his life was barely saved by the quick thinking of an Indian girl named Leather Belly. After all those miles and so many close calls, Sam figured his safe return with all that money in his belt was nothing short of a miracle. But he would let Molly continue to believe the undertaking was an easy one. Maybe he would need another loan someday.

Sam was equally pleased at Molly's reception of Snake Woman. She didn't show any of the normal prejudice against Indians. But he supposed a woman in Molly's business didn't get far looking down her nose at people.

Molly seemed to understand when Sam told her that Snake Woman was mourning the death of family members and friends wiped out in a smallpox epidemic, then scalped and mutilated by people unknown to Sam. Sam said he thought the old woman might be willing to talk about the scalping once she got over her mourning.

"What do you want to know?" asked Molly, getting at the heart of things.

"Who did it," responded Sam.

"But why?"

"I want to know that too," Sam responded, changing the meaning of her comment. "I want to know why they did it."

"So you can get revenge."

"I don't know. I just have to know." Sam looked at his feet, feeling foolish that he couldn't express in words what he felt compelled to do. "Haven't you ever felt like you just had to do something, not for any specific reason, but just because you had to do it?" he asked.

Molly nodded, allowing him to continue.

"I couldn't leave her there to die."

"I can understand that," said Molly reassuringly.

"No," said Sam, "I don't think you do. She's an old woman. Lost her family. Is no longer useful to her people. Her time is past. I could have left her to die, if that was all."

"What are you talking about?" asked Molly.

"The bodies. The children. The old people. The women. Dug from their graves and scalped, then left scattered about on top of the ground for the birds to peck at."

Molly put her hand to her mouth in unpretended horror.

"She knows," said Sam, pointing to Snake Woman. "And maybe someday she'll be able to talk about it. By keeping her alive, I've kept a horrible secret alive."

"So you can get revenge," repeated Molly.

"I don't know," said Sam, raising his voice, not wanting to be pushed any further into something he didn't understand. "I just have to know, if possible. That's all." He paused, then continued.

"Maybe I'll want to seek revenge. Maybe I'll just let it go. I don't know. First I have to hear what the old woman knows."

"Did you know the Indians? asked Molly. "The ones who were scalped."

Sam turned away.

"Yes."

"Were they your friends?"

"No."

Molly was waiting for Sam to say more, but he remained silent. He was thinking how he and Lance had passed out the firewater to Curly Bear's people, then practically stolen their horses in exchange for more firewater. At the time it had seemed like such a clever thing to do. Even afterward, it had just seemed like one exciting part of a grand adventure.

But after finding those same Indians dead and mutilated in that draw, the trading whiskey for horses had taken on a different meaning. Though Sam insisted to himself that this thinking was wrong, the feeling wouldn't leave him that he and Lance had somehow been accomplices in the murder and mutilation of Curly Bear's people. Sam could find no logic to connect the trading of firewater for horses to the smallpox epidemic and eventual scalping. Still, the guilt feelings were there, like an infected wound getting steadily worse.

Molly turned to Snake Woman and began to direct her toward the kitchen. She sensed when it was best not to continue a conversation.

"As soon as I can, I'll let you know where I'm staying," said Sam. "So you can contact me when she decides to talk about it."

Molly nodded, continuing to guide the old woman into the kitchen.

As Sam reached for the door, he wondered what had happened to the bold young man who had entered that same door several months earlier. The certainty that had dominated his life was gone. He didn't know if that was good or bad, or whether or not it would ever return.

Chapter 32

Flaming Bear Chaser didn't like being tied up, but there was no alternative. In a big city like Salt Lake, a dog couldn't be allowed to run free. Stray dogs were frequently shot.

The dog was tied to a post behind Bill Child's livery stable and freighting business on South Temple and Second West. Sam had a temporary arrangement to stay in the loft, but he didn't mind. He liked being close to his horse and dog. The hay loft would do fine until he figured out exactly what he was going to do.

After the dog and horse were safely put away at the livery, Sam headed for the nearest banking institution, Zion's Bank on Main Street, where he deposited the bulk of his money, making sure he kept enough in his pocket to transform himself into the new Sam Storm.

Upon leaving the bank, he headed for the nearest ZCMI store to outfit himself, for the first time in his life, in factory-made, store-bought clothing, including a silk-lined hat. Not very many young men his age had over seven thousand dollars in the bank. He fully intended to look and act the part of the successful young businessman about town.

But even before he entered the store, he was distracted from his purpose by an unusual street-front display of Indian-crafted items. There were tables covered with authentic buckskin shirts, dresses, quivers, shoulder pouches, belts, bows and arrows, cradle boards, moccasins, rawhide saddles and ropes, buffalo robes, headdresses, and teepee covers heaped in piles on the ground. One of the teepees was stretched over lodgepoles to show what teepees looked like set up.

An enthusiastic young man wearing a black silk hat was selling the Indian items to browsing customers. Sam was compelled to take a closer look.

"Which tribe?" asked Sam as he began to unfold one of the teepee covers, looking for any sign of identification. He didn't know what he was looking for.

"Shoshone," replied the clerk with confidence, almost arrogance, like he was an important expert on the American Indian.

"How much?" asked Sam.

"The teepees range from twenty to thirty dollars each depending on size and condition. That one, I think, is twenty-five dollars."

Sam looked up at the clerk.

"A Shoshone wouldn't sell his teepee for twenty-five dollars."

"And why not?" asked the clerk, obviously surprised by Sam's comment.

"There's fourteen or fifteen buffalo hides in that teepee. Half a winter of tanning and sewing for a squaw, plus the value of the hides. Not even a drunk Indian would sell a teepee like that for twenty-five dollars."

It was obvious the young clerk was unaccustomed to pointed questions about his wares, but he recovered quickly.

"What makes you think these items were purchased from Indians?"

"What?" asked Sam.

"The items before you are not common trade goods, but the spoils of war, relics of the Indian wars, taken in battle. That's why these items are so valuable as collectibles, and why the prices are so reasonable."

"What Indian wars are you talking about?" asked Sam, hardly believing what he was hearing. "There aren't any Indian wars going on."

"Though you are wearing buckskins," replied the clerk condescendingly, "it is very obvious you don't know anything about the country north of here. The Shoshones are battling the Nez Perces, the Flatheads are continually attacking the Bannocks, the Utes kill Crows by the hundreds, and all of them regularly launch campaigns against the Blackfeet."

The clerk spoke with enthusiasm and authority, and with a loud voice. Several spectators had gathered to listen to the debate.

"You don't know what you are talking about," said Sam. "Tell me where this stuff really comes from."

"The proof of the Indian wars is before your eyes. Don't tell me you think these items grow on trees."

"This stuff didn't come from any battle between Shoshones and Nez Perces," said Sam with sarcasm in his voice. "There are no bullet or arrow holes in the shirts, and there aren't any blood stains. You don't suppose that instead of fighting this stuff was won in a game of strip poker?"

The spectators laughed, but not the young clerk. He wasn't used to being ridiculed over his limited knowledge of Indians.

"Then how do you explain the scalps?"

"What?" asked Sam in surprise.

"The scalps. I doubt an Indian would offer his scalp in a game of strip poker."

The clerk pointed to a post near the rear of the display. Sam hadn't noticed it earlier. Hanging on the post were dozens of glossy, black scalps.

Without saying anything more, Sam walked over to the post for a closer look. The clerk was gloating in what he thought was victory over the ignorant stranger.

"Don't handle unless you intend to buy," scolded the clerk as Sam ran his hand through the bundles of scalps. Sam ignored the clerk and pulled out several to inspect more closely. More people had gathered to watch the confrontation between Sam and the clerk.

"The skin isn't totally dried out yet on some of these," said Sam.

"Fresh from the Indian wars, just as I said before."

"How much?" asked Sam.

"Only three dollars for the larger ones. All of them are long, thick, and glossy. Well-salted to prevent rot and keep the worms out. Terrific buy."

"Uh-huh," said Sam. "Never met a warrior yet that would sell his scalps for any price, certainly not for three dollars."

"The little ones are only two dollars."

"The little ones?"

"At the bottom of the pole."

Sam removed one of the little scalps from the bottom of the pole. "Why are these smaller?" he asked, his hand beginning to shake.

The clerk didn't notice the increased intensity in Sam's emotions. "Indians are like people," he responded, "some blessed with more hair than others."

"But the hair on this little scalp is finer, not as coarse."

"A scalp is a scalp," said the clerk, shrugging his shoulders.

"No," said Sam, stepping toward the clerk, still holding the little scalp in the palm of his shaking hand. "This scalp is no ordinary scalp. It's from a child, probably a little girl."

Sam thrust the scalp over his head, and shouted for all to hear, "Terrific buy. Only two dollars for this scalp, fresh from the head of a little girl. For three dollars more you can get her mother's scalp. A matching pair."

"Shut up," shouted the clerk, lunging at Sam.

The clerk was about Sam's age and size, perhaps a little taller. But the clerk in the silk hat was no match for Sam, who instinctively side-stepped the awkward charge, at the same time grabbing the clerk's arm and pushing the young man onto the ground, the silk hat bouncing to one side and uncovering a thick patch of red hair.

At first the spectators pushed in to get a better look at the scuffle, but when those in the front saw the flash of Sam's knife they pushed back, some beginning to call for a policeman, thinking Sam was going to kill the young man.

It wasn't until Sam thrust the bloody patch of red hair above his head that the spectators realized what had happened.

"Here's a scalp taken in battle," shouted Sam. "Just don't hang it on the same pole with the scalps of women and children."

Sam threw the scalp on the ground and got to his feet. The clerk stayed on the ground, holding the top of his bloody head, sobbing. He was not seriously hurt, at least not in Sam's eyes.

Sam wiped the knife on his leggings, inserted it back in the sheath, and turned to walk away.

"Raise your hands above your head. The jail is that way," said the policeman who had just pushed through the edge of the crowd. His left hand was pointing up the street. His right hand held a pistol.

Sam raised his hands above his head and began walking up the street. Some of the spectators followed Sam and the policeman. The rest gathered around the clerk with the bloody head.

Chapter 33

"Anybody ever escaped this place?" asked Sam of his only cellmate, an old cowboy who had been locked up for disturbing the peace while intoxicated.

"None that I know of . . . at least none that lived."

"Oh?" said Sam, encouraging the old man to continue.

"Any hand that escapes from here takes the chance of getting old Port on his tail. Might as well be kill't in the escape."

"You mean Porter Rockwell?"

"Yep. Kill't more than a hundred men, they say. Nobody messes with Port."

Sam turned toward the barred window of the red brick cell. He had been in jail nearly three days and was getting restless. He hadn't seen a judge yet, and none of the jailers seemed to know what was going to happen to him. Nobody had ever scalped a store clerk in Salt Lake City before. The guards told him the scalped clerk had been released from the hospital the day before with a big bandage on his head and had mysteriously left town for an unknown destination before any of the newspaper reporters could interview him.

Now Sam was just waiting for he knew not what. Would they send him to prison? Would they fine him if they found out he had nearly eight thousand dollars in the bank? Would they try to force him to leave town? He didn't know.

He wondered about the scalping and how he could have done such a thing in broad daylight on the streets of a busy city. He had never scalped anyone before, not even in the close calls with the Indians up in the Bitterroot Mountains. He and Lance had discussed scalping techniques on several occasions, but only out of interest, never with the intent to actually do it.

He had scalped the clerk in a fit of anger, without any forethought or plan. It had just happened, triggered by the sight of the wet scalps and the haunting memories of those Shoshone women and children dragged from their shallow graves and scalped. Sam knew the clerk hadn't done the scalping, but the man's persistent attempts to establish commercial value on the scalps of women and children was more than Sam could stand with the memories of that grotesque graveyard still fresh in his mind.

Sam wondered about the actual scalping of the clerk. It had been an easy thing for him to do. Maybe too easy. Even fun. But that wasn't the right word. The frustrations over what he had seen at Curly Bear's camp had been building in him. The clerk had fanned the flames. The scalping had been a partial release of many days of gnawing frustration. It had felt good to finally do something about those haunting memories, too good.

Still, it had been the wrong thing to do. He determined that in the future he would take a firmer control of his emotions and actions. He wondered if news of the scalping would make the papers, how Kathryn Cannon would respond, if her pious father would forbid her to see this savage who scalped people on the streets of civilized communities.

Sam's thoughts were interrupted by the clanking of metal, the turning of a key in the door lock. Sam turned toward the door as it opened. The guard ushered Brutus Young into the cell and locked the door behind him.

"Good to see you, Storm," said Brutus, extending his chubby white hand.

Sam nodded and took the hand.

"See you've repented," laughed Brutus, looking in the direction of the cowboy.

"What?" asked Sam, not understanding.

"The old man still has his hair."

Sam didn't laugh with Brutus and the cowboy.

Brutus made himself at home, sitting on the edge of one of the cots. Sam remained standing.

"You'll be getting out of here soon, Storm," said Brutus. "Possibly this evening."

"But I haven't even seen the judge yet."

"I told them you were an old friend," continued Brutus, "from a solid Mormon family, the son of Dan Storm. Everybody around here has heard of your father."

"But I scalped a man in broad daylight in downtown Salt Lake City. They won't turn me loose just because my father is Dan Storm."

"I told them you had just returned from Indian country and that you were totally exhausted from the long journey, that you thought one of the scalps had come from an old Indian friend of yours, that after a few days rest you would be all right. I assured them it wouldn't happen again."

"Wait a minute," said Sam. "Why are you doing all this for me? Remember, I'm the fellow who stole your carriage and tried to steal your girl."

"You returned the carriage and the girl accepted my engagement ring. You haven't done me any harm, Storm. Besides, I like you."

"But what about the clerk, the one I scalped? Isn't he pressing charges?"

"No, he's fine," said Brutus reassuringly. "Not too happy about losing the skin and hair, but he'll survive. The store gave him a nice raise, two brand-new imported wigs, and transferred him to St. George. He's already on his way down there.

"Oh yes," Brutus said as an afterthought. "I killed the story in the papers too. Would appreciate you staying away from reporters. The company doesn't like this kind of publicity."

"What about the scalps?" asked Sam, beginning to feel he was being swept under the carpet.

"Oh, that was an awful thing," said Brutus with as much sincerity as he could muster. "We didn't know some of them were from women and children. I assure you they have been destroyed."

"Good," said Sam, hoping he was hearing the truth.

Brutus stood up, smoothing out his cotton trousers with his pudgy hands, then removing his pocket watch to catch the time. He called for the jailer to open the door.

"Got to be going, Storm," he said. "The little wife is having an early supper tonight."

It took a moment for the words to register, but when they did, Sam was stunned. Brutus was already married! Several thoughts flashed through his mind. The horse-trading expedition. All the money in the bank. The plan to win Kathryn away from Brutus. All too late. They were already married! Sam felt cheated. He sat on the edge of the bed.

"But you weren't going to be married until later in the fall," was all he could get out.

Brutus looked at Sam for a moment, then began to laugh.

Sam stood up, feeling an overwhelming urge to smash that laughing mouth with his clenched fists. But he remembered the scalping and his decision to maintain better control. He concentrated on releasing the tension in his fists, while noticing for the first time the wedding band on Brutus's left hand.

Brutus stopped laughing and took a step back, sensing the intensity in Sam's face. Quickly he began to explain. "Phyllis is fixing supper. We were married three weeks ago."

Sam looked up at the pudgy businessman, hardly able to believe his own good fortune. Brutus had married someone else!

"She's a little on the heavy side and isn't blessed with the good looks Kathryn has, but she's the sweetest little thing you ever met. A great cook. Her father is on the board of directors of ZCMI."

Sam grinned. He couldn't help it. What kind of fool was this Brutus Young, that he would give up a queen for an opportunity to make a few points with his boss? What a fool!

"How did Kathryn take it? I mean, you marrying Phyllis?" asked Sam, trying to contain a growing desire to laugh.

"Oh fine," said Brutus. "At first she didn't like the idea, but she's fine now."

"That's good to hear," said Sam, his mind whirling with new possibilities.

"But very busy," continued Brutus.

"Busy?"

"Wedding preparations. You know how women go overboard on those kinds of things."

"Whose wedding?" asked Sam, beginning to feel that maybe he had laughed too soon.

"Her own, of course."

"Who's she marrying?" asked Sam, all the feelings of good humor suddenly gone.

"You have indeed been in the wilderness a long time. Don't you remember? Kathryn and I are engaged."

"You just said you married Phyllis."

"That's right. And I'm marrying Kathryn too, at the end of October."

Sam sat back down on the bunk, beginning to wonder if he was dreaming.

"Don't look so surprised," counseled Brutus as the jailer opened the door. "Your father has more than one wife. I have been selected to enter the principle too."

"Kathryn will be my second wife," were Brutus's last words as he disappeared through the door.

"I wouldn't bet on that," hissed Sam to himself as the jailer's big key clanked the door bolt back in place.

Chapter 34

Many thoughts were running through Sam's mind as he drove his new carriage eastward on South Temple toward the home of Willard Cannon.

He thought of his own family in American Fork. He hadn't been home in almost two years. He missed his father, Dan Storm, and riding into the hills with him looking for stray cattle and horses, hunting for deer and elk. He missed the home cooking and conversation with his mother, Caroline, and her sister-wife, Sarah, and thought how fortunate he had been to have been raised by two mothers. They had spent many hours reading to him and educating him. And he missed his little brothers and sisters and wrestling and playing with them. He determined to pay them a visit as soon as this matter with Kathryn Cannon reached a conclusion.

Sam wondered about Kathryn and her engagement to Brutus Young. He still found it hard to believe that she really intended to become the second wife, the plural wife, to Brutus. She deserved, and could get, so much more. He wondered what she could possibly see in the plump dry goods broker.

There were a lot of things Sam didn't understand about polygamy. All over Utah, it seemed, young beautiful women were becoming the plural wives of men old enough to be their fathers, even their grandfathers. It was beyond Sam's comprehension why a young, attractive woman would marry a bearded fat man twice her age when there were plenty of young, single men available. When he returned to American Fork he would ask his father's opinion on the subject.

Sam wondered what it would take for Kathryn to change her mind about the upcoming marriage. He wondered if she shared any of the same feelings for him that he had for her. He wondered if his plan to win her hand was too deceptive, not direct enough. He wasn't sure. He only knew that he couldn't wait, he had to move ahead whether he was ready or not. The wedding date with Brutus was approaching quickly. There was no time to lose.

His plan was a simple one. He had stopped by the day before and asked Kathryn to help him choose a home to purchase. He said he had narrowed the field down to two homes and asked her if she would come with him the next day to look at them. He needed the advice of a woman. Today he was picking her up to go look at the two homes. Nothing had been said the day before about her marriage plans or about her engagement to Brutus.

As the carriage moved along the tree-lined streets, Sam thought about his friend Lance, somewhere up in the wilds of Montana with his Blackfoot bride, Kicking Woman. And Leather Belly, the Indian girl Sam had renamed Grizzly Fire Woman. He wondered if he had made a mistake in leaving her behind. She had saved his life in the grizzly attack. She was resourceful, hard-working, and never complained. And he liked her, sometimes more than Kathryn.

He marveled at the differences between Kathryn and Grizzly Fire Woman. While Kathryn played lawn tennis and attended operas, Grizzly Fire Woman tanned buffalo hides and made pemmican in a stick wickiup. He laughed out loud when the thought occurred to him that maybe he could become a polygamist and marry both of them—a society lady from the big city and an Indian squaw from the wilderness. No, that wouldn't do. He had made his choice. Kathryn would be his woman. The only problem was that she had not made that same decision.

During the summer his memories of her had begun to fade. It had become harder to remember what she looked like. The mild scent of her perfume, the touch of her hand, the sound of her voice—all had become memories of memories. But that had changed in the few minutes he had seen her the day before. She was more beautiful than he had remembered, more charming, as they would say in the city, easier to like. He had a feeling that she liked him too, though he couldn't put his finger on anything specific.

But while the memories of Kathryn had faded during the summer, there were other memories that didn't fade. Memories that Sam wanted desperately to forget. The bodies of those scalped Shoshone women and children were as clear in his mind as if he had seen them again that very morning. An Indian walking along the street, fresh dirt beside a hole in the ground, the feel of a cold wind against his face—any of these things would trigger fresh and vivid memories of those scalped bodies.

He thought about the old Shoshone squaw, Snake Woman, and wondered if she would ever talk about the scalping, if she would be able to tell him who did it. He wondered if those were the same scalps he had seen for sale at the store-front display. He wondered what he would do if he found out who had taken the scalps. He wondered why he was so concerned, even haunted, by those poor dead Indians. Indians had been killing and scalping each other for hundreds, perhaps thousands, of years. He should forget the incident, but he couldn't.

Sam pulled his carriage to a stop in front of Kathryn's house and tied his horse to a white post with an iron ring bolted to the top. As he walked toward the door, his feet rustled through red and yellow maple leaves cluttering the cobblestone walk. It was a brisk fall afternoon, perfect for a carriage ride through the streets of Salt Lake City.

Sam was relieved when Willard Jr., Kathryn's little brother, answered the door instead of her father. Sam didn't like being under the scrutinizing eyes of her father, though he felt he had impressed the old man with all the talk the day before about buying a new home and becoming a distributor of fine horses and carriages. Sam hadn't really given much thought as to what he would do once he settled down in Salt Lake, but when Willard Cannon asked, he had to come up with something fast, and dealing in fine horses was something he had always liked. He wasn't sure why he threw in the part about the carriages.

Young Willard held his palm against his mouth to muffle a cough as he welcomed Sam into the house. Willard Jr. didn't appear healthy. He was frail and thin. His normally pale face was red, perhaps with fever. The boy looked like he belonged in bed. Still, he pushed for conversation with Sam.

"You've been in Indian country, haven't you?"

"Yes," responded Sam. "Just got back. Is your sister ready?"

"She'll be down in a minute. I've got some real moccasins." He pointed to his feet.

"What kind are they?" asked Sam. "Which tribe?"

"Brutus said they were Shoshone."

"Brutus gave them to you?" said Sam.

The boy nodded, then held his hand to his mouth to muffle another cough.

"Why did you scalp the ZCMI clerk?" asked the boy after he had finished coughing.

Sam liked the boy's directness, but he hesitated a moment to gather his thoughts. He noticed the oil lamp by the door, the same one where he had held his hand over the flame a few months earlier. He looked at the scar on the palm of his hand.

"He was selling scalps."

"You scalped him for that?" said Willard Jr.

"The scalps came from women and children."

The boy's eyes widened. "Brutus didn't tell us that."

"It's true."

The boy paused for a minute to digest the new information, then continued.

"What was it like? I mean, scalping the clerk. Was it hard? Did you get blood on your hands?"

Sam grinned and drew his knife. "Lay down on the floor, I'll show you."

The boy raised his hands to the side of his head and stepped back. "No, just tell me."

"Come here," said Sam reassuringly. "I won't hurt you. I'll use the back side of the knife to show you where to cut. Promise I won't hurt you."

The boy didn't take long to make up his mind. There was something in Sam's manner that won his trust. He dropped to the floor in front of Sam and rolled over on his back. Sam dropped to one knee, taking a hold of the boy's hair in one hand and with the other holding the dull side of the knife against the boy's forehead.

"You pull the hair tight, like this," said Sam, "then you cut—"

Suddenly the room was filled with the shrill scream of a terrified woman.

Sam spun around. The boy sat up, trying desperately to explain to his stepmother that he was all right, that the man who had scalped the store clerk wasn't doing the same thing to her stepson.

But the woman just stood there and screamed, unable to hear or comprehend any explanation. The boy scrambled to his feet and rushed toward her. Sam returned the knife to its sheath, cursing his bad judgment in attempting to show the boy how a scalp was taken.

Kathryn soon joined the shrieking woman to see what was the matter. Sam thanked his stars that the old man was gone, as was the other wife.

The woman finally stopped screaming when she realized the boy was not harmed. Still, she looked at Sam suspiciously, still unconvinced he hadn't been attempting to scalp the boy, who had only been saved by her intervention.

Sam apologized for the misunderstanding, trying to sound as gentlemanly as possible.

He looked at Kathryn and motioned toward the door. "We need to get going if we're going to be back by dark."

"I don't think your father would want you going anywhere with this man," said the stepmother, still not trusting the young man whom she had seen holding a knife to her stepson's forehead just moments ago.

"I know," said Kathryn, as she put her arm in Sam's and accompanied him to the door.

Chapter 35

"You are still engaged to Brutus," was Sam's first comment as the carriage glided along a tree-lined street toward the first of two houses Sam was considering buying.

"Is there something wrong with that?" responded Kathryn, looking straight ahead past the trotting horse.

"I can think of one good reason," said Sam, sensing he was heading in the wrong direction with this discussion, but unable to stop. "Her name is Phyllis, Brutus's first wife."

"You don't think I should become the second wife of Brutus Young?" Kathryn said coolly, continuing to look ahead.

"It doesn't bother you?"

"Didn't you tell me one time that your father married your mother and another woman in the same ceremony?"

Sam nodded, slapping the horse on the rump with the reins to make it trot faster.

"Have your mother and that other woman been happy, married to your father?"

"Of course," responded Sam, "but with you and Brutus, it's different."

"Is it?" Kathryn said. "I believe plural marriage is ordained of God. Don't you?"

"I don't know," responded Sam honestly.

"Do you think your mother and father were living in sin?"

"Of course not," said Sam.

"Then you must believe in the principle."

"Maybe so," said Sam thoughtfully.

"But," he continued. "I just can't see you becoming the second wife of Brutus Young."

"Why not?" said Kathryn, turning to look at Sam for the first time. Sam couldn't understand why she seemed so good-natured about the coming marriage.

"Do you love him?" asked Sam.

"Yes, I think I do," said Kathryn, looking ahead again.

"I'm beginning to think that maybe you deserve each other," said Sam, suddenly irritated by Kathryn's behavior.

"Would you mind explaining that?" said Kathryn, a note of anger in her voice too. "Besides, what makes you think you're a better catch than Brutus?" she added.

Sam paused a moment, gathering his thoughts, wanting to be precise and accurate with his words so there would be no misunderstanding.

"I think you deserve something better than to be the second wife of Brutus Young. Maybe it isn't me, but I don't think Brutus is for you."

"The authorities of the Church have approved the marriage. I don't remember my father being so happy about anything in years."

"Do you feel trapped?" asked Sam without thinking, but finally catching Kathryn by surprise.

Kathryn didn't respond, continuing to look forward over the back of the trotting horse. It wasn't until Sam noticed the slow crawl of a tear down her cheek that he knew he had finally cracked the shell.

"You don't have to go through with it."

"That's easy for you to say."

"I suppose." There was silence for a few moments.

"It would break my father's heart if I didn't go through with it."

"And if you do go through with it, whose heart will be broken?"

"Not yours, I'm sure," said Kathryn, getting angry again.

"I was talking about you, not me."

"You don't know me."

"And you don't know me."

"That's for sure."

"Then why did you come out with me today?" asked Sam.

"The excitement, I suppose."

"Excitement? We're going to look at a house. That doesn't sound very exciting."

"I mean being with you. A man who borrows money from prostitutes, sells firewater to Indians, scalps store clerks, and has enough money to buy a new house."

Sam found himself blushing. He hadn't realized she knew so much about him. Salt Lake society had an effective grapevine. He was pleased the conversation was finally going in a lighter direction, but Kathryn ended that with her next question.

"Why did you scalp that clerk?"

Sam pondered her question a moment, then asked, "Do you really want to know?"

Kathryn nodded.

Sam looked at her. "I mean, would you really like to know?"

Kathryn nodded again.

Sam pulled the horse to a halt.

"What are you doing?" asked Kathryn.

"There's a woman I would like you to meet."

"I thought we were going to look at a house."

"The house can wait." Sam turned the horse west onto a street that would lead them to the other side of town.

"Where are we going?" asked Kathryn.

"I want you to meet an old woman, a Shoshone squaw."

Chapter 36

"I was gone when it happened," said Molly Skinner. She was shaking her head, looking down at the lifeless body of Snake Woman. The old squaw was wrapped in a green blanket, only her face exposed, eyes closed. The wrinkled, leathery skin had lost its color. The long black hair was wrapped neatly behind her head.

"The police didn't even arrest the man. They said he fired the gun in self-defense," Molly continued. "The stranger was coming up the walk when Snake Woman—seated in a lawn chair in the front yard—grabbed a spade and tried to flatten his head. She was too frail, though. He sidestepped the spade, drew his pistol, and shot her in the chest. That was all."

"Who was he?" asked Sam. Kathryn was at his side.

"J. W. Wilson, according to the police. A freighter. Never heard of him before. An older man with a cane."

"Why did she attack him?" asked Kathryn.

"Nobody knows," said Molly. "The girl who saw it said the old woman just came out of her chair screaming, grabbed the spade and ran toward him. It didn't appear he did anything to provoke the attack."

"Not here in Salt Lake," said Sam. "But maybe up in the Snake River country. Maybe in Curly Bear's village. I don't know, but I would sure like to talk to this J. W. Wilson."

"First," said Molly, "let's see that this poor woman gets a proper burial. I was going to call for a carriage, but we can use yours."

It was almost dark, the sun already below the horizon, when Sam threw the last shovelful of dirt from the bottom of the new grave.

"I'll fetch a lantern," said the man in black who had helped Sam with the digging. Sam crawled out of the hole and brushed off his clothing. Molly and Kathryn were standing beside the new pine box, the final resting place for Snake Woman.

"I'm not a bishop or an elder, but maybe I should say a few words before we lower her down," said Sam, looking toward the two women for their approval. Both nodded for him to proceed.

Sam looked down at the pine box. The aroma of fresh pitch filled the air. No breeze to carry it away.

"I don't know who you were except that your name was Snake Woman," began Sam. "I don't know what other names you may have had as you lived among the Shoshones. I don't know who your man was, if he was kind or mean to you. I assume you had children you loved and who returned that love, but I don't know that either.

"I don't know what burdens you have had to bear, only that the one of recent weeks was a heavy one, when you were found beside the mutilated bodies of your loved ones.

"I don't know what secrets you are taking into the grave with you, but if you can hear me, if you have a spirit watching your body being lowered into the dirt, I want you to know that in me you have a friend, one who won't desert you even in death.

"In my dreams I can still see the desecrated bodies of your loved ones, dragged from their graves, scalped and left for the birds to peck on."

Sam put his hands on his hips. His fists were clenched, turning the knuckles white. Words were coming with increasing difficulty.

"As we lower you into a grave that will not be disturbed, I promise you I will not forget what I saw. And if I can, I will avenge those desecrations. I promise you that, before God and these witnesses."

The man in black returned with the lantern which he placed on the fresh mound of dirt while he and Sam lowered the pine box into the hole.

After dropping off Molly, Sam and Kathryn were silent for a long time as the carriage carried them home. Kathryn was the first to speak.

"This all started when I asked you why you scalped the clerk. I still don't understand."

"When I saw those scalps hanging on a pole in that store," said Sam, after taking a moment to gather his thoughts, "some of them so new they were still moist, some of them so small they had to come from children, the thought occurred to me that maybe they had come from Curly Bear's village, that maybe they had come from Snake Woman's children. I shouldn't have done it, but I just flew into a rage, and that clerk got in the way. I don't know why I scalped him, except that scalping was on my mind at the time. It was the wrong thing to do."

"Then I can tell Father you've repented," said Kathryn good-naturedly, trying to add a little cheer to a somber mood.

"Yes," said Sam, suddenly smiling and looking over at her. Just as quickly his smile disappeared. "At least until I find J. W. Wilson."

Neither said anything as Kathryn scooted closer to Sam, putting her arm in his.

When Sam pulled the horse to a halt in front of her house, she asked, "Will I see you again?"

"Do you want to?"

"Very much," Kathryn said quietly, looking down at her lap.

"I'll pick you up tomorrow afternoon when I'm through at the police station."

"Police?"

"J. W. Wilson. Got to find out what they know about him."

Kathryn ran up the leaf-covered walk as Sam turned his horse around and headed back down the street.

Chapter 37

"What did you find out about the man who shot Snake Woman?" asked Kathryn as Sam helped her into his carriage the next afternoon.

"The police didn't know anything about J. W. Wilson," responded Sam, "except that he was the man who shot an old squaw who tried to hit him with a shovel. No address. No official report. Not that big of a deal. Just another Injun getting out of line. Nobody at the police station could tell me any more than I already knew."

"What are you going to do now?"

"I don't know, not for sure. But if you want to help, next time you see Brutus, ask him if he's ever heard of J. W. Wilson. Maybe I'll ask him that myself."

"What makes you think Brutus might know him?"

"Could be the fellow who sold those green scalps to Brutus. Snake Woman must have recognized him, or at least thought she did. Maybe J. W. Wilson did some of the digging up and scalping on those dead Shoshones. Maybe he tried to sell the stuff to Brutus."

A few minutes later Sam pulled the carriage to a stop in front of a colonial style two-story red frame home with freshly painted white trim and shutters. The home was surrounded by spacious lawns and yellow-red maple trees. There was a "for sale" sign on the front lawn.

"You're not thinking of buying this!" exclaimed Kathryn, turning to Sam, a look of total surprise on her face.

Sam nodded in the affirmative, obviously pleased at Kathryn's reaction.

"But I thought . . ." she continued as she turned and looked at the house again. "I thought it would be a little shack, a log cabin or something. This is practically a mansion! You don't have enough money to buy this, do you?"

Sam nodded, then without saying another word got out to tie the horse to a white hitching post topped with a brass ring.

"Like to see the inside?" he asked as he helped Kathryn out of the carriage.

"That would be nice," she said.

The brick walkway was spotted with red and yellow leaves, and the grass hadn't been trimmed in over a month. Still, there was an elegance about the place that put it in the class with the finest homes in Salt Lake.

"Are you sure you can afford this?" ventured Kathryn, still finding it very hard to accept the idea that this young adventurer and former railroad worker could possibly purchase such a home.

Without answering, Sam left her behind on the walkway and strode across the lawn to the "for sale" sign. Grabbing the wooden sign with both hands he pulled it free and tossed it in some bushes.

"Already bought it," announced Sam, removing the soil from his palms by rubbing them together. "Closed the deal this morning. It's all mine. No mortgage, either."

"But how did you pay for it?" asked Kathryn.

"With money," joked Sam, smiling.

"And how did you get the money?" she persisted. "I mean, taking a few horses to Canada couldn't produce enough money to buy a house like this."

Sam returned to Kathryn, taking her by the arm and guiding her toward the front door.

"Pushing a herd of ponies through Blackfoot country is not an easy thing. Few men who know that country would dare such an undertaking. Lance and I did. We succeeded. And the Royal Canadian Mounted Police rewarded us fairly."

Sam was proud of how brave and resourceful he had described himself, without mentioning the use of firewater in obtaining the horses.

"Where's Lance now?" asked Kathryn as they entered the empty house.

"Stayed in Montana. Settled down with a Blackfoot squaw called Kicking Woman."

"Why didn't you stay with them?"

"I was tempted," said Sam, not sure of the direction the conversation was headed.

"Lance wanted you to stay?"

"Yes, but more than that, there was this Blackfoot squaw . . . but that's a long story. What color rug do you think would go best in this entryway?"

"What was her name?" asked Kathryn, refusing to change conversation.

"Grizzly Fire Woman," responded Sam, not sure if bringing another woman into the conversation would help or hinder his efforts to win Kathryn's affections.

"A very impressive name," said Kathryn, running her right forefinger along a dusty rail. "I'll bet she is very beautiful, for an Indian."

"Yes, she is," said Sam. "A little chubby perhaps, but very healthy and good-looking—and she can ride a horse better than most men."

Sam and Kathryn were slowly moving up the stairway, her forefinger still sliding through the dust.

"What else can she do?" asked Kathryn. Sam thought he noticed a hint of jealousy in her voice.

"Unarmed, she drove off a grizzly bear that was attacking me. Doused it in hot fat and set it on fire."

"Remarkable."

"They used to call her Leather Belly."

"What?" asked Kathryn, taken totally by surprise and beginning to laugh.

"I thought it was funny too. That's why I changed her name to Grizzly Fire Woman."

"Leather Belly," laughed Kathryn as they walked slowly across the balcony toward the master bedroom.

"Did you ever think of bringing her down to Salt Lake with you? I'll bet she would love this house."

"I doubt it," responded Sam, sure now that he had made Kathryn jealous, but not sure if it had been the right thing to do.

"If she didn't like the house, you could put up a teepee for her in the backyard," laughed Kathryn. Sam laughed too. In one sense the comment seemed degrading to Grizzly Fire Woman, but it was also funny—a smoky buffalo-hide teepee didn't belong in the backyard of one of Salt Lake's finest homes.

"If you like this Leather Belly so much," said Kathryn as they entered the master bedroom, "why did you leave her?"

Sam wasn't ready to answer her question, not yet. "Her name is Grizzly Fire Woman, not Leather Belly, not anymore."

"I'm sorry, I forgot." Kathryn walked over to the window. "You were the one who changed her name?"

"Yes, I did," said Sam.

"If I were an Indian," said Kathryn with a sudden burst of enthusiasm, turning to face Sam, "what would you call me?"

Sam grinned, sensing a prime opportunity to do something significant, but he wasn't sure what.

"Let me think about that for a minute," he said, thoughtfully grabbing his chin and turning away. "Hmmm, if you were a squaw, what would be an appropriate name?"

Kathryn waited patiently, idly examining the flower pattern on the wallpaper while Sam considered possible names.

"I've got it," said Sam, turning to face her.

"Caribou Woman."

After what seemed a long pause Kathryn responded with a tentative, "That's interesting."

"Have you ever seen a caribou?" asked Sam.

"No."

"I have. In Canada. A caribou is one of the most beautiful, most majestic animals alive."

Kathryn beamed, thoroughly enjoying the flattery.

"A caribou is almost as big as an elk," continued Sam. "They have big horns like an elk, but the bones are finer. The eyes are big and dark, deep and sensitive. Beautiful animals." Sam paused.

"Please continue," urged Kathryn, smiling brightly.

"A caribou," began Sam, this time talking slower and with more deliberation than before, "is probably the dumbest four-legged animal alive. And I'm not excluding sheep."

Kathryn stepped back, raising one hand to her mouth in total surprise.

"A caribou is too dumb to run from a hunter after two of its companions are gunned down. A caribou is too dumb to stay out of a river that will wash it over a cliff. A caribou is too dumb to effectively use its big horns to protect its young from wolves."

"What did I do to deserve such a cruel attack?" asked Kathryn. There was emotion in her voice, and Sam thought he saw a tear in her eye. Immediately he regretted having been so harsh.

"Look," he said. "I didn't mean to hurt you, but this thing with Brutus—becoming his second wife. Sounds awful stupid to me. I don't think you even love the clown."

"What makes you an expert on how I feel about anything?" asked Kathryn, the tone of hurt in her voice having given way to anger.

"It's just impossible for me to swallow the idea that you are head over heels in love with a chubby dry goods broker whose first love is business, buying, and selling."

"Brutus is a good man," argued Kathryn. "He's in church every week. He sings in the choir. He is a praying man, too. A good example. More than I can say for you. When's the last time you attended a sacrament meeting?"

"About a week before I headed north with those packhorses loaded with firewater for the Injuns," responded Sam impulsively.

"Do you believe in God?" asked Kathryn, taking the offensive.

"Sure," said Sam.

"Do you pray to him?"

"Sometimes when I'm by myself. Never been much of a hand at praying in church," responded Sam in a sincere manner, looking directly into her face.

"Why did you come back here, from Montana?"

"To see you."

Kathryn looked away to the window.

"Why did you want to see me?"

"I think you know the answer to that question," he said softly.

Kathryn stepped toward the window, mustering the strength to ask the next question.

"Do you want to marry me?"

"Is that a formal proposal?" asked Sam, grinning at the chance to have some fun with Kathryn. She spun around, anger flashing in her eyes. If she had had something in her hand she would have thrown it at him.

"No," she said with contempt in her voice. "I love Brutus and intend to marry him."

"Then why did you come here with me today?"

"I was just trying to find out why you are making such an ass out of yourself."

"I'll tell you why," said Sam, determined not to get in a shouting match with this woman he felt so attracted to. He stepped closer to Kathryn. They were facing each other.

"Every time I look into your eyes, or touch your hand, I feel drawn toward you, in a very forceful way. Some of your friends would call it the Spirit of God. Some would call it love. There are some who would call it lust. I don't know what it is. I only know it's real. And I think you feel it too, right?"

"Maybe," said Kathryn, looking down at her feet, unwilling to admit that she had the same feelings.

"I don't know if we are right for each other," continued Sam. "Maybe things won't work out for me in your world. I've bought this house, and I intend to make a living trading and training fine horses. But maybe it won't work. Maybe I'll want to go back into the wilderness with Lance. Maybe I'll get the urge to leave civilization and roam the open prairie with an Indian maiden by the name of Grizzly Fire Woman.

"But then again, maybe I won't want to leave. Maybe things here will agree with me. Maybe you and I could be very happy together. I don't know."

"So, what do you want from me?" said Kathryn, looking again into his eyes.

"Time. All I want is a little time. I don't want any promises. Just time."

"How much?"

"Till spring, maybe. Put off the wedding until spring. Give us a chance to get to know each other better. I'll even take you to church, if you won't expect me to sing in the choir. Maybe things will work out. Maybe they won't. But by spring we should know."

"This is crazy," said Kathryn, looking away again, but visibly moved by Sam's sincerity.

"Until spring?" he pushed.

"I don't know."

Sam took her hands in his.

"Postpone the wedding until spring."

"I'll think about it," she hedged.

Without warning, Sam bent over and kissed her on the cheek. He didn't let go of her hands, nor did she pull them away as she stepped back in surprise.

"You shouldn't have done that."

"You don't think I should have given you a kiss? Why not?" asked Sam, grinning.

"It's too early. Brutus didn't kiss me until after we were engaged."

"In that case, I'll just take it back," said Sam. Before Kathryn realized what he had said, he was kissing her again, this time full on the mouth. This time she didn't withdraw as quickly as before.

"You agree then to postpone the wedding until spring?"

Kathryn nodded and turned toward the door. Sam followed, delighted at how things were working out.

Chapter 38

At first everyone thought it was just another of the many sicknesses that had plagued young Willard from early childhood. The chills, the headache and backache, the nausea and vomiting, and the fever. For a boy that seemed to be continually sick, there was nothing new or noteworthy about a reappearance of these common symptoms. It wasn't until the third day when the red spots began to appear on his face and arms that anyone began to think the unthinkable.

One of the stepmothers insisted young Willard was having a reaction to some bottled strawberries he had eaten. Everyone hoped she was right. But when the spots spread to his trunk and legs and began to fill with pus, the doctor was called to confirm the worst. Willard Jr. had smallpox.

The house was quarantined and no one was allowed to leave. Signs were posted to the front and back gates to warn visitors to stay away. Daily, a neighbor left a box of supplies on the front porch containing fresh fruit, milk, bread, mail, and medical supplies. After the neighbor left the yard, one of the Cannons would take the box inside. The empty box would be returned to the porch, sometimes with messages to be delivered for those quarantined inside the house.

Sometimes there was a message to be delivered to Sam Storm, the young adventurer who was building stables behind his new home a few blocks away. Sam enjoyed receiving the handwritten notes from Kathryn and was always genuinely interested in hearing the latest on how young Willard was getting along. Sam had already had the disease as a child and would have gladly visited the Cannon residence, but the quarantine required that no visitors enter the house because it was feared by the most prominent doctors that even immune individuals could carry the disease germs away from the home with them.

At first Kathryn's letter discussed nothing but Willard's sickness. The high temperature, the delirium, the increasing number of spots, the swelling, the pus, and the grief of Kathryn's father over the possibility of losing his only son. It was a tragic time for the Cannon family. Kathryn seemed to find relief in writing the letters to Sam. He answered most of them, trying to offer what comfort he could but feeling helpless, wishing somehow he could do more.

After the quarantine had been in effect about a week, Sam received a letter with some very unusual, unexpected news. Brutus Young had broken the quarantine and begun his own concerned vigil at the foot of the boy's bed.

"No one was more shocked than I," Kathryn said in her letter to Sam, "to see Brutus break the quarantine. Everyone knew he liked Willard Jr., always bringing him gifts, like all those Indian things: bows, arrows, moccasins, and a buckskin shirt. But no one expected Brutus to break the quarantine. He knew he wouldn't be able to leave the house until after the quarantine, but he came anyway, even though it is his busiest time of the year.

"The first thing Brutus did upon entering the house was insist on joining with my father to give the boy a blessing with consecrated oil. I think all of us were very wrong about Brutus when we accused him of being all business. He is certainly more concerned about the well-being of my little brother than his business interests."

Sam didn't know what to make of the letter. Something was wrong, but he couldn't put his finger on it. Was Brutus involved in a clever attempt to win back Kathryn's affections? He hadn't seemed very upset, according to what Kathryn said, when she told him she wanted to postpone the wedding until spring, that she wasn't absolutely sure she wanted to go through with it, especially since she was now relegated to the position of second wife. She told him she needed more time to think it over, and he said he was agreeable to that. Sam didn't place Brutus above trickery, but it just didn't seem like Brutus to leave his business during the busiest time of the year, unless he was sincerely concerned about the boy. But that didn't seem like Brutus, either, to care that much about the little brother of his former fiancée.

The thought occurred to Sam that maybe he should have broken the quarantine and joined the Cannon family. Having had the disease as a child and being immune, he could have been useful to the family, maybe even found favor with the grieving father. But it was too late now. He had missed that opportunity. With Brutus on hand, there was no room for Sam. He had no alternative but to wait and see what developed. He continued to build his stables.

Four days passed before he received the next letter from Kathryn. This one began with more news about Brutus.

"You wouldn't believe Brutus," she began. "He doesn't eat. He doesn't sleep. He insists on administering to Willard daily. Brutus is the first to cheer when Willard shows the littlest bit of improvement, and the first to moan when the boy gets worse. Unfortunately, the moans are more frequent than the cheers. The temperature refuses to go down. The pox are getting bigger every day. The worst is yet to come, and Willard is getting weaker by the hour. Please remember Willard in your prayers."

Since leaving home to work on the railroad, Sam had never been very regular with personal prayers, but he began to pray frequently that Willard would survive the smallpox.

"Lord," said Sam, kneeling in the sawdust in one of the stalls in his newly completed stable, "I haven't been very faithful. I've sold fire-water to the Injuns. I swear a little, and haven't been to church in over a year. I promise I'll be a lot better if you'll heal this boy. I'll quit swearing, pay my tithing, and even start going to church. I'll even sing in the choir, if that's what it takes. But please help young Willard to whip the smallpox. The boy hasn't had much of a life, being sick all the time. He deserves better. Help him overcome this so he can have a better life . . ."

The words came easier than Sam thought they would. It gave him a good, wholesome feeling to know he was saying a sincere prayer. He began to pray frequently, the health of young Willard always the main subject of his prayers.

But the prayers didn't work. Fifteen days after the spots first appeared, Willard Cannon, age sixteen, died. Two days later he was buried.

Sam attended the funeral but otherwise left the Cannons and Brutus alone to mourn the loss of Willard. A little more than a week following the funeral, Sam received a note from Kathryn requesting that he come see her.

It was a gray afternoon when Sam pulled his carriage to a halt in front of the Cannon home. The first winter snow was sifting down through the chilly, still air. Though the air was cold, the ground was not, at least not enough to hold the tiny snowflakes, which disappeared on contact. But the snow didn't feel cold to Sam. The anticipation of seeing Kathryn once again warmed him to the point where nothing felt cold, not even the snow.

Before Sam could tie the horse's head, he noticed that Kathryn had emerged from the house and was headed in his direction. He waited for her.

A bulky white scarf covered her glossy black hair, which was tied in a bundle at the back of her head. Her cheeks were already pink from the chilly air. Her eyes were dark and sober. A tan shawl covered her strong shoulders, and there were no petticoats to hold her wool skirt away from her legs as she walked quickly toward him. She had never looked so beautiful.

"Let's go for a ride," she said when she was close enough for him to hear.

Sam secured the tie rope to the harness and stepped forward to help Kathryn into the carriage. It felt good to touch her hand once again.

"I prayed for your brother," said Sam, as the carriage began to move up the street. It felt so good to have her beside him once again.

"Everyone did," said Kathryn.

Sam urged the horse into a trot, not sure what he should say next. Maybe enough had been said about Willard. Maybe they should talk about something else.

"We were wrong about Brutus," said Kathryn.

The last thing Sam wanted to talk about was Brutus Young. He didn't respond.

"He's stopped working," she continued, "at the job he loved so much. He and my father sit together for hours, talking about Willard. Sometimes I think Brutus is taking the death harder than Father. I have never seen so much compassion in a man. I have never seen a man so devastated by the death of a loved one."

"You mean Brutus?" asked Sam.

"Yes. We were so wrong about him."

"I guess so," said Sam, unable to think of anything else to say.

There was silence, an awkward silence.

"Would you take me back home?" asked Kathryn.

"Sure," said Sam, turning the carriage around.

"Did you finish the stable?" asked Kathryn.

"Yes."

More silence.

"I don't want you to call on me anymore," said Kathryn as the carriage came to a stop in front of the Cannon home.

"You don't?" said Sam awkwardly.

"Brutus needs me."

"So do I."

"I am going to marry Brutus."

"You promised you would wait until spring."

"Things have changed."

Without waiting for Sam to help her down, Kathryn jumped out of the carriage and ran toward the front door. Sam watched her disappear behind the door, then clucked for the horse to start moving. The snowflakes were bigger now and felt very cold.

Chapter 39

It was still dark when Sam jerked the diamond hitch tight on his second packhorse. He was leaving Salt Lake for good. Now that Kathryn had definitely decided to marry Brutus, there was no longer anything to keep Sam in the city. He had lost all interest in developing a business in fine horses and carriages.

Sam hadn't been home to see his parents and brothers and sisters in American Fork for over a year. He missed them and would have probably gone home had it not been for something he had learned in a recent meeting with Brutus Young.

He had gone to see Brutus in an effort to follow up on the J. W. Wilson lead, to find out if Brutus knew anything about the man who had killed Snake Woman.

Brutus was no longer a chubby, pink-faced businessman. He was lean and pale, with bloodshot eyes and a worried look on his face. Sam still found it hard to understand how a man like Brutus could be so devastated by the death of Kathryn's little brother. The death had changed Brutus dramatically. And he was not faking or pretending.

Brutus swore to Sam that he didn't know anything about a J. W. Wilson, that he had never even heard the name, as far as he could recall. When Sam persisted with questions, Brutus admitted that all the Indian souvenirs had been purchased from one man. Dick Boggs.

Brutus said that Boggs brought several wagonloads of Indian souvenirs to him during the summer, stuff that had been gathered from warring Comanche tribes on the Great Plains. None of it had come from the Shoshone tribes of the Snake River country.

When Sam mentioned how he and Lance had seen Boggs enter Curly Bear's village early in the summer, Brutus just stared at Sam, a sick look on his face like he had just been caught stealing money out of somebody's cash register.

Brutus said Boggs had left town several weeks ago, promising to return in the spring with more Indian souvenirs. The one-legged Missourian had said something about wintering in Bozeman, a Montana Territory mining town.

"No Comanches around there," said Sam in parting.

From the conversation with Brutus, Sam concluded that J. W. Wilson was probably mixed up with Boggs in this souvenir gathering, and that if he found Boggs, J. W. Wilson wouldn't be far away.

He also knew he didn't have much time if he hoped to reach Bozeman before the mountain passes filled with snow. If he waited until spring, there was no telling where Boggs might disappear to. From Bozeman it was possible to follow the Missouri River to St. Louis, or Clark's Fork and the Columbia Rivers to the Pacific Ocean, even in winter. Sam decided to head for Bozeman right away, to get over the passes before the first heavy snows.

When the packhorses were loaded and ready, Sam made one last tour of his new home, the one he had bought for Kathryn. He was carrying a kerosene lantern to light his way in the predawn darkness. He noticed the rail where Kathryn had wiped away the dust with her finger. He also noticed the wallpaper Kathryn had inspected so carefully. Sam stopped in the master bedroom where Kathryn had promised to postpone the wedding with Brutus, where Sam had kissed her. That had been a great day.

Then the boy became ill and Brutus became such a fervent mourner that Kathryn reversed her decision about the marriage, refusing any further contact with Sam.

Sam felt empty, frustrated, unhappy, the fool. As he headed back down the stairs, he decided this brief stay in Salt Lake was a part of his life he wanted to forget. He wanted to forget this house. He wanted to forget Kathryn.

Sam placed the lantern on the only table in the house. There was some white writing paper, a pen, and a bottle of black ink on one side of the table. He began to write a parting note to Kathryn. Maybe the note would help loosen some of the knots in his heart. He didn't know. He only knew that he wanted to speak to her before leaving, and since she refused to see him, using pen and paper was the only alternative. Sam's writing hand was heavy and forceful, and his emotions spilled onto the paper. When finished, he folded the note and slipped it in his shirt pocket for later mailing.

Sam remembered from childhood stories the log cabin his father had built on a hill in Nauvoo, Illinois, overlooking the Mississippi River. He remembered how his father, Dan, had built that cabin in anticipation of marrying his mother, Caroline Logan, and how when she refused him, Dan had burned the cabin to the ground before heading west with the first pioneer company.

Sam had always wondered why his father had burned a perfectly good cabin. Now he thought he could understand. He also felt an urgent need to rid himself of everything that reminded him of a woman who wanted nothing to do with him. He wanted to cleanse his soul of her memories. He wanted to make her sorry about what she had done. Yes, he could understand why his father had burned that new cabin, the one he had worked so hard to build.

Sam had just closed the back door when he looked down at the lantern. He stopped.

Why not? he thought.

He reopened the back door and blew out the lamp. A moment later he climbed into the saddle and grabbed the lead ropes to the two packhorses. Pulling his saddle horse to a stop beside the open back door, he struck a wooden match and tossed it inside. It went out. He tossed in a second match. This one ignited the oil he had just spilled on the kitchen floor. As the flames began to spread, he turned his horse toward the street, digging his heels into its ribs.

A few minutes later he heard bells ringing at a distant firehouse. He wondered if the firemen would get there in time to put out the fire. It didn't really matter. He had more important things to do than to worry about a little fire. He had to get to Bozeman and find Dick Boggs before the passes filled with winter snow.

Chapter 40

"Did the note say anything about why he set it on fire?" asked Brutus. He was in Kathryn's parlor, working out final details for the wedding. The color had returned to his cheeks, and the dry goods broker seemed to be regaining his former cheerfulness. He was eating again, and rapidly gaining back the weight he had lost during the boy's illness.

"Not a thing," said Kathryn.

"But that home was worth nearly eight thousand dollars and he just burned it down. He must be crazy."

"I suppose so," responded Kathryn, a distant look in her eye. She was thinking back on the note Sam had sent her after the fire. It had been addressed to Caribou Woman. That was the first insult. The letter was full of innuendoes, double meanings, and outright bluntness. He had wished her a long and happy life with the dry goods broker, but had also expressed doubt that that would be possible. Sam said he was heading north to find Grizzly Fire Woman, a woman with the courage to do what in her heart she knew to be right.

Sam expressed sincere regret over her brother's death but said Kathryn had been wrong in letting Brutus's mourning move her so deeply. She resented Sam's judgment of the man who had grieved so bitterly over her little brother's death.

Upon finishing the letter, Kathryn burned it, hoping the act would in some way help extinguish memories of the handsome young adventurer. But even as the letter burst into flames, she was overwhelmed with the insignificance of what she was doing. She was burning a piece of paper. He had burned down an entire house, practically a mansion. How much had he really loved her? She would never know. There were a lot of things she would never know about Sam Storm.

Kathryn forced herself back to the present. She looked at the man she would marry in just a few days. He was bouncing back quickly. Still, she marveled at how Brutus had suffered as her brother passed away. A father or brother couldn't have suffered more. She loved Brutus for that. She would always love him, she thought.

Kathryn stepped forward, taking in her hand a package from the table. It was wrapped in white paper and bound with a red string. She handed it to Brutus.

"What's this?" he asked.

"A little gift," she responded.

"Too early for wedding presents."

"I know, but he would want you to have it," she said, referring to her little brother.

Brutus untied the string. The package was soft. He unraveled the paper in eager expectation, then froze, his pink face losing its color when he saw what the package contained.

"I know he would want you to have them," Kathryn said, not understanding what had become a look of horror on Brutus's face. He was looking at the pair of buckskin moccasins he had given the boy several months earlier.

Brutus continued to stare at the moccasins. Finally, Kathryn reached out and removed the moccasins from the package.

"He was so proud to have them," she said, holding the soft, smoky leather against her cheek.

"Don't hold those against your face!" shouted Brutus without warning, reaching out and grabbing the moccasins and rolling them up in the white paper.

"What's wrong?" demanded Kathryn.

Brutus stared at her. He was searching for words. Had she not known better, she could have easily interpreted the look on his face as one of guilt.

"I suppose they bring back memories of things I want to forget," he said meekly, looking down at his feet. "Memories about your brother."

"Look, I've got to go now," he said. "I'll see you tomorrow. Things will be better after we're married."

"I hope so," said Kathryn as she watched him walk toward his carriage. "I hope so."

But as Kathryn went about her afternoon chores, she couldn't forget Brutus's reaction to the moccasins her brother had loved. He should have been touched by such a gift. Instead, he had found them revolting, especially when she had held them against her cheek.

For the second time since Kathryn had known Brutus he had not been predictable. The first time was his deep involvement and mourning in her brother's death. Now, his revulsion to her brother's moccasins. Something wasn't consistent. Something was wrong. Something was confusing.

Kathryn slipped out the back door without saying anything to anyone and ran to the barn. She saddled her horse, mounted, and headed out the back of the lot so no one would see her.

A few minutes later she arrived at the huge pile of ashes that had once been Sam Storm's new house. She didn't know why she had come, only that she felt like it. As though somewhere in those ashes there might be an answer, something to explain or clarify the confusion that was welling up inside her, a helpless feeling that she was being pushed toward some unknown horror.

Not caring about blackening her shoes and the hem of her skirt, Kathryn kicked her way though the ashes. What kind of man would burn down a beautiful house over lost love? What kind of man would scalp a store clerk in a big city? What kind of man would take care of an old wrinkled squaw, swearing a tearful oath over her grave?

Sam said Snake Woman's loved ones had been dug from their graves, stripped, and scalped. How could a woman bear something so horrible? But maybe that wasn't so horrible as helplessly watching those same people die of smallpox. Kathryn could understand what that was like.

Why did Snake Woman go after that man with a shovel? Why did he have to kill her? Why did Brutus buy scalps and sell them? Were those scalps really from children as Sam said they were?

Could Brutus somehow be connected in all these horrible things? Of course not. He had too much compassion. That he had proved. But why had he acted so funny when he saw the moccasins?

Kathryn didn't feel any better as she rode home. Too many questions. Not enough answers. But most of all, that feeling that something was horribly wrong. Maybe Brutus was right. Maybe things would be better once they were married.

Chapter 41

It was a cold November morning when Kathryn, her father and stepmothers, and a small group of relatives gathered in the Sugarhouse Ward building for a quiet marriage ceremony. Completion of the Salt Lake Temple was still more than twenty years away. Later, most Mormon weddings in the Salt Lake area would be performed there.

Brutus was at the church too, with his first wife, Phyllis. The plump, red-faced young woman was already showing the bulge of a first pregnancy.

While first marriages were often surrounded by the customary pomp and ceremony, plural marriages, even in Utah, were generally quiet, even secret. Eastern newspapers were too willing to publicize such events to eager, outraged readers. Federal politicians were falling over each other sponsoring popular antipolygamy legislation. And federal judges assigned to the Utah Territory were eager to jump into the national limelight by clamping down on anything having to do with polygamy. As a result the Mormons tried to be as discreet and secret as possible in an effort to avoid the exploitation of their sacred practice by politicians and newspapers.

Before the ceremony began, a young scribe with bushy sideburns and thick glasses sat down with Kathryn and Brutus to record the vital statistics. He was armed with an impressive pen and ink set. He recorded the information in a big blue book. He wrote down their full names, ages, native towns, counties, and states. He wrote deliberately and carefully, frequently dipping his pen into the ink bottle.

When the scribe was finished, Kathryn, Phyllis, and Brutus were asked to come to the front of the room and stand in a row, facing Bishop Glenn Hill, an older man with thick, snowy hair who had come to the valley with one of the first pioneer companies.

Kathryn was dressed in a blue satin dress, flushed full with petticoats about the bottom, form-fitting around the waist and chest to show off her womanly figure, but modest about the neck. A white shawl was draped loosely about her shoulders. Her long black hair was tied in a tight knot on top of her head, unnatural and stiff. Sam would not have approved. Brutus didn't seem to notice.

The bishop guided plump little Phyllis to the middle position, the grinning Brutus on her right and Kathryn on her left. The three of them were facing the bishop, the rest of the guests behind them, standing and sitting, quietly waiting for the ceremony to begin.

Kathryn looked back at her father and stepmothers, who gave her polite, reassuring smiles. As she looked back at the bishop, tears began to well up in her eyes. She didn't have a handkerchief, so she was forced to sniff.

But her tears were not tears of joy. That was the problem. She wasn't feeling any joy at becoming the second wife of Brutus Young.

It had seemed so right, after her brother's death, to want to marry Brutus. He needed her, and her father had wanted the marriage so badly. But now her feelings had changed, and it was too late to turn back. She hadn't slept the previous night, not because of the usual con cerns of a new bride, but rather the memories of Brutus's revulsion to her brother's moccasins. Something was wrong with the man she was about to marry, and she couldn't put her finger on it.

The bishop began, speaking to Phyllis.

"Are you willing to give this woman to your husband to be his lawful and wedded wife for time and for all eternity? If you are, you will manifest it by placing her right hand within the right hand of your husband."

Kathryn felt Phyllis's hot, moist hand close around her right hand, pulling it toward Brutus. A moment later her hand was swallowed up in Brutus's clammy paw, while Phyllis put her right arm around Brutus's left arm as if she were going for a walk with him.

"Do you, Brother Brutus Millhouse Young," began the bishop, looking at Brutus, "take Sister Kathryn Cannon by the right hand to receive her unto yourself to be your lawful and wedded wife, and you to be her lawful and wedded husband for time and for all eternity . . . ?"

Kathryn's head was spinning. Tears were streaming down her cheeks, and her nose was running. She had tried so hard to please her father. When Brutus had so dreadfully mourned the death of her brother, she had come to the rescue, driving Sam off to Montana. What was supposed to be the happiest day of her life was quickly becoming the most miserable.

"Do you, Sister Kathryn Cannon, take Brother Brutus Millhouse Young by the right hand, and give yourself to him, to be his lawful and wedded wife for time and for all eternity . . . ?"

Kathryn felt Brutus's hand tighten on hers. She didn't like it. She wished he would let go. He would if she had that moccasin in her hand, the moccasin that had repulsed, even frightened him, a few days earlier—like it had some kind of disease or . . .

That was it! Suddenly the pieces began to fall into place. It was like a fresh blast of cold air suddenly clearing away the cloudiness in her mind and in her heart.

Suddenly Kathryn was aware of Bishop Hill asking her a question, something about making a covenant before "these witnesses of your own free will and choice?" A moment earlier, Brutus had said yes to the same question. The bishop was waiting for her to answer. She could feel Brutus's hand tightening its grip even more.

Kathryn looked over at Brutus, who was dry-eyed and grinning.

"The moccasins carried the smallpox!" she shouted. "You knew it." She jerked her hand free and wiped off the sweat on the side of her dress. "You grieved because you killed him, not because you really cared about my brother! You murderer!" She was screaming.

Brutus turned pale, frozen like a statue, mouth open, staring in disbelief at Kathryn. Poor little Phyllis, both hands over her face, was beginning to cry. Kathryn could hear a growing murmur behind her.

The only calm face in the room was that belonging to Bishop Hill. Though totally taken by surprise at Kathryn's outbreak, it was by no means the worst thing that had ever happened, and he was ready to do whatever was necessary to handle the situation. But he wasn't sure yet what action might be required, though his knees were slightly bent, readying him for sudden movement if necessary, a natural stance for a man like Bishop Hill when faced with a stressful situation.

"Please take me home," pleaded Kathryn, stepping forward, putting her hand on the bishop's arm.

"I can't go through with this," she said, "and I can't face my father and all these people. Please take me home, now."

The bishop responded, not so much to her words as to the pleading in her face. A moment later he helped her onto the carriage seat beside him and slapped the reins firmly on the horse's rump, leaving the stunned Brutus, the crying Phyllis, and the startled friends and family behind.

"Do you want to talk about it?" asked the bishop after the horse rounded the first corner and the church was out of sight.

"I tried so hard," she sobbed, "to do the right thing. But he knew about the smallpox."

"I don't understand," said the bishop.

"Brutus gave my brother moccasins taken from Indians who died of smallpox. Willard caught it and died. Brutus knew where the pox came from but didn't say.

"Thinking Brutus really cared about my brother," she continued, "I drove someone else away—the man I ought to marry, the man I want to marry."

"You can probably get him back, and everything will work out just fine," said the bishop reassuringly.

Kathryn shook her head. "No. He burned his house and headed off to Montana, looking for a Blackfoot squaw named Leather Belly. I've lost him."

"Sam Storm, is he the one?"

Kathryn nodded.

"I know his parents," said Bishop Hill.

"You do?"

"Married them. On the Sweetwater, in a snowstorm."

"You did?"

"Good people. Bet the boy is too. Don't think you could go wrong with him."

Kathryn didn't respond. Bishop Hill handed her his handkerchief to wipe her nose. They rode in silence for a while.

"What are you going to do?" asked the bishop as they approached the Cannon home.

"I'm going after him."

"Young Storm?"

She nodded.

"The road to Montana is no place for a lone woman," said the bishop. "Bandits, Indians, men without principle. Winter is approaching. The passes may be closed."

Kathryn didn't respond, but the bishop guessed by the set of her jaw and the look of determination in her eye that she was not seriously heeding his advice.

"Kathryn," said Bishop Hill, as the carriage came to a halt in front of her house. "There's a freighter named Jake Smith. Lives in Centerville. He's leaving for the Montana gold fields in a few days, taking supplies to the mines at Helena, right in the middle of Blackfoot country. Good brother. You can trust him."

"Jake Smith?" asked Kathryn, making sure she got the name right.

"In Centerville." The bishop winked at her.

"You won't tell?" she said.

"I won't."

"Promise?"

"I promise."

Kathryn leaned over and kissed the bishop on the cheek, then jumped out of the carriage and ran toward the house, trying to remember the name of that chief. Blackotter or something. No. Blackweasel. That was it. She would find Blackweasel's band, and Sam Storm.

Chapter 42

Finding Blackweasel's camp on the banks of the Beaverhead River was an unexpected bonus for Sam. He had considered looking for the band after his visit to Bozeman, but it had never occurred to him that he might run into the camp before reaching Bozeman.

The camp was in an open meadow surrounded by cottonwood trees, just a short distance from the willow-lined river. There were eight or nine skin teepees. Half a dozen fresh buffalo hides were pegged out on the yellow grass, flesh side up. Long strips of red meat were drying on willow racks over all of the outside cookfires. Several buffalo quarters were hanging from tree limbs. It appeared Blackweasel's band was having a successful fall hunt, that there would be plenty of food to see the small Blackfoot band through the coming winter.

Leather Belly and Kicking Woman recognized Sam as he entered the camp and ran to him, squealing with delight. Kicking Woman, big with her and Lance's first child, was awkward and clumsy in running to meet Sam. Leather Belly, or Grizzly Fire Woman, had changed too. She was thinner, more of a woman, less of a girl. Sam was glad to see her.

Sam learned that Lance had gone to Bozeman for supplies and was due back at any time. Since Sam had already crossed the high passes and a storm was threatening in the premature darkness of an already gray afternoon, he decided to wait out the storm at Blackweasel's camp. It would be good to see Lance again. But even more, he looked forward to spending some time with Grizzly Fire Woman.

It was dark and snow was falling when Sam heard the first shrill war whoop. He knew that because of the muffling effect of the falling snow it wasn't as far away as it sounded. He grabbed his rifle and stepped out into the snowy darkness. Blackweasel and some of his warriors had heard the cry too and were emerging from their teepees. The war cry sounded again, this time closer. Sam pumped a bullet into the chamber of his rifle.

When the war cry sounded a third time, Sam noticed a familiarity in the voice. So did Blackweasel.

"Claw," grunted the old chief as he crawled back into the warmth of his teepee. Lance Claw was returning from Bozeman.

Not wanting to spend another night out in the storm, Lance had continued his journey after darkness, knowing he would soon be home.

A few minutes later Sam and Lance crawled into the teepee. Lance was jubilant at seeing his old friend again, but he was even more jubilant about what had happened in Bozeman. Reaching into the pockets of his buffalo coat, Lance pulled out handfuls of gold coins. Hundreds of dollars worth. "Should have seen the old buzzard's face when I beat him," he said. "I won it all. Every last gold piece. Reaching into his pack, Lance pulled out a beautiful full-length beaver coat and tossed it to Kicking Woman.

"Won that, too. Cleaned out the old buzzard."

Lance began to tell Sam and the women about the great poker game in Bozeman and how the "half-breed from Blackweasel's band cleaned out all those smart palefaces." He described the last hand, how everyone had bet so much, and how he had won it with aces and eights, two pair.

"The old one-legged, one-eyed buzzard was furious!" laughed Lance. "Should have heard him curse. Took all his money and the very coat off his back, that one there," he said, pointing to the beautiful beaver coat he had just given to Kicking Woman.

The reference to the one-legged, one-eyed old buzzard reminded Sam of the man he was looking for in Bozeman. Dick Boggs.

"Do you remember the old buzzard's name?" asked Sam.

"Yeah," said Lance. "Olson, or Wilson, or something like that."

"Try to remember."

Lance thought a minute.

"Wilson. That was it. J. W. Wilson. Do you know him?"

Sam's mind was spinning. J. W. Wilson was the man who shot Snake Woman. Now Lance was telling him J. W. Wilson was an old man with a wooden leg and one eye, a description that fit Dick Boggs who, according to Brutus, was in Bozeman.

Sam asked Lance to describe the old man once again. When the half-breed finished, Sam was sure that J. W. Wilson and Dick Boggs were the same person. Dick Boggs had killed Snake Woman, probably because she recognized him as one of the men who dug up and scalped her loved ones. Brutus, knowingly or unknowingly, had lied about the green scalps not being Shoshone.

The next morning there was over two feet of snow on the ground, too much to allow travel by horse, and since it was still early in the winter season, Sam didn't want to set out on snowshoes, taking the risk that a few warm days would melt the snow and leave him without a horse. He decided to wait a few days.

Besides, he needed time to think things out. How was he going to approach Boggs? While it appeared that Boggs was definitely involved in the desecrations at Curly Bear's camp, Sam still didn't know exactly what that involvement was. Had Boggs actually dug up the bodies and scalped them? Or had he just bought the scalps and clothing from other Indians who had done the dirty work? Had Boggs just stumbled accidentally onto the camp devastated by smallpox on the way to Salt Lake and seen an opportunity to increase his profits? Or was there a more calculated involvement?

Sam knew he didn't have the whole picture. He also knew Boggs wouldn't willingly volunteer information. He couldn't just gun Boggs down without knowing more. But how could he learn more?

Sam explained his problem to Lance, who up until now hadn't been aware of the smallpox epidemic in Curly Bear's camp.

"Us Injuns have ways to make white men talk," was Lance's simple reply. He was grinning. "Bring him here. He'll talk."

Sam knew Lance was referring to the vicious tortures Indians inflicted on each other. And he knew Lance wouldn't hesitate to inflict the cruelest of tortures on Boggs.

Sam thought about what he had seen at Curly Bear's camp, his nightmares, his promise to Snake Woman as he buried her in the ground, the profiteering Boggs had enjoyed through Brutus Young, the smallpox epidemics wiping out Indian villages. And there was no doubt but what Dick Boggs had answers to many of the unanswered questions.

"I'll bring him," said Sam.

"Want me to help you?" asked Lance.

Sam nodded.

"We'll leave for Bozeman as soon as the snow melts."

Chapter 43

But the snow didn't melt, not right away. The storm was followed by plunging temperatures, and before warmer air began to melt the snow, a new storm dumped another foot on the ground. It was early November, though, and Sam still expected a thaw of sufficient duration to allow travel by horse.

There was plenty of meat in camp, so the men felt no urgency to hunt. During the days they worked on weapons and peeled bark from young cottonwood trees to feed their horses, which were having difficulty pawing down through the deep snow to get grass. The women worked on hides, made articles of clothing, gathered firewood, and cooked. The children played with their sleds on a nearby hill—sleds made from long buffalo rib bones bashed together at one end with strips of rawhide. After dark everyone gathered around the warm fires inside the teepees, eating and telling stories.

Sam spent much of his time with Grizzly Fire Woman. In the evenings they were never alone. Six to eight people lived in each teepee. Among the Indians there was no such thing as nighttime privacy, unless a couple wanted to venture out into the freezing night.

Sam and Grizzly Fire Woman were frequently alone during the days, however, when they wandered off into the woods to strip cottonwood bark for the horses and gather firewood.

Sometimes they talked about the horse-stealing raid at the Nez Perce camp over on the Salmon River, where Sam and Lance had freed Grizzly Fire Woman and Kicking Woman from their captors. They talked about the ride over the Bitterroot Mountains, the attack of the grizzly bear. Both enjoyed remembering the exciting adventures they had experienced together. But mostly they just enjoyed being together, gathering the bark and firewood, occasionally touching, looking into each other's eyes.

Sam guessed, from the way Grizzly Fire Woman looked at him and her eagerness to be with him, that she wanted to be his woman. Sam felt the same way about her, especially when he thought about Kathryn becoming the second wife of Brutus Young. But still, he felt some reluctance, and he wasn't sure why. Maybe he wasn't sure he wanted to live the life of an Indian. Sometimes he yearned to return to Utah Valley, where he was raised, settle on some land as his father had done, build a log cabin, grow crops, and raise a family. He didn't think Grizzly Fire Woman would fit well into a white pioneer society. It wasn't the different way of life that bothered him. She could adjust to that. The problem was how she would fit into a white society that didn't like Indians. Every settler knew someone who had been killed, kidnapped, or scalped by Indians. Everyone had had livestock or personal belongings stolen by Indians. Indians were second-class citizens, heathens, people to be avoided. Sam wasn't sure he wanted to bring Grizzly Fire Woman into that kind of world. And he wasn't sure he wanted to live in her world, where his friend Lance Claw seemed to be so happy.

The second storm was followed by another cold spell, and it was ten days before the snow finally began to melt. Sam and Lance made preparations for their trip to Bozeman. They had decided to lure Boggs out of town, where they would take him captive and bring him back to camp.

Several times Sam had asked the question of Lance, "How do you intend to make him talk?"

Lance always gave the same reply, grinning as he said, "You'll see."

On the morning they were to leave, Kicking Woman became ill. She had severe chills, a headache, and a backache. Had she not been heavy with child, Lance probably would not have been as concerned. Sam and Lance decided to postpone their departure until the next morning when, hopefully, she would be feeling better.

But Kicking Woman was worse the next morning. The chills continued, accompanied now by nausea, vomiting, and what seemed a very high fever. The trip to Bozeman was postponed.

When Sam invited Grizzly Fire Woman to go with him to gather firewood, she shook her head to indicate that she didn't want to. She pulled her buffalo robe more tightly around her shoulders, saying it was too cold outside. Sam was surprised by her answer because a mild south wind had been blowing throughout most of the night and most of the snow had melted. He reached across the small cookfire and placed his palm on her forehead. It was hot, too hot. It was later reported that several of the children in the camp suffered from the same symptoms.

The village became very silent as the smaller children who were still feeling well were sent out to play. The women began to work on hides and gather firewood, and the men tended to their horses, but nobody was talking. Every adult face was as sober as death. No one wanted to be first to speak the unspeakable. It was still too early to be sure, but any hope of escape was rapidly disappearing.

It didn't take Sam long to figure out what was wrong. Too many villages had been devastated. The symptoms always began with the chills and headaches. But no one could be sure until the red spots appeared. When that happened they would know the smallpox was upon them and would be lucky if only half the people in the village died.

Sam gathered firewood by himself. He would have to forget about Boggs for a while. Sam had had the pox as a child and survived, as most white people did. He wouldn't get it again. He could help.

Sam hadn't prayed since before Kathryn's brother's death, but as he gathered the firewood, he knelt in a patch of wet snow and prayed again.

"What did these people do to deserve the smallpox?" he asked God.

"If you don't intervene, most of them will probably die," continued Sam. "I'll do anything you ask if you will make these people well."

He listened for a few moments, hoping for some kind of answer, something he had never done before, but the heavens were silent.

Sam remembered how his father had often given blessings to his wives and children using olive oil, but Sam didn't have any oil, nor did he have the higher priesthood required to perform such blessings. He had never felt so helpless in all his life.

The next morning red spots were discovered on Kicking Woman's face and arms. More of the women and children and one of the men had the chills. There was no longer any doubt that a smallpox epidemic was upon the village. Though no one had died, some of the women began to mourn, wailing the pain in their hearts to the empty skies.

That evening as they were crouched around the fire in silence, Kicking Woman thrashed helplessly on her buffalo robe, clenching her new beaver coat around her body, Sam was suddenly possessed with a thought that released a surge of adrenaline in his veins. His face reddened. His fists clenched.

"You said you won the very coat off his back," said Sam, referring to the beaver coat Lance had won from Dick Boggs, alias J. W. Wilson, in the poker game.

"That's right," said Lance, surprised at the question but even more surprised at the intensity in Sam's voice.

"Was he wearing it?" continued Sam.

"No, we were inside where it was warm."

"Had he been wearing it?"

"No. He had a buffalo coat hanging on a peg by the door."

"Where did he get the beaver coat?"

"He went across the street to a shack where he was staying and fished it out of a pile of things in the woodshed behind the shack."

"Did you go with him?"

"You bet. Didn't want him skipping out on me."

"What did he say when he gave you the coat?"

"'Give this to your squaw. She'll love it.'"

"Did he seem reluctant to give you such a valuable coat?"

"No. He was grinning. He seemed eager to give it to me, like I was an old friend or something."

"Did you wonder why he acted that way to someone who had just cleaned him out in a poker game?"

"No."

"Did he say anything else?" persisted Sam.

"Yes. He asked where I was wintering."

Sam turned and crawled out of the teepee and stood up. He needed some fresh air. He needed to think.

Lance followed. He was curious now. He wanted to know what Sam was thinking. "Tell me what's going through your mind," he demanded.

Sam was silent for a moment, looking up at the stars, breathing deeply the cool night air.

"Remember when we first came upon Curly Bear's camp, on the Snake River?" began Sam.

Lance nodded.

"Remember the old man in the wagon who was trading with the Indians?"

"You called him Boggs, right?"

"Dick Boggs. He also uses the name J. W. Wilson. He's the fellow you played poker with."

"What are you getting at?" asked Lance, getting impatient.

"It wasn't very long after we saw Boggs on the Snake that Curly Bear's camp was wiped out with smallpox."

"Many villages have been wiped out with smallpox this year."

"I wonder how many of them traded with Boggs prior to the outbreak of the epidemic," continued Sam.

"What are you saying?" demanded Lance. He was getting angry too.

"The smallpox broke out in Curly Bear's village shortly after Boggs sold them some trade blankets. Kicking Woman broke out in chills just two weeks after you gave her that beaver coat from Boggs."

"You think I brought the pox back with me from Bozeman?" Lance was shaking as he spoke.

"I think Boggs knew that coat was infected when he gave it to you."

Lance dove into the teepee. A moment later the beaver coat came flying out through the opening, followed by Lance, a rifle in one hand, his coat in the other.

"Where are you going?" demanded Sam.

"There's a son-of-a-bitch in Bozeman that's going to get his head blown off."

Lance reached for a bridle hanging on a tree limb. Sam grabbed Lance's arm.

"We can't go now, not while all these people are sick."

"What do you mean *we*? I'm the one that brought that beaver coat into camp. I'm the one that's going to take care of Wilson, or Boggs."

"Kicking Woman may have a better chance of pulling through if you're here to care for her, to encourage her. Even if she doesn't make it, you should be with her."

Lance jerked his arm out of Sam's grip and threw his rifle on the ground. Clenching his fists and looking toward the sky, the half-breed screamed with all his strength. Sam dropped to his knees and entered the teepee, followed a few moments later by Lance, his face still red with emotion.

"Were you exposed to it as a child?" Sam asked Lance.

"No," said Lance, getting control of himself in front of the women.

"If I get it," said Lance, looking into the fire, "and don't pull through so I can finish my business with Boggs . . ." He hesitated, looking up directly into Sam's face. "Will you finish it for me?"

Sam nodded.

"Swear it."

"I swear," said Sam quietly. "But you're going to pull through. We'll handle Boggs together."

"I hope so," said Lance, looking back into the fire.

Chapter 44

Everyone in Blackweasel's camp who did not come down with the smallpox was busy caring for those who did. Some of the older people had survived the first smallpox epidemic of 1838 that had wiped out nearly half of the entire Blackfoot tribe. They were immune now and were the ones providing most of the care for the children and young people coming down with the disease.

The spots appeared three or four days after the beginning of the chills and headaches, accompanied by high fever. Nausea and vomiting preceded the spots, too. The spots first appeared on the face and arms, eventually spreading to the trunk and legs. Gradually the spots raised, becoming pus-filled blisters, reaching maximum size about the fourteenth day. If the victim survived, the blisters began to dry up, leaving scabs and sometimes scars. Occasionally the fever became so intense the victims tried to crawl into snow banks or icy rivers, the shock usually bringing an early death. Sometimes the victims would try to kill themselves with self-inflicted wounds or by jumping from cliffs.

Sam spent as much time as he could with Grizzly Fire Woman, talking to her, cooling her feverish forehead with a damp rag, helping her about. But as the disease spread and some of the victims became delirious in the advanced stages, Sam's help was needed everywhere—fetching water from the stream, cutting up meat for the soup kettles, gathering firewood and tending the various fires, moving victims, and even washing in the stream an ever-increasing amount of soiled clothing and buffalo robes, the result of severe vomiting and diarrhea. Sam did everything that needed to be done without complaint and with very little rest or sleep.

Lance had become sick too, but he continued to help Kicking Woman until he was too weak to lift his arms. On the ninth day, Kicking Woman lost her baby, which Sam buried in the meadow beyond the circle of teepees. He dug the little grave with the only shovel that was available in the camp.

About the fourteenth day some of the victims began to die. Sam, being the strongest person not stricken with sickness, was selected to dig the graves with the only shovel in camp. He was thankful to be selected for the task. The hard work was somewhat of a distraction from the horror that surrounded him, an outlet for the frustration over watching his friends waste away and not being able to do anything really effective to help them.

In five days Sam dug eleven graves. One cold, windy afternoon while he was digging, he heard someone call his name. Looking back toward the village he saw one of the old women waving to him with one arm, while frantically pointing toward the river with the other.

Sam dropped his shovel and started running toward the river. About halfway there he spotted a woman wading into the icy current. She was already in up to her waist. It was Grizzly Fire Woman. Sam doubled his speed. She had been delirious with fever throughout most of the day, but he would never have guessed she had the strength to reach the river, let alone wade into the strong current.

Sam raced into the water without breaking stride. By the time he reached Grizzly Fire Woman, she had lost her footing and was going under, her long black hair floating above the icy blackness of the water. She was gasping for air as Sam pulled her from the water and cradled her in his arms. After wading from the water, he ran back to the teepee in an effort to get out of the cold wind as quickly as possible.

Gently, Sam placed Grizzly Fire Woman on an open buffalo robe and began to change her soaked clothing. She had been mostly incoherent for several days, but the icy water had revived her, at least temporarily, enabling her to talk.

"Cold water feels good," she said. "Takes away fire."

"Too much cold water is not good," said Sam. "Don't go back to stream. Do you understand me, Grizzly Fire Woman?"

"Grizzly Fire Woman a good name, better than Leather Belly," she said weakly, looking up into Sam's face as he dabbed the moisture from her body with a wad of soft deerskin. A dry doeskin dress was draped across his knee. The wet dress was in a soggy heap on a flat stone by the fire.

Grizzly Fire Woman's stomach was gaunt and hollow from nearly two weeks of sickness. The outline of every rib was clearly defined, but her thighs and breasts were still full and womanly. In addition to the female contours, however, Sam was just as aware of the ugly red blisters erupting through her beautiful bronze skin. He couldn't tell which was stronger, his grief for Grizzly Fire Woman or his hate for Dick Boggs.

"What will happen to me?" she asked, continuing to gaze into Sam's face.

"If you don't hurry and get well, we'll have to change your name to Spotted Belly." Sam forced a smile at this weak attempt at humor, but inside he was choking on his grief.

She smiled too, weakly reaching up to fondle the bear claw necklace she had made for Sam.

"And after I get well?" Grizzly Fire Woman asked.

"You'll be my woman. We'll have our own teepee. Next summer we'll go to a high valley surrounded by snowcapped peaks. There will be so many deer, elk, and buffalo that I will never have to leave on hunting trips. I'll even build you a white man's cabin so you'll be more comfortable in the winter." Sam paused, trying to sense if he was telling her the right things.

"Tell me more," she urged, a weak smile still on her lips, a faraway look in her eyes, as though she could see the things he was describing.

"And we'll have lots of children, little boys with willow bows and arrows running about the woods and meadow, pretending to be warriors. And little girls making clothes for their dolls, helping you about the cabin. Maybe Kicking Woman and Lance will be our neighbors. Our children will play with theirs. . . ."

Sam continued talking as he helped Grizzly Fire Woman into the dry dress and made her as comfortable as possible on the buffalo robe. Several times she tried to add to the picture he was painting with comments of her own, but each time her voice trailed off into incoherence, her strength rapidly evaporating before Sam's eyes. Though briefly stimulating, the icy waters of the Beaverhead River had taken their toll. Grizzly Fire Woman died in Sam's arms.

He held her for a long time, not wanting to let go, not wanting her body to grow cold. She had faced a raging grizzly to save his life. She had been a good friend, and had it not been for the smallpox she would have become his mate for life, perhaps for eternity, the mother of his children. He just couldn't let her go, not without doing something. But what could he do?

Nothing.

He just sat there by the teepee fire, holding her across his lap. Beyond thinking, beyond reasoning, but not beyond feeling.

The next morning, Sam buried Grizzly Fire Woman in the grave he had been digging the day before. She was wrapped in a buffalo robe, still wearing the grizzly claw necklace matching the one Sam was wearing.

Kicking Woman, in spite of losing her child, managed to hang on until the fever broke and the blisters began to dry up. Lance pulled through too, but his emaciated body was little more than a shadow of its former self.

After three weeks the worst was over. Most of the sick Indians who had lasted it out were beginning to hobble about the camp. There hadn't been any new cases in almost ten days.

Blackweasel, who like Sam had had smallpox before, began to make preparations to move what was left of his camp. It was time to leave the memories of horror behind, the filth, too. A year or two of rain, snow, wind, and sun, and it would be a good place to camp again, but now the place was too filthy even for a dog.

On the morning of the departure, Sam was helping Lance take down his teepee when Lance said, "You haven't forgotten Boggs."

"No," said Sam, continuing to roll the heavy buffalo hide cover away from the poles. "That's why I'm not leaving with you this morning."

"You know how much I want to go with you to Bozeman," said the half-breed.

Sam nodded. "But you can't. I understand. Kicking Woman needs you for a while. Besides, you're too weak to be of any use to me."

Lance didn't argue. It took all the strength he had just to help take down the teepee.

"Should Boggs slip past me, we'll both go after him in the spring. But hopefully it'll all be over by then," said Sam as he pushed over the long pole holding the rolled-up hide above the ground.

"Will you leave for Bozeman today?" asked Lance.

"No. I'm not going to Bozeman," said Sam, turning to face the surprised half-breed.

"I don't understand. That's where Boggs is."

"Remember when he gave you the beaver coat and asked where you were camped? What did you tell him?"

"In a meadow about a mile above where the Beaverhead and Ruby Rivers come together."

Sam dropped to his knees and began to roll up the teepee cover.

"I don't need to go to Bozeman to find Boggs. He's coming here, wagon and all. And soon, before the big snows come."

Lance looked at Sam, not saying anything.

"And when he starts digging up those graves," Sam nodded toward the meadow, "I'll be watching from that bunch of trees." Sam pointed toward a grove of ponderosa pine on the hillside just above the meadow.

For the first time since the sickness, Lance grinned. "Do you think you can pull the trigger?" he said. "You've always been a little soft about those kinds of things."

"I'll be the first to admit that some of the evidence on Boggs is what lawyers would call circumstantial," replied Sam. "But when that old man shows up in this camp with a shovel in his hand, his guilt will be sealed before God, as far as I'm concerned."

Sam glanced in the direction of Grizzly Fire Woman's grave, then reached out and grabbed Lance by both shoulders. Looking his friend straight in the eye, he said, "You don't have to worry about me not pulling the trigger on Dick Boggs."

"Will you promise to bring me his scalp, so I can hang it on my lodgepole?" asked Lance.

Sam started to laugh, the first time since Grizzly Fire Woman had died.

"What's funny?" said Lance.

"Boggs is bald."

"Then I'll hang a piece of skin from the top of my highest lodgepole."

"I won't scalp a bald man," said Sam as he wrapped his powerful arms around the bulky teepee cover, lifted it, and began walking toward the nearest packhorse.

Chapter 45

Sam didn't build a fire, night or day. He knew Boggs wouldn't drive his wagon into camp without a prior close check from the top of a hill to make sure everyone had left. That's why Sam had sent his horses with Lance. He couldn't take the chance that Boggs might see or hear a horse. Blackweasel's band was headed upstream in search of a fresh place to camp. There were plenty of big meadows and lots of cottonwood trees all along the Beaverhead River, so Sam didn't think the band would go far, especially with so many still weak from the sickness. He figured they would go five or ten miles at most. Sam planned to join them as soon as he finished with Boggs.

Sam made sure the Indians left some of the teepee poles in place where they could be easily seen from a distance. He also made sure the excess clothing, bedding and other articles left behind by the Indians in their hurry to get away were left in the open, where they would be easy to see. He wanted Boggs to think he would find easy pickings in Blackweasel's camp.

Sam fixed himself a shelter from an old teepee cover, covered with brush for camouflage and lined with several buffalo robes. He didn't have any trouble keeping warm without a fire, though the nights were very cold. Most of the snow had melted during the warm spell, but the northerly winds had brought in more cold air, sometimes cold enough to fill the stream with floating ice. But there was no new snow to protect the ground from the bitter north wind.

During the epidemic, Sam had been too busy to sleep. Now there was nothing to do but sleep, wait and watch. And think.

The beaver coat he was wearing helped him think about Dick Boggs and the smallpox epidemic. He wondered how many Indian villages had unknowingly received the smallpox germs from Dick Boggs. He wondered how many Indians had died from the disease spread by Dick Boggs.

Sam also wondered if Boggs would have gone to so much trouble to spread the smallpox had there not been a ready market for the Indian souvenirs in Salt Lake City. He decided Boggs probably would not have been spreading the disease had there not been good profit in it.

The next question was how much Brutus Young knew about the Indian products he was buying. Surely the ambitious dry goods broker would have been suspicious about Boggs's ability to obtain wagonloads of discarded Indian items with such regularity. It was certainly possible Brutus knew the full story. If so, Brutus was equally guilty, perhaps more so. As much as Sam hated Boggs, he couldn't deny the simple logic that places as much guilt on the man who pays the money as on the man who pulls the trigger. Sam realized that if he killed Boggs he might never know the extent of Brutus's involvement.

Yet he remembered his promise to Snake Woman and what he had sworn to Lance. Sam knew he would take care of Boggs. There was no choice. But if he could do it in a way to find out the true extent of Brutus's involvement, that would be the way to do it.

Yet, did he dare try to take Boggs prisoner? Boggs was tricky, mean. If there was any man alive who knew how to weasel his way out of a tight situation, Boggs did. There were many unanswered questions. The only thing Sam knew for sure was that if he tried to take Boggs alive he would be taking a chance the old man might turn the tables on him.

Sam thought about other things too, about a society where men like Boggs and Brutus could prosper at the expense of so many innocent people. He wondered about a God that would allow so many innocent people to suffer and die to satisfy the greed of a few evil men.

He thought about his own fervent prayers and how they had not been answered or even acknowledged, as far as he could tell. He began to wonder if there was even a God in heaven. He had been taught all his life to have faith, and he had believed, but when things got tough, when people were dying and he turned to God in sincere prayer, nothing had happened. The heavens had remained closed.

Midway into the first night, from the dark confines of his lonely vigil, Sam began to pray again.

"Lord," he began. "All my life I've been told you hear and answer prayers. I'm beginning to wonder about that, and I think you know why." Sam hesitated. He had never prayed like this before. It felt strange trying to talk to God, instead of just asking for stuff.

"I know I haven't been that faithful, especially when I traded the firewater to the Injuns for those horses," he continued, speaking out loud, his face pointed skyward. "But I wasn't praying for myself these last few times—I can understand why you wouldn't want to give me anything. I was praying for people who were dying from smallpox. With all the sincerity of my heart I was asking you to help those poor people. You did nothing. Can you give me one good reason why I should continue believing in you?"

Sam paused again, listening for an answer to his prayer. He could hear the cold wind in the pine boughs. Nothing else.

"Look," said Sam beginning again. "I don't mean to sound rude or proud, but recent events in my life have pushed me beyond the blind faith stage. That blind faith I learned at my father's knee wasn't enough when those people were dying.

"Maybe you don't want anything to do with me because of what I'm about to do. I'm going to kill a man. But you know the details better than I do. I wouldn't be surprised if you were delighted to see someone finally get rid of Boggs. But maybe you don't want the devil getting someone like Boggs to team up with.

"But what about me? You know what's in my heart. Can't you give me some kind of sign, so I can know that I should continue believing in you? I would like to know if you really care about those poor people in this meadow that I had to cover up with dirt."

Sam continued through most of the night, pleading, reasoning, listening. He had no desire to sleep or eat, though he needed both after the long siege with the smallpox.

"I give up," were Sam's last words when it was almost dawn. "When I'm off doing something you don't like, just remember I tried to get something going between you and me. I really did. I tried, and you refused to meet me partway. I hope you don't forget that. I won't."

Sam rolled over onto his back and closed his eyes, trying to relax, determined to get a little sleep before dawn. He felt sick, as though he might throw up. His body was weak and frail from too little nourishment, too little rest, and too much emotional drain. He was too spent to sleep.

"I must sleep," he told himself, keeping his eyes closed. He tried to clear his mind, to not think about anything.

Such were his efforts when he became aware of a cool wetness on both cheeks. Tears were pushing out of the corners of his closed eyes. At the same time he began to feel a welling up in his chest, the kind of feeling a child has when he or she is about to cry. Great sobs forced their way into his throat. He hadn't cried for many years, but he was doing it now. His entire body was suddenly flooded with emotion he could neither control nor understand. The feeling was warm and penetrating, pushing away the weariness, leaving a feeling of well-being and strength. The tears continued to flow after the sobs subsided.

Sam couldn't gauge how long the experience lasted, and he knew he hadn't seen a face or heard a voice. But there was no doubt what he had felt. He concluded his prayers had been answered, in a way he didn't fully understand. Maybe someday.

"Thank you, Lord," were Sam's last words as he fell into a deep, peaceful sleep.

For three days and three nights, Sam waited and watched. He was certain Boggs would come, and he knew exactly what he would do when Boggs started digging up the graves.

It was midway through the morning of the fourth day when Sam thought he heard the sound of iron clanking on stone. Listening intently, he heard the sound again. A few moments later, he could hear the clicking of shod hooves against rocks.

He crouched closer to the ground and pumped a cartridge into the chamber of his Winchester 30-30 repeating rifle. The graves were less than fifty yards away. He would have to be very still if he didn't want to be seen or heard.

A few minutes later Sam spotted an old wagon lumbering along the edge of the river, the same kind of wagon he and Lance had seen the previous summer in Curly Bear's camp. But it was impossible to identify the lone driver as Dick Boggs. The man was bound up tight in a heavy buffalo coat. A wide-brimmed hat was pulled down over his head. The face was nothing more than a brown-black blur under the drooping rim of the hat. A black mule was pulling the wagon.

After passing the teepee poles, the wagon came to a halt only a few yards from one of the graves. The driver climbed down and began to limp toward the back of the wagon. He limped like a man with a wooden leg. It had to be Boggs.

The man hobbled to the rear of the wagon, where he grabbed a shovel before moving toward the nearest grave. There was no longer any doubt in Sam's mind but what the man was Dick Boggs come to rob the graves—the graves of Indians he had infected with his beaver coat. Sam raised the rifle just a little and aligned his sights with Boggs's chest.

It was an easy shot, no chance of missing. Sam had the urge to just squeeze the trigger and get it over with. But no, he would follow his plan, for better or worse. He continued to wait as the old man began to dig, first breaking through the frozen crust, then sinking the shovel into the soft mud below.

After a few minutes of digging, his breath now steamy in the cool winter air, Boggs stopped for a rest, leaning forward on the shovel, raising his wooden leg to rest on the edge of the grave. His strong, good leg was holding the bulk of his weight.

Sam took careful aim. Hitting a man at fifty yards was easy, but hitting a knee at that same distance requires excellent marksmanship. Sam held his breath and squeezed carefully.

The explosion of the rifle echoed back and forth across the little valley, and the startled Dick Boggs found himself flat on his face in the mud of the shallow grave.

Sam ran forward, pumping another round into the chamber. By the time Boggs wiped the mud out of his eyes, he found himself staring into the muzzle of Sam's rifle.

Boggs had lost his hat in the fall, and the greasy white skin on the top of his bald head was the cleanest part of his body. His red beard was oozing with brown muck, as was the front of his smelly buffalo coat. Even the black patch over his bad eye was coated with brown ooze, and he was spitting more muck from between his crooked yellow teeth.

"Want your coat back?" asked Sam.

Boggs appeared to recognize the coat, but it took him a moment or two to figure out who the young man was who was wearing the coat.

"You're the Storm kid," were Boggs's first words, seeming to ignore the bloody mess just above the good knee. Sam had missed his intended mark, inflicting only a flesh wound, though a nasty one.

"Does Brutus Young know how you are getting the Indian stuff you sell him?" asked Sam, at the same time checking the hammer on his rifle to make sure it was ready to fire.

Boggs ignored the question, pushing himself to a sitting position where he could see the tangled mess of bloody flesh. He cursed his bad fortune.

"What about Brutus Young?" persisted Sam. "Did he know you were spreading smallpox among the Indian villages?"

"Of course he knew!" shouted Boggs, irritated by the question. "He bought the stuff and cleaned it up."

"Is there any reason I shouldn't kill you right now?" asked Sam, realizing Boggs might have been lying about Brutus in an effort to shift at least some of the blame away from himself.

"The back of the wagon," said Boggs. "If you saw what's there, you wouldn't kill me."

"What's in the wagon?" demanded Sam.

"Go look."

"No. Tell me," insisted Sam, taking a step closer, shoving the rifle barrel into Boggs's face.

Boggs turned to look at the wagon. Sam glanced in the same direction, suspecting a trick, but not totally sure. That was all the distraction the sly old man needed. He grabbed the barrel of Sam's rifle and jerked it forward, pulling Sam off balance while shoving the barrel into the mud. By the time Sam reacted, regaining his balance and jerking the rifle out of the old man's grasp, the damage had been done. The barrel was full of mud.

"Go ahead, pull the trigger," dared Boggs. "It'll blow up in your face."

Sam knew enough about guns to know Boggs could very well be right. The end of the barrel had gone several inches into the thick mud.

As if from nowhere, Boggs suddenly had a long skinning knife in his hand. He lunged forward, thrusting the knife ahead of him. Sam jumped back, just missing the sweep of the razor-sharp blade.

Before Sam could regain his balance, he saw out of the corner of his eye that Boggs had drawn the knife back behind his right ear and was about to throw it. Sam rolled to one side just as the knife shot forward. It hit him, penetrating the beaver coat and inflicting a nasty slice across his ribs.

Still on his knees, Sam looked over at Boggs, who was cursing the ineffectiveness of his throw while reaching into his coat for what Sam guessed was another knife. Sam leaped away, heading for the nearest willow bush, where he could break off a stick and clean out his rifle barrel. As he did so, he watched Boggs crawl toward the front of his wagon, pushing himself along the ground with the help of his wooden leg. The wounded leg wasn't totally useless, either.

By the time Sam had worked the mud out of the rifle barrel, the determined Boggs was pulling himself over the front wheel onto the wagon seat where his own rifle was resting.

Sam could feel a warm stickiness across his middle as he took quick aim and fired just as Boggs was cocking back the hammer of his rifle. Both rifles fired almost simultaneously. While Boggs's bullet buried itself into the dirt, wide and low of its intended target, Sam wasn't sure where his bullet went. Boggs rolled over backward into the back of the wagon as the startled mule lunged forward, turning away from Sam, toward the river. Sam figured the forward thrust of the wagon was more likely the cause of Boggs rolling into the box than the bullet from Sam's rifle. Sam had fired too quickly to be sure his bullet had found its mark.

The mule pulled the bouncing wagon onto the wagon path beside the icy river and headed back the way it had come, full speed, Boggs safely out of sight in the back of the wagon. Sam looked down at the growing circle of red where the knife had sliced his ribs. The wagon would soon be out of sight, and it appeared he would lose a lot of blood if he ran after it.

Sam raised the rifle to his shoulder again, pumping another cartridge into the chamber, taking careful aim at the galloping mule. There was no other way to stop the wagon.

Carefully, he squeezed off the round. The mule appeared to leap higher than normal as the rifle went off, then fell back into its normal gallop. But it didn't go more than twenty yards before its front legs buckled. Had it not been moving along at a full gallop, the wagon would have just stopped, but at full speed, the momentum of the wagon pushed the front wheels over the mule's back legs, tipping the wagon toward the icy river.

The capsized wagon ground to a halt at the water's edge, dumping all of its contents, including the wounded, cursing Boggs, into the icy current. Boggs started scrambling toward the bank until one of Sam's bullets shattered a chunk of floating ice right in front of his face. Turning, Boggs splashed toward the center of the stream where the current was fastest, having decided he preferred the company of the icy water to that of the angry young man with the rifle.

The last Sam saw Boggs, the old man was frantically trying to keep his head above the surface as the icy current carried him around a bend in the stream and out of sight.

Knowing Boggs wouldn't last long in the freezing waters, Sam looked down at his wound. The blood was flowing freely. Holding one arm tight against his side, he took one last look at Grizzly Fire Woman's grave, then started walking upstream. He hoped Blackweasel's camp wasn't very far.

Chapter 46

Boggs was hanging onto a floating bedroll, still in the swiftest part of the current, when Jake Smith spotted him. Smith's five freight wagons and a small herd of horses had just stopped to make camp not more than a mile below where Boggs had fallen into the water. Though Boggs couldn't have been in the water more than five or six minutes, he had already passed out from the cold, and only his instincts enabled him to hang on to the floating bedroll. His blue hands seemed permanently locked on the folds of the buffalo hide and probably wouldn't have released their grasp even in death, or so it appeared.

Jake and two of his men waded into the shallow part of the stream to get as close to the main channel as possible. They carried long poles, which they used to intercept the floating Boggs as he passed by. They succeeded in drawing him toward them, out of the main current, and a moment later they dragged the half-frozen Boggs ashore.

It was a lucky day for Boggs. One of the wagons was carrying a bathtub ordered by a Helena saloon. Some of the freighters had been heating bath water for a beautiful young woman who had been traveling with them from Utah. She had been nearly two weeks on the trail without bathing, and the freighters had promised to prepare a hot bath for her at the Beaverhead crossing.

The quick-thinking freighters eased the unconscious Boggs into the big bathtub, not bothering to remove his clothing or even his boots, and began dumping the steaming cauldrons of hot water over him. A few minutes later the old man was revived and cursing with pain as the feeling returned too quickly to his extremities. The bath water quickly turned pink as the blood began to flow again from the wound in Boggs's leg. But the pinkness soon gave way to brown as the hot water, with the help of a little lye soap, began to release a half-year's accumulation of grease and dirt from Boggs and his clothing. The warm stench of wet dog permeated the air.

A few minutes later Boggs was in dry clothes, wrapped up in a dry buffalo robe on a cot in the cook tent, which was heated by a blazing cast-iron stove. The young woman with long black hair was tending his wound. She said her name was Kathryn Cannon, which somehow sounded familiar to Boggs, but he couldn't remember where he'd heard it. Her face looked familiar too. She said she had been a nurse at one time at a Salt Lake hospital and would have his leg fixed up in a jiffy. Boggs was grateful for the care. He couldn't get back on his feet too soon. Young Storm probably figured he was dead and had gone upstream to Blackweasel's camp to nurse the knife wound. Even before Kathryn had finished sewing up the wound, Boggs was plotting his revenge on Sam Storm.

Making small talk to put her patient at ease while she worked on the wound, Kathryn mentioned she was looking for the camp of a Blackfoot Indian by the name of Blackweasel.

"What?" said the startled Boggs, sitting up.

"Oh, you know of him?" responded Kathryn.

"Yeah," said Boggs. "He's camped upstream, not more than six or seven miles, I'd guess. What business do you have with that thievin', filthy Injun?"

Kathryn didn't catch the hate in Boggs's voice. She was overwhelmed at the unexpected news of Blackweasel's camp was so close. She answered his question.

"Looking for my fiancé who is supposedly wintering with Blackweasel."

Kathryn didn't figure she was lying calling Sam her fiancé. After all, he had proposed to her. She just hadn't told him yes yet. Besides, she had discovered a double benefit to calling Sam her fiancé since leaving Salt Lake. Going north into the wilderness to be married gave a girl a lot more respect than going north chasing an old boyfriend. And the news that she was engaged tended to stop the men from making serious advances, though they flirted incessantly.

"What's his name? Maybe I know him," asked Boggs, his heart pounding in his chest.

"Sam Storm," said Kathryn.

The cunning Boggs looked down at his leg, thinking. He had to be careful, couldn't show his hand.

"Never heard of him. Must be new to this country," he said matter-of-factly. Then, changing the subject, "How long before I'll be on my feet again?"

"A few days," she answered quickly, her mind now on more important matters. "A clean wound, not very deep. You haven't told us your name," said Kathryn, getting up to leave. She needed to talk Jake Smith out of a saddle horse.

"Ken Jones, they call me," lied Boggs. "Been prospecting near Virginia City."

Kathryn didn't catch the phony name. She was thinking that if she got an early start the next morning, she might be in Blackweasel's camp by noon. She would get the men to heat some clean water for the tub. She would look her best for Sam.

Chapter 47

Sam was picking lint and dirt out of the nasty knife wound when Lance crawled into the teepee. Though not yet his former self, Lance was gaining strength daily, as was Kicking Woman. It was late afternoon.

"You got a visitor," announced Lance.

"Is it Dick Boggs?" asked Sam without laughing at his own weak attempt at humor, and without looking up from the wound.

"A woman."

"The only woman I want to see is under five feet of dirt at the old camp."

"She's beautiful."

"Leave me alone," said Sam, turning away.

"Want me to tell you who she is?"

"Not interested."

"Caribou Woman."

Sam stopped picking at the wound. He had never mentioned that name to Lance, or anyone. Only Kathryn. Impossible. He looked up at Lance, who nodded toward the door and shrugged his shoulders.

"Wouldn't have believed it, either," said Lance. "Take a look. It's her."

Sam crawled out of the teepee and stood up. It was Kathryn, all right. She was mounted on a big gray gelding. She was wearing a red wool coat, blue cotton trousers, and cowhide boots. Her head was bare, but a long white shawl was wrapped around her neck and chin.

Her cheeks were flushed from the cold winter air. She looked good.

"How did you get here?" asked Sam, shaking his head, still finding it hard to believe his eyes weren't playing tricks on him.

"Had some second thoughts about your marriage proposition. Thought I'd ride up and have a talk with you," Kathryn said lightly.

"But this place is over four hundred miles from Salt Lake. It's winter. The passes are filling with snow," stammered Sam.

"You sound like my father."

"But what about Brutus, the wedding?"

"Last I saw Brutus, he was standing at the altar, looking like a stuck pig in front of the bishop and all the wedding guests."

"You didn't marry him?"

"Aren't you going to help me down from this horse?"

Sam stepped forward, reaching up. But as he did so he winced, his face twisting in pain.

Kathryn jumped down without any assistance.

"Knife wound across my chest," explained Sam. "Not serious."

"Let me see," said Kathryn, the nurse in her taking over. Without asking for permission, she lifted up the front of Sam's buckskin shirt to examine the wound.

"A little cleaning and stitching, you'll be as good as new," she said. "Good thing I showed up to take care of you."

A few minutes later Sam was stretched out on a buffalo robe, his chest bare except for the grizzly claw necklace. Kathryn was carefully cleaning the wound in preparation for sewing up the loose flesh. A needle and thread were resting in her lap.

"Never suspected my nursing skills would be in such demand up here," she said to make conversation. Sam didn't respond.

"Patched up a bullet hole yesterday," she continued. "Today a knife wound."

"Bullet hole?" inquired Sam.

"An old man, shot in the leg. The freighters I was traveling with found him floating down the middle of the river, hanging onto a floating buffalo robe."

Sam sat up, ignoring the flash of pain across his chest.

"You know him?" she asked.

"I shot him and dumped him in the river," explained Sam. "Do you know who he is?"

"Said his name was Jones, I think, from Virginia City."

"Did he have a wooden leg and a patch over one eye?"

Kathryn nodded.

"Damn," said Sam. "I figured the cold water would have taken care of him."

"It would have," said Kathryn, "had they not found him when they did and thrown him in a tub of hot water. Who is he?"

"Dick Boggs," explained Sam. "He lied to you about his name."

"Is he the one who was selling all that Indian stuff to Brutus?"

"Right," said Sam. "All those items that were infected with the smallpox germs."

"The moccasins Brutus gave my brother?"

Sam nodded. "Good thing Boggs didn't know who you were."

"But he did," said Kathryn. "He told me where to find Blackweasel's camp. When I told him I was looking for you, he said he had never heard of you."

"How bad was his wound?" asked Sam.

"A flesh wound. Should keep him down for a few days."

"Where were the freighters headed?" asked Sam.

"Helena."

"Were they going to take Boggs with them?"

"Jake wouldn't leave a wounded old man alone on the trail, especially not in winter."

Sam turned toward Lance, who was just entering the teepee.

"Boggs survived my bullet, and the river. He's on his way to Helena with some freighters."

"I'll start getting the horses and gear ready," responded Lance, reacting quickly to the news. "When do you want to leave, tomorrow?"

"Yeah," said Sam. "Shouldn't be any problem catching up with him before they reach Helena. He knows I'm wounded too, so hopefully he won't be in too big a hurry to disappear." Lance crawled back outside to begin getting things together for the journey.

"Sure you need to go after him?" asked Kathryn when they were alone again.

"Do you know where Boggs got all that stuff he was selling to Brutus?"

"From Indian villages that had been devastated by smallpox."

"Do you know how those Indians came in contact with the pox?

Do you know how Boggs was able to provide Brutus with a regular supply of Indian products?"

"What are you getting at?" asked Kathryn.

"Boggs was systematically taking the disease to Indian bands, trading them infected blankets and articles of clothing. Then returning a few weeks later to gather the spoils."

Kathryn put her hand over her mouth, too stunned to speak.

"The only unanswered question is whether or not Brutus knew how Boggs was getting the stuff. Boggs says he did, but I don't know if that's the truth."

Kathryn explained how Brutus reacted to the moccasins she had given him.

"He knew the stuff was infected," said Sam, "but I'm not sure he knew how Boggs was taking the disease to the Indian villages."

Both were silent for a time, contemplating the horror Boggs had inflicted on Indian villages.

"How's Grizzly Woman, the squaw that used to be called Leather Belly?" asked Kathryn cautiously.

"Her name was Grizzly Fire Woman. I buried her at the old camp."

"Smallpox?"

Sam nodded, then told Kathryn about the beaver coat Lance had won in the poker game, and how the resulting smallpox had devastated Blackweasel's camp. How Boggs had confirmed his guilt by showing up with a wagon and shovel after the surviving members of the band had left. While Sam described his confrontation with Boggs in the old camp, Kathryn finished cleaning the wound, threaded the needle, and began sewing the skin back in place.

"What about us?" asked Kathryn, after most of the stitches were in place. She knew the time was not yet ripe for such a discussion. But she also knew that with Sam taking off after Boggs the next morning, there might never be a better time to bring up the subject that had been foremost in her mind during the four-hundred-mile journey to this wild north country.

"Some things have changed," said Sam, looking up at the sky through the open smoke flaps. "I would have married Grizzly Fire Woman had she lived. Tomorrow I'm going after the man who killed her. And when I catch him, I'll kill him."

"I don't blame you."

"And after I'm finished with Boggs, I'm going after Brutus."

"You're going to kill him?"

"I'm going to find out to what extent he's involved in this thing. If he knows how Boggs was getting the stuff, and the law won't take care of him, then I will."

"What about us?"

"I'm no longer the starry-eyed kid who bought that house for you in Salt Lake."

"But you are the same idealistic young man who burned it down."

"When this is all over I'm not going to be a trader of fine horses and carriages in Salt Lake."

"Do you think that matters to me?"

"I'm just not sure anymore."

"Your feelings toward me have changed?"

"You were raised with a silver spoon in your mouth, lawn tennis, and frequent visits to the opera."

"That wasn't my fault," protested Kathryn, sensing that Sam had indeed changed and that she had come on too strong too soon.

"The timing isn't good," said Sam, his voice cold and distant. "Grizzly Fire Woman is hardly cold in her grave. Tomorrow I'm going after the man who killed her. You may very well be the most beautiful woman in Salt Lake, and I'm flattered that you would ride four hundred miles to see me, but you didn't exactly catch me in a romantic mood. Am I making sense?"

Kathryn jerked the needle harder than necessary as she tightened the last stitch. Sam grimaced at the pain. Kathryn smiled in insincere apology.

After gathering her things, she started crawling toward the door.

"Where are you going?"

"Back to Salt Lake," responded Kathryn, stopping but not turning to look at Sam. She didn't want him to see the hurt in her face. And she didn't want to cry in front of the man who had just rejected her.

"How? It's almost dark, and it looks like snow tonight."

"I figured Blackweasel or Lance would find a place for me to stay the night. Tomorrow I'll ride over to Virginia City. Shouldn't have any trouble finding some freight wagons on their way to Salt Lake." Kathryn was pleased with how quickly she had planned a sensible retreat.

"When this is all over," said Sam, his voice softening, "I'll look you up. Things might be different then."

"Suit yourself," snapped Kathryn as she crawled out of the teepee.

"Thanks for patching me up," shouted Sam after her.

Chapter 48

It snowed during the night, but not very much. A few inches at most. In the early morning while Sam and Lance were preparing their gear for what could be an extended journey in pursuit of Dick Boggs, Kathryn was taking a walk along the banks of the Beaverhead River, sorting out her thoughts and feelings. Two of the Indians had agreed to accompany her to Virginia City, but they had had some trouble finding and catching their horses and wouldn't be ready to leave until later in the day.

Sam's coolness and rejection had been hard to take, but as Kathryn thought about it, he had treated her no worse than she had treated him in Salt Lake. At least Sam had left the door open, saying he would look her up when he returned to Salt Lake. He was right; the timing was bad. Had she dropped in on him several weeks or months later, things might have been different. It would probably be best to return to Salt Lake. Sam needed more time to get over Grizzly Fire Woman's death, and he needed to finish this business with Boggs.

That worried her as much as anything. The old man she had patched up hadn't seemed dangerous. Not with a wooden leg and a patch over one eye. But after finding out how Boggs had deliberately spread smallpox among the Indians, she knew her initial impression had been wrong.

Kathryn was a little over half a mile upstream from camp when she was startled by a white snowshoe rabbit racing down the path toward her. She held still as it bounded by. She wondered what had startled it, and looked ahead into the thickening willows.

"Good morning, Kathryn," said a voice that was strangely familiar.

"I guess that's everything," said Sam, jerking tight the last diamond hitch on the pack saddle.

"Wish we had more ammunition," said Lance.

"Maybe we can pick some up on the way, from a prospector, maybe a trapper," suggested Sam.

Lance nodded and turned toward his teepee. "I'll say good-bye to Kicking Woman, then we can be on our way."

Sam just stood there holding the horses. Before entering the teepee, Lance turned to Sam. He had been aware of Sam's moodiness since the little blowup with Kathryn the night before. He knew it would be good if Sam could clear the air between him and Kathryn before their paths went in different directions.

"Don't you think you ought to say good-bye to Kathryn?" said Lance. "Saw her walking upstream a little while ago. Wouldn't take a minute for you to ride up there and have a few words with her."

Sam had been thinking the same thing. He had slept very little during the night. Kathryn had sure picked a bad time to drop in on him. She thought they could just start where they left off in Salt Lake. But they couldn't. So many things had happened, and were happening. Still, Sam felt bad he had been so hard on her. Lance was right. It would be good to have some parting words with her, to patch things up. With time, maybe he and Kathryn could get things going again.

After tossing the lead rope of the packhorse over a tree limb, Sam swung into the saddle and reined his buckskin mare toward the river. In the new snow it was easy to spot Kathryn's trail headed upstream. He knew the trail belonged to her because there were no other tracks in the new snow and Lance had said he had seen Kathryn walking upstream. Sam followed.

Sam was wondering what he should say to her. He figured he should apologize for his abrupt behavior the day before. Maybe even promise to come and see her as soon as the business with Boggs was finished. He decided against inviting her to remain in the Indian camp until he returned.

Sam was contemplating how to phrase his apology when he entered a clump of willows. He pulled the horse to a sudden halt, carefully studying the tracks in the snow. Kathryn's tracks were no longer the only ones in the new snow. A larger boot track, a white man's boot, now accompanied her smaller tracks. But something was wrong with the new tracks.

Sam glanced ahead through the thickening willows, wondering who the other person could be. There were no other tracks coming from the camp. Seeing no one, he dismounted to take a closer look. He spotted a round hole in the snow, then another a foot further up the trail. Sam realized what was wrong with the new boot tracks. There were only half as many as there should have been. The round holes in the snow had been made by a wooden leg.

Sam reached back and quietly pulled his carbine out of the scabbard. He pumped a bullet into the chamber while looking forward through the willows, thinking how stupid he had been in underestimating Boggs. Instead of fleeing to Helena with the freighters, Boggs had come upstream after the kid who had shot him in the leg. Instead of finding Sam, however, the old man had stumbled onto Kathryn.

In the new snow it was easy to see from the tracks that Kathryn was in front, probably with the barrel of Boggs's gun in her back, as the trail led upstream through the willows. Expecting an ambush at any moment, Sam moved cautiously forward until he found the horse tracks. The boot tracks disappeared where Kathryn and Boggs had mounted. The horses had headed upstream at a gallop. Sam couldn't guess where they were headed.

Taking one last look at the snow for any additional evidence that might be available, Sam spotted a patch of red, possibly blood. He crouched for a closer look and picked up a piece of white material, possibly a piece of the white shawl Kathryn had been wearing. It was stained with blood.

Sam leaped upon his horse, keeping the rifle in his hand instead of returning it to the scabbard. He resisted the temptation to follow Boggs immediately. He didn't have any idea where the old man was going, or how long it would take to catch him. Digging his heels into the horse's sides, he galloped back to camp.

"Boggs has Kathryn," shouted Sam as he jerked his horse to a halt in front of Lance's teepee. The half-breed was still inside. "I'm going on ahead. Follow me with the packhorse."

By the time Lance crawled out of the teepee, all he could see was the rear end of Sam's buckskin horse as it lunged up the trail.

Chapter 49

Holding Kathryn at gun point, Boggs tied a dirty rag over her mouth and bound her hands behind her back. Then he helped her onto his packhorse, Kathryn straddling the sawbuck, her legs in front of the partially full canvas bags that were hanging from each side of the sawbuck. The canvas bags contained soiled Indian clothing. As an afterthought, Boggs ripped off a corner of Kathryn's shawl, then slashed her arm with his skinning knife to bloody the piece of shawl before throwing it down on the new snow. It was the perfect piece of bait to make sure Sam followed.

In approaching Blackweasel's camp that morning, it had been Boggs's plan to merely hide in the willows, hoping for a chance to get a shot at Sam. But that plan had had one big flaw. After shooting Sam, he would probably end up with a bunch of angry Blackfeet on his tail.

Finding Kathryn wandering up the trail was an unexpected bonus, an opportunity to lure Sam away from the camp. Kathryn was just the bait Boggs needed, and a beautiful piece of bait at that.

And Boggs knew exactly where he would take Kathryn. Before getting involved with the smallpox and Indians, he had been working a silver mine in a little box canyon between Bannock and Virginia City, not more than ten miles upstream from Blackweasel's new camp. The mine shaft was nestled in the side of a cliff overlooking a little shack. The entrance to the shaft was a perfect place from which to ambush anyone approaching the shack. A narrow path on the side of the cliff was the only way to reach the shaft.

For the first time she could remember, Kathryn feared for her life. With her hands tied behind her back, it was all she could do to keep her seat as the packhorse trotted and galloped along the rocky trail. Her hands were tied too tight. They were cold, almost numb from lack of circulation. And the sawbuck quickly wore painful blisters in soft places.

Kathryn had no idea where she was being taken. She only knew that Boggs wanted Sam to follow. But even with the bloody piece of shawl on the trail, she had her doubts. Sam had been about to head in the other direction with Lance when she began her walk upstream. She hadn't expected to see him again. Maybe she wouldn't be missed until long after Sam and Lance were on their way downstream.

Maybe that was best. Boggs wanted to be followed. Whoever followed would be walking into some kind of trap with Kathryn as bait. Kathryn realized she might never see Sam again, or anybody else, for that matter. She knew Boggs wasn't above killing her, not if there was some benefit for him in doing so.

After about two hours of hard travel, Boggs led Kathryn's horse off the main trail and into the entrance of what appeared to be a box canyon. Much of the snow had melted by then, so to make sure his trail wouldn't be missed, the old man ripped off another piece of shawl, reopened the wound on Kathryn's arm to soak up some fresh blood on the cloth, and hung the material on a bush that marked the turnoff point.

Kathryn spotted a little log shack with a dirt roof at the far end of the canyon at the base of a high cliff. The thought of being alone in that shack with Boggs was almost more frightening to her than death. She couldn't help but wonder what tortures, what abuses, a man like Boggs was capable of. Earlier, she had hoped that for the sake of his own safety Sam wouldn't discover her trail. Now, she hoped he had—that somehow he would find a way to avoid the apparent ambush and save her from Boggs.

Boggs tied both horses to a rail in front of the shack. After Boggs had cut her arm and bound her wrists too tightly, Kathryn was braced for rough treatment. To her surprise, he was suddenly very gentle as he helped her down from her horse and guided her toward the little plank door.

The windowless cabin was dark inside, and before Kathryn's eyes could adjust to the darkness, Boggs gently pushed her to a sitting position on a cluttered bunk against the north wall, leaving her hands tied behind her back. The bedding smelled of rancid fat and rat droppings. But the sick feeling welling up in Kathryn's chest was not a result of the smell. It was the fear, the awful anticipation, of what might happen.

Boggs bent over a little wood stove and shoved in some paper and sticks, which he ignited with a wooden match. "Soon be so warm in here you'll want to take your clothes off," he grunted as he shoved some bigger pieces of wood onto the fire.

Standing upright, Boggs turned to face Kathryn. He was grinning. The firelight leaking from the stove provided just enough light for her to see the outline of his broken brown teeth as he grinned.

"Almost wish I hadn't left a trail for young Storm," said Boggs as he hobbled toward her, his wooden stump of a leg thumping on the packed dirt floor. He reached out and took hold of her arm as she instinctively withdrew. With his other grimy hand, Boggs jerked the gag down from her mouth.

"How would you like to spend a winter here with ol' Dicky?" He laughed. Kathryn froze, her eyes wide with fright.

"We'll talk about that later," said Boggs, "but first we got to take care of Storm—unless there's something else you'd rather do, something that might keep old Dicky's mind off Storm for a bit . . ."

Kathryn spit in his face. It was an instinctive action, surprising her almost more than it did Boggs, who abruptly turned to one side. Without bothering to wipe the spit away, he hobbled to the corner of the shack where he picked up a coil of rope, slipping it over one shoulder. He returned to Kathryn, roughly grabbing her arm and pulling her to her feet. After jerking the gag back in place over her mouth, Boggs pushed her toward the door.

Kathryn felt a wave of relief as she bent over to avoid bumping her head on the doorjamb and stepped outside into the daylight.

But the relief was short-lived as Boggs slipped his rifle from its scabbard, then escorted Kathryn around to the rear of the cabin, where they began climbing the trail to the mine shaft in the side of the cliff.

Chapter 50

"Think I'll try for a gut shot," growled Boggs. He was leaning against a huge pine beam just inside the entrance of his mine. "A gut shot brings a slow, painful death." Kathryn was sitting with her back against the far wall, hands still tied behind her back, the gag still over her mouth.

The floor of the shaft was about forty feet above the valley floor, with a sheer drop-off from the mouth of the cave to a pile of boulders at the base of the cliff—boulders that had been pushed from the shaft as it was dug.

From where she was seated in the shadows just inside the mine, Kathryn had a clear view of the log shack and surrounding meadow. The horses were still tied to the post in front of the shack, and smoke was drifting from the pipe chimney. It would appear to Sam as he approached that Boggs and Kathryn were in the cabin. As Sam neared the cabin, he would be an easy target for Boggs.

Kathryn began to think that perhaps she had done the wrong thing spitting in Boggs's face. Maybe she should have forced herself to be more agreeable, even seductive. Maybe she could have distracted Boggs, giving Sam more time. Maybe she could have saved Sam's life. Now it was too late.

"Bet you would like to get rid of that gag," grunted Boggs. "Then you could yell a warning to him. You'd like that, wouldn't you?"

Kathryn just stared at Boggs, refusing to answer his question, determined not to let his taunting get the best of her.

"Would you like me to take that gag off?" said Boggs.

Kathryn knew he was teasing and didn't answer.

Boggs walked over to her, reached down and, to her amazement, removed the gag.

"Know why I did that?" he asked.

Kathryn shook her head, at the same time glancing at the meadow to see if Sam was coming. She could warn him now.

"I'll tell you why," he continued. "So I can have a little fun with the lady who spit in my face, find out how much she really loves that Storm kid. Bet you don't love him as much as you think you do."

Boggs dropped to his good knee in front of Kathryn, then taking one end of the long rope, he wrapped it around Kathryn's right leg several times and tied a tight knot. Then, getting to his feet, he hobbled back to the far side of the cave, where he tied the other end of the rope to the base of the heavy pine beam.

"Go ahead and warn him," he smiled, looking back at her. "But if you do," he growled, his voice suddenly getting loud and mean, "I swear I'll push you off the cliff." He paused, still glaring at her, waiting for his threat to sink in.

"The rope is thirty feet long. Break your fall about ten feet short of the rock pile, jerking your leg off at the hip. You'll drop gently on the rocks, breaking a few bones, then lie there and die with the blood and guts running out of the hole where your leg used to be." Boggs watched intently as his words sank in.

"And if you don't yell a warning to young Storm," Boggs continued, "I'll shoot him in the guts when he gets close to the cabin.

"Your choice is clear, white woman. Shout a warning and you'll get your leg jerked off. Keep your mouth shut, and you'll watch your lover catch a bullet in the belly."

Kathryn was hardly able to think. Her head was spinning as if she was about to pass out. But she couldn't allow that, not now.

"Hope he doesn't come right away," Boggs hissed. "Hope he gives you plenty of time to think over what you're going to do." He laughed.

Kathryn forced herself to look away from Boggs, down at the cabin and meadow. She prayed Sam wouldn't come, that nobody would come. Eventually she would find a way to get away from Boggs, if he didn't kill her. If only Sam wouldn't come, not now. She almost wished Boggs hadn't taken the gag off and given her such a horrible choice to make. Maybe Sam would wait until nightfall, then approach the cabin under cover of darkness. When he discovered no one was in the cabin, he would find the trail leading to the mine shaft and know where she was. That would be the right thing to do. But would Sam think of that, not knowing beforehand about the shaft?

Suddenly Kathryn's eye caught some movement, not at the far end of the meadow as she had anticipated, but in some tall sagebrush on the downhill side of the cabin. On foot, and not more than thirty feet away, Sam was charging toward the cabin.

Kathryn glanced over at Boggs, who had seen the movement too, and was raising his rifle to his shoulder. She looked back at Sam who had already reached the cabin door, breaking it in with his shoulder, then disappearing inside before Boggs could fire.

"Damn," cursed Boggs without taking the rifle down. "I'll get him coming out."

If only the cabin had a back door, thought Kathryn. But it didn't. There was only one way for Sam to come out, right in front of Boggs's rifle sights.

A few seconds later, Sam appeared in the doorway, looking first right, then left.

Boggs prepared to fire.

"Look out!" screamed Kathryn. "Up here. He's going to shoot!"

The explosion of Boggs's rifle shattered the silence, just as Sam ducked back inside the cabin. The bullet shattered the jamb above the door. Sam was untouched.

Boggs began to laugh. Taking the rope in his hand, he began to hobble toward Kathryn. There were tears streaming down her cheeks, but there was defiance in her face. She raised her chin and spit at him again, but he was too far away for her insult to reach him. The tears continued streaming down her cheeks.

Boggs stopped, then turned toward the cabin.

"Got a friend of yours up here," he shouted. "Come outside and throw down your gun. There's a thirty-foot rope tied to one of her legs. Going to push her off the cliff if you don't do as I say, now!"

"Don't come out!" screamed Kathryn. "He'll kill you."

"If you don't come out," yelled Boggs, "I'll push her off the cliff."

Sam appeared in the doorway, throwing his rifle ahead of him, into the snow.

"That's better," yelled Boggs. "Now come up here. Follow the trail. Keep your hands over your head." Sam started walking toward the trail as Boggs grabbed Kathryn by the arm and forced her to her feet. Boggs pushed her forward to the very edge of the cliff, in front of the big pine beam where the other end of her rope was secured.

"You can prolong your life by not fooling around," he hissed. "By not moving. One little move and over you go."

A minute later Sam was standing beside the big beam, Kathryn only a few feet away. Boggs was standing at the other side of the shaft opening, his rifle pointed at Sam, hammer back.

"You and me are a lot alike," growled Boggs. "A few days ago you were ambushing me. Now I've got you in my sights, but I won't blow it like you did."

"That's where the similarity ends," said Sam, hoping to get Boggs in an argument to buy some time. "You've got a wooden leg and a patch over your eye."

"Thanks to your old man," bellowed Boggs, the anger boiling up inside. "Every time this stump starts hurting I remember that bear trap your old man set for me. And I vow someday I'll pay him back. And every time I have trouble seeing something, or judging a distance, I remember that dog your old man set on me, his fangs digging my eye out. And I vow your old man will pay some day.

"That day has come, Storm. I wish it were your old man instead of you standing in front of me, but I'll enjoy it just the same. Think I'll send him your scalp, wrapped around your eyeballs. Love to see his face when he opens it."

"You're sick," challenged Kathryn.

"One last thing," said Boggs, ignoring Kathryn's comment, still speaking to Sam. "Give me that bear claw necklace before I blow you over the cliff."

"So you can sell it to Brutus?" challenged Sam, fingering one of the claws on the necklace Grizzly Fire Woman had made for him.

"A matched pair would bring a lot of money," said Boggs, waiting for the meaning of his comment to sink in.

"A matched pair?" questioned Sam.

Boggs opened his shirt, revealing a bear claw necklace identical to Sam's.

"Got it off a poxed squaw last night," explained Boggs, pleased with the knowledge that his words carried a lot of hate and pain. Kathryn remembered the soiled Indian clothing in the canvas bags on the packhorse. Boggs had stopped off at Blackweasel's old camp to dig up some spoils.

Sam had had all he could stand of Dick Boggs. He reached to remove the necklace, as if he were going along with Boggs's request, then after faking a sudden movement to the right, he lunged at Boggs with all his strength.

Sam wasn't sure if he had been hit or not when the rifle exploded. He only knew that his momentum had not been impaired by a bullet and that he would reach Boggs before the old man could pump another bullet into the chamber. With adrenaline flowing, Sam grabbed the rifle, jerked it out of Boggs's hands, and flung it over the edge of the cliff.

By the time Sam turned back to Boggs, the old man had already drawn his long skinning knife and was preparing to lunge at Sam, who backed up a step, picking up a fist-sized rock.

Sam backed another step, then another as Boggs inched forward, the long razor-edged blade flashing in the afternoon light. Sam continued to back up until he had passed between Kathryn and the big beam. He was careful not to tangle his feet in the rope. With Kathryn on his left and the beam on his right, Sam refused to retreat any further. His fist tightened on the rock.

Boggs passed the knife from his right hand to the left, then back to the right, inching forward and looking for an opportunity to strike.

Neither Sam nor Kathryn anticipated Boggs's next move. Feigning a knife thrust toward Sam, the old man suddenly swung the knife in a wide arc to his right, just missing Kathryn's throat as she instinctively jumped back. At the same time, Sam threw the rock with all his might, striking Boggs squarely in the chest, driving the old man back a few paces.

Seconds suddenly seemed like minutes as time slowed down. The sight of Boggs stumbling backward became a secondary consideration. Kathryn was screaming. In her attempt to avoid the knife thrust she had lost her balance. Her feet were in the loose rock at the very edge of the cliff where the sheer drop-off began. Her hands were still tied behind her back, preventing her from reaching out for help or balance. Kathryn was falling out into space, and there was nothing Sam could do to stop her. There was no time, not even to think. When her feet left the loose rock Kathryn would be gone, forever.

What happened next was an instinctive reaction more than a conscious decision. There was no time for conscious thought.

While Kathryn was still teetering on the loose rock, Sam dropped to his knees, grabbing the loose coils of the rope. He found the section closest to the end tied to Kathryn's leg and wrapped it quickly around his left wrist before taking a firm hold with his hand, at the same time wrapping his right arm around the heavy pine beam.

By taking up the slack in the rope, Sam broke Kathryn's fall before it hardly began. She felt the pull of the rope as she began to fall, turning her upside down and holding her in a hanging position just over the edge of the cliff. She was out of sight, maybe a foot or two below the ledge, and somewhat bruised from the slam against the cliff face as the rope broke her fall. Otherwise, she was all right—except for the paralyzing fear of being so close to death and being totally helpless to do anything about it.

Sam began to tug on the rope, hoping he had the strength to pull Kathryn back up with one arm. But as soon as he began to inch the rope in, he became aware of Boggs again. Having recovered from the rock's blow, the old man was creeping forward, the long skinning knife still in his hand.

Sam was helpless to do anything. If he let go of the rope, Kathryn would fall to her death. If he continued to hang on, he would be defenseless before Dick Boggs and his knife.

Boggs stepped closer. Sam looked right and left, but he didn't know what he was looking for. In his confusion over what to do, his grip on the rope relaxed, just a little, just enough for the rope to begin slipping through his hand. Sam tightened his grip, stopping the movement of the rope.

Boggs began to laugh, stepping even closer.

"Better let her go," taunted Boggs. "Plenty more women where she came from." Sam continued to hang on, a determined but desperate look on his face. He could hear Kathryn sobbing.

"If you don't let go, I'm going to slit your throat," warned Boggs. "As your blood runs out you'll begin to lose your strength, the rope will begin to slip, you'll let go, and she'll fall to her death." Grinning, the old man moved one step closer.

Something Boggs had said started racing again and again through Sam's mind. The rope will begin to slip. *That's it,* thought Sam. *Our only chance.*

Sam loosened his grip on the rope just a little, allowing it to slip between his fingers. Faster. His plan was simple. Let all the rope out. Kathryn could hang just as comfortably thirty feet down the cliff as she could in her present place just over the edge. But with all the rope played out, the heavy beam would be holding Kathryn, freeing Sam to deal with Boggs.

Sam let the rope out even faster. There wasn't much time. His hand was burning as the rope wore through skin and flesh.

Sam looked up at Boggs, who was watching the rope, trying to figure out what Sam was up to.

Trying to anticipate what Boggs might do next, Sam changed to a sitting position, pushing his feet out in front of him, toward Boggs. Sam was ready now to kick at Boggs should the old man decide to come at him before all the rope was out.

Having figured out what Sam was doing, Boggs didn't waste any time deciding what he would do. He moved close, fully aware that Sam could kick at him and possibly kick the knife out of his hand if he got too close. But he had something else in mind.

Just when Boggs was almost in kicking range, when Sam was getting ready to strike out with one of his boots, Boggs did the unexpected again. Reaching down, he picked up one of the remaining coils of rope and cut it with his knife, laughing.

Sam's plan was spoiled. The end of Kathryn's rope was no longer tied to the beam. The end would soon slip through Sam's hand and she would fall to her death.

"What are you going to do, kid?" asked Boggs. "Let her go and fight me like a man? Or hang on until I slit your throat?"

Sam could see Kathryn falling to her death on the boulders below. Logic told him she would die no matter what he did. He might as well let go now so he would have a chance to save his own skin. That is what she would want him to do. Hanging on wouldn't do her any good. Not now.

Still, there was something about the conscious act of letting go of the rope, even though it seemed the logical thing to do, that was beyond Sam's ability to do. He couldn't let go.

"What are you going to do?" taunted Boggs, just out of reach of Sam's boot.

Sam raised his chin and spit at Boggs, at the same time continuing to hang onto the rope.

Boggs moved in. Sam kicked simultaneously with both feet, striking Boggs in the stomach. Almost instinctively, the old man wrapped his arms around the boots to prevent a second kick. Sam tried to pull his feet free but couldn't. Every movement was loosening his hold on the beam and his grip on the rope. Boggs knew it and leaned backward, pulling Sam away from the beam and rope.

Sam didn't know what else to do but hang on and grit his teeth. He knew only one thing, that he would not let go of the rope or the beam as long as there was strength in him to hang on.

Suddenly there was a snapping, in his head. Like something cracked. He felt it. But when it happened again, Sam thought maybe he was hearing it. Suddenly Boggs let go of his boots. Sam forced his eyes to focus on Boggs, who was reeling about, blood streaming from his nose and mouth.

Again the crack. This time Sam realized he had been hearing the report of a rifle. Someone from down below was pumping lead into Dick Boggs. The old man dropped forward to his knees, again within range of Sam's boot, but closer to the edge of the cliff. Sam kicked again. Boggs lost his balance and disappeared from sight.

Sam's attention was back on the rope and Kathryn and how he could get the loose end secured to the beam. He no longer had the strength to pull her up. He couldn't hang on much longer. But he couldn't let her go. Not now.

"Help," he called. He hoped that whoever had fired those shots was running up the trail. It seemed like an eternity, but eventually Sam became aware of footsteps behind him.

"Don't let go now," cautioned a voice. It was Lance.

Lance grabbed the rope and together they began pulling Kathryn up the cliff, calling to her that everything was going to be all right.

She was bruised and battered, and the skin was worn raw where the rope was tied around her leg.

As soon as Kathryn was safe on the ledge, with Sam untying the rope, Lance headed back down the trail. "Got a little business to take care of with Boggs," he said in parting.

Sam glanced over the cliff. Below on the boulders he could see the twisted body. It wasn't moving. He turned to Kathryn. "You going to be all right?"

She nodded. He sat down beside her, both with their backs against the heavy beam, both too spent to talk. It felt so good, just to be alive and know that life wasn't going to end at any moment.

After a while Kathryn began to pick some rock particles out of an abrasion on her shoulder. Sam looked at the bloody mess that had once been the palm of his left hand.

"Isn't it wonderful that it's over?" said Kathryn.

"Feels great," said Sam.

"Think I can still make it to Virginia City by dark?" asked Kathryn.

They were both laughing when Lance reappeared, tossing a bloody piece of skin at their feet.

"What's that?" asked Kathryn.

"Boggs's scalp," said Sam. "Lance is half Indian."

"But there's no hair on it," said Kathryn.

"Being bald doesn't get special privileges for a man like Boggs," responded Lance. They all laughed.

"Found this on him," said Lance, tossing the bear claw necklace in Sam's lap. "Think it's the one Grizzly Fire Woman was wearing. Thought you would want it."

"Thanks," said Sam.

Without warning and before she could respond, Sam reached over and placed the necklace over Kathryn's head. She looked at him. She knew the story of the matching necklaces and what they meant to Sam.

"Are you sure you want me to have this?" she asked.

"I'm sure," he said. "But on one condition."

"What's that?"

"That you forget the trip to Virginia City."

"It's a deal," Kathryn said, holding the shiny black claws out where she could get a better look at them.

About the Author

Until someone else steps forward, it appears *The Storm Testament* series author Lee Nelson is the only man in modern times to kill a bull buffalo from the back of a galloping horse with a bow and arrow.

No, Lee is not a lunatic bent on suicide, but a best-selling author intent on gathering authentic research. Digging through dusty journals, starting fires without matches, and even chewing on raw buffalo is part of Nelson's research in writing historical/adventure/romance novels unparalleled in authenticity and originality.

Lee was born high in the Rocky Mountains in Logan, Utah, later graduating from high school in California. After studying at the University of California at Berkeley, he served a mission for the LDS Church in southern Germany. Lee has a bachelor's degree in English literature and an MBA, both from Brigham Young University.

Lee Nelson has more than thirty published books, including ten historical novels in *The Storm Testament* series.

0 26575 73746 2